KU-083-378

STRIKING MURDER

HIGHLAND
LIBRARIES

WITHDRAWN

STRIKING MURDER

by

A. J. Wright

HIGHLAND
LIBRARIES

HIGHLAND
LIBRARIES

170005256

WITHDRAWN

Magna Large Print Books
Long Preston, North Yorkshire,
BD23 4ND, England.

British Library Cataloguing in Publication Data.

A catalogue record of this book is
available from the British Library

ISBN   978-0-7505-4460-3

First published in Great Britain by Allison & Busby Limited in 2016

Copyright © 2016 by Alan Wright

Cover design © Christina Griffiths/bookdeluxe
Cover illustration © Gordan1/JonnyJim/iStockphoto/
Geoff Pickering/Fotolia by arrangement with Allison & Busby Ltd.

The moral right of the author is hereby asserted in accordance with
the Copyright, Designs and Patents Act, 1988

Published in Large Print 2017 by arrangement with
Allison & Busby Limited

All rights reserved. No part of this publication may be reproduced,
stored in a retrieval system, or transmitted in any form or by any
means, electronic, mechanical, photocopying, recording or otherwise
without the prior permission of the Copyright owner.

Magna Large Print is an imprint of Library Magna Books Ltd.

Printed and bound in Great Britain by
T.J. (International) Ltd., Cornwall, PL28 8RW

*All characters and events in this publication,
other than those clearly in the public domain,
are fictitious and any resemblance to actual persons,
living or dead, is purely coincidental.*

For my grandsons, whom I love beyond measure
Olli, Harri and Freddie

'Can one go upon hot coals,
and his feet not be burnt?'
Proverbs 6.28

'He that diggeth a pit shall fall into it'
Ecclesiastes 2.8

'When you strike at a king, you must kill him'
Ralph Waldo Emerson

PROLOGUE

Wigan, Lancashire
1893

He thought he heard something and looked round.

No one.

His imagination, then. The hiss of the gas lamp, per-haps. Or something beast-like slouching from beyond the closed doors. Carefully he made his way along the terraced street, thankful for the snow, still falling, that kept them indoors. Yet he cursed the bitter chill of the night, and thought enviously of the place he had left. His only comfort was that this wouldn't take long.

He would make damned sure of that.

As he passed each window he caught glimpses, through the threadbare fabric of the curtains, of what lay beyond: a man slumped in a chair, head bowed forward in an attitude of sleep; a filthy child torment-ing an even filthier dog; a wife stirring an earthen-ware pot on the range beside a feeble fire.

He smiled grimly. They had thought, if they could hold out until winter, he and the others would admit defeat and welcome them back with open arms. But winter was here, fierce and merciless, and it would keep them huddled close, like bears in a wintry cave, until they accepted the inevitable.

He gave an involuntary grunt at the thought of what they would do to him if they knew he was here, in this street, and moved quickly on, towards his destination.

13

Not far now.

And this time, there would be no mistake. He would settle this thing between them once and for all.

A few more yards, and the end was in sight. He saw the window and the shadow on the curtain.

But then something else caught his eye. A dark figure ahead, waiting in the mouth of a small alleyway on the far side of the street. It reached out a dark, gloved hand and beckoned to him frantically, a furtive gesture veiled by a gasp of breath cloud. He heard his name hissed urgently. What the blazes?

For a second he was afraid. And then, by the dim glow of a street lamp, he saw who it was, and his eyes narrowed in anger and confusion. 'What the hellfire are you doing out here?' he snarled, a feral whisper.

The figure said nothing, merely retreated into the darkness of the alleyway.

He glanced up and down the long terraced street. Not a soul.

He muttered a curse and entered the alleyway.

CHAPTER ONE

Father Kevin Brady had never been what you might call a man of fancy. He had seen too many sudden or lingering deaths to believe in anything other than what lay before his eyes. Tonight, in a bitterly cold, cheerless room, he had been in the presence of yet another expiry, this time the lamentable drawing out of a bundle of wasted bones that had once flexed iron muscles deep underground. He had known the old collier for nigh on thirty years, had listened to his confession and shaken his head many times at the grey and sad ordinariness of sin. Yet the cold glaze in the collier's eyes as he gripped his hand like a drowning man had confirmed for him once more the chill finality of that moment. Even the man's last discernible utterance, that had brought spiritual solace to his wife, carried an ambiguity not lost on the old priest: *'Jesus!'*

Now, as he made his way home, careful not to lose his footing on the thick, hard snow, he reached out to fumble against the chalky brickwork of the alleyway that ran at the back of the long row of terraced houses. His hand felt wet, and he remembered how, in summer, the walls often oozed slime, like pus from the crevices in the bricks, where the ordure from the pail closets beyond produced a sickly, rank-smelling dampness. From the muted stench all around him, he gathered the muck men were long overdue. It wasn't a task he envied – especially in those hot summer months – and yet, with a wry smile, he reflected how, in the old debating classes he used to enjoy so much in the seminary, he'd have drawn some metaphysical link between the two callings of priest and muck man. Both deal with the filth of man, both get closer to it than they would like, and both help to clear the mess, leaving closet, or soul, clean once more.

He stopped to wipe a smear of slime down his topcoat.

The moon had long ago drifted behind thick cloud, and the subsequent gloom had settled on the place like a heavy shroud. Even the occasional screech from invisible windows a few yards away, as some marital dispute kept the combatants awake, seemed muffled, deadened by the density of an approaching storm.

Not more snow, surely? He leant his shoulder against a wall and allowed himself the sad luxury of a sigh.

'*Father Brady's here now,*' the old woman had said to the dying man, as if somehow he carried with him the mysticism of revival.

He recalled the look in the children's eyes, huddled in the furthest corner of the room, as far from the terror on the bed as they could get, yet fearful of what lay on the dark stairs beyond the door. Their eyes flickered with hope as they registered the white of his collar and the magic he performed every Sunday with a piece of bread and a goblet of wine. Perhaps, tonight, he could show them some more of that mystic art...

Suddenly, an oil lamp flared above his head and brought him back to the present. He looked up, saw the looming shadows of a bedroom, the curtains drawn back so that he could catch some of the light from the lamp. A black, monstrous shape moved grotesquely along the bedroom wall, distorted even more by the swirls of ice that had laced themselves along the window. It stood upright, its elongated head held high. He recognised the attitude and smiled, hearing the faint sound of the piss rattling in the pot.

Now, as he looked down the alleyway, thanks to the dim yellow cast by the lamp, he could see the curve in the wall that led to a narrow ginnel – the one he'd missed in the darkness.

With a shivered nod of gratitude to the unknown source of light, he pushed himself from the wall, felt once more the slithering wetness of slime against his flat palm, and walked quickly towards the narrow gap that led to the terraced street.

As he was emerging onto the long sweep of terraced houses, he heard something, a faint gnawing that somehow repulsed him. Then there was a skittering and a squeaking behind him. In the blackness of the narrow archway he had just traversed, he must have disturbed a nest of rats – all along the tunnel-like gap, there were obscure cancerous cavities in the walls, some as small as the palm of his hand, and others large enough for a grown man to hide in. Now, disturbed by his intrusion, it would take them a while to settle, and they could well spread themselves along the low channels below the kerbstones, slithering in and out of the mounded cobblestones looking for scraps of waste in the covering darkness.

'You'll be lucky,' he said aloud.

To his right, he saw the dull haze of a gas lamp. Slowly, he made his way down the deserted street, his bearings recovered now that he could see at least some signs of where he was. The uneven flagstones were treacherous, and he reached out to steady himself against the jagged sills of the houses.

What time would it be now? He had arrived at the old miner's home as the clock in the front room had struck twelve. That had been a good two hours ago. He reached the glare of the gas lamp and put his hand beneath his coat, to the small waistcoat pocket where he kept the fob watch his da had given him so many years ago, as a gift for entering the priesthood.

It was as he pulled it out, and peered down to register the time, that he caught his breath. His right hand was wet, glistening in the light from above.

A cold shiver ran down his spine.

He remembered the slime on the alley wall.

Since when has slime been red, Kevin? Sure an' it isn't slime at all.

He swallowed hard, threw a horrified glance back the way he had come. In his mind he retraced his steps, back down the dark ginnel, left into the alleyway, a few yards further back – to a wall covered with blood.

And he called to mind something else. Something he had heard.

The gnawing of rats in the blackness.

The gunshot cracked the crisp morning air, like a bone snapping.

'That bugger's mine!'

'We'll see then!'

The two boys, no more than ten years old, hared off towards the bank of the canal, their heads held far back and their arms pumping the air like pistons. Some of the men turned from the pigeon shoot to watch them race across the field, their breath freezing in the grey air.

'Little 'un, for a bob!' one man shouted, raising his bowler to show himself in the crowd.

'I'll have yon lanky 'un!' shouted another, who pushed past those beside him and shook hands with the first.

'Done!'

And so the wager was made. More of the men swivelled their gaze round, ignoring the rasp of the wooden slats, the laboured flap of pigeons' wings and the next crack of gunshot, to watch the two youngsters race to the canal bank. Although their pace was slowed by the thick snow, they moved with all the eagerness of both youth and hunger, and, urged on by the ironic cheers of the spectators, the smaller of the two boys reached the bank first, where, with a wild whoop of victory, he hurled himself over the edge. The spectators heard the dull clang as his iron clogs landed on the thick ice.

'It's not done yet,' yelled the supporter of the 'lanky 'un'. 'Not till he has it in his hand.'

''Course,' said the other. The smile on his face held the confidence of a man about to become a shilling richer.

The taller boy now leapt over the edge of the bank, and for a few seconds the tension among the watching men grew. Some coughed, some gave encouraging cries, and some even thought of breaking from the others and rushing over to see just what was happening. It was more entertaining than the pigeon shoot.

Then an arm appeared above the bank's edge. The taller boy was clambering up, and the cheering that greeted his appearance was quickly replaced by a communal groan when he pulled himself fully up onto the bank. Both hands were empty.

Then, to his left, a small arm was thrust into

the air, the hand clutching the dead pigeon, whose head flapped loosely to and fro in the boy's excitement.

'The little sod!' the second man said. He took out a shilling and slammed it down into the up-turned palm of the grinning victor.

The men cheered as the small boy struggled to negotiate the steep bank, but eventually he made it, holding the dead pigeon close to his chest now.

'I slurred too far,' grumbled the taller boy. 'Yon ice is bloody thick.'

'That's three of 'em I've got,' said the other as they made their way back to the semicircular crowd watching the pigeon shoot.

Another shot tore through the air.

'Me mam'll be pleased. Pigeon pie, eh?' Tommy Haggerty pulled open his threadbare jacket and stuffed the bird close to his chest, along with the others he had already bagged.

The sideshow over, the men turned to the real business of the morning, and watched impatiently as the two armed combatants continued with the pigeon shoot. There had already been too many grumbles about the unfairness of the day's com-petition – pigeons' wings tended to freeze in the cold air, and when they flew from the boxes their flight was slow and laboured, rendering them the easiest of targets against the white roofs of the nearby streets and the grey skies beyond.

'A blind man wi' palsy could get fifteen out o' fifteen in this bloody weather!' one disgruntled spectator had observed.

Tommy, content with his haul for the day, ignored the communal gloom of the men, bade a cocky farewell to the taller boy and walked quickly through the mounds of snow to the main road. He tried to picture the smile on his mam's face as he pulled out the three birds, one after another, just like the clown they'd seen at the circus last summer.

Before the strike.

Tommy skipped past the crowd huddled outside the entrance to the alleyway. He barely noticed the two policemen in their great coats and helmets standing on guard, rubbing their hands furiously, and keeping the more curious away from the alley. He felt the still-warm feathers of the birds safely tucked away inside his jacket. Pigeon pie. His favourite.

'Mam!' he yelled as he burst through the front door. 'Mam! Guess what I got!'

Silence. Only the tumble of glowing coals settling in the grate, sparks soaring upwards in a crazy spiral as they caught the draught from the closing door. He ran into the kitchen, but she wasn't there, either. Now where could she be?

He shook the question from his head, pulled out the pigeons and laid them carefully on the kitchen table. She'd only be next door, or next door but one. When she eventually did walk through the door, the birds would be the first things she would see. He stroked them as if they were merely sleeping, smoothing out the feathers to cover the tiny holes where the shot had entered, and sat on the chair, swinging his pale, scuffed legs and sitting on his hands to ward off the chill.

Hurry up, Mam.

Michael Brennan sat at the kitchen table, warming his hands on a mug of strong tea while his wife, Ellen, swept away the crumbs that were left from breakfast. She glanced at him and smiled with just a hint of censure as their five-year-old son, Barry, stared in wonder at the frosted art on the kitchen window.

It had been in the early hours when he had walked into their room complaining of the cold and rubbing his eyes.

'Why are you fightin'?' he had asked.

'We're not fightin'.'

His dad's voice had sounded strange in the dark.

'You was. I 'eard me mam cryin'.'

Then he'd heard his mam giggle and knew she was all right now.

'Come on, buggerlugs,' said his dad. 'Hop in.'

Now, Brennan took a sip of tea and gave a grunt of pleasure, wiping the moisture from his thick moustache.

'Can we go to the park today?' the child asked.

Ellen Brennan turned from the sink and frowned. 'It's bitter. Best build up that fire and stay in. We've enough coal for that, at any rate.'

'Dad?'

Brennan looked across at those sparkling blue eyes. 'Well, I reckon if we wrap up properly...'

Ellen wiped her hands on the tea cloth. 'And if he catches a chill you'll be up all night damping his brow no doubt.' Her tone belied the rebuke in the words.

Barry clamped his hands together, his usual display of delight.

The harsh knock on the front door froze his smile. Knocks like that took his dad away from him.

'Who on earth?' Ellen gave her husband a sharp look, as if somehow he had orchestrated both the promise and its imminent breach.

Brennan rose, ruffled his son's shock of hair, and went to the front door. A large uniformed constable stood on the pavement, his helmet clutched to his breast as if fully expecting to be invited in. The red flush on his cheeks suggested an urgency that made Brennan's heart lurch.

'What?'

'Beg pardon, Sergeant. Only you're needed, like.'

Brennan could feel his son's disappointed gaze between his broad shoulder blades.

'I'm not on shift, Constable Jaggery. Or don't you check the duty roster?'

The constable shifted uneasily and looked down at his boots, at the scuffed snow stubbornly refusing to melt. 'I did, sir. Only it's Captain Bell hisself, like.'

Brennan frowned. 'Well come in, Constable. Come in. You're turning the whole house into a meat safe!'

Once inside the Wigan Borough Police Station, Detective Sergeant Michael Brennan removed the thick woollen muffler and his greatcoat, thrust them unceremoniously into the arms of Constable Jaggery, and made his way past the duty desk, where a uniformed sergeant was busy scribbling something into a heavy ledger.

'His lordship's in his office, Michael,' he said

23

without raising his head.

Brennan saw his mouth twitch in scorn.

'Looks like he's had his arse stung an' all.'

Brennan smiled, more in acknowledgement of the lurid image that flashed in his head than in any sense of anticipation at meeting the chief constable.

Captain Bell was one of those men who rarely smiled. When he did it was usually the harbinger of something singularly unpleasant. He had spent many years in the army, and had seen service in what might be regarded as the social extremities of the Empire, India and Ireland. As an ex-military man, he had brought a rugged efficiency and respect for uniform to the police force. It was therefore beyond doubt that he took his duties seriously, and had a genuine belief in the efficacy of policing and the almost biblical necessity for the rigour of punishment; but somehow, in his steadfast pursuit of a social and moral rectitude, he seemed to have lost something on the way – a warmth, a softness, a humanity. Some wag had once described him as possessing all the flexibility of a narrow gauge tramline.

Brennan walked quickly down the long corridor. The room at the end – the one with an ornate, smoked-glass window subtly tinctured with reds and greens suggestive of a miniature cathedral – belonged to the chief constable. He knocked and waited, feeling almost like a recalcitrant choirboy about to face the minister.

'Come in!' snapped a voice from within.

Captain Bell was seated behind his immaculately polished desk. Once again, Brennan was struck by the fleeting impression of death as he contemplated his superior's gaunt features. A pallid hue suffused his skin, which appeared to have all the consistency of rather thin vellum, stretched taut over cadaverous cheekbones. His eyes were cast down in the attitude of close reading, his pince-nez perched on the extremity of a hawk's beak. The man was a living *memento mori*.

After a few seconds he looked up. 'Please accept my apologies, Sergeant.'

'Apologies, sir?'

'For disturbing your Sabbath. Believe me, I wouldn't have done so if it had been anything less ... disturbing.'

'Disturbing, sir?' He saw the tic in Captain Bell's cheek at the unintended echo of his words.

His superior gave a sigh and steepled his hands. 'Constable Jaggery told you there's been a murder?'

'Yes, sir, body found in Scholes in the early hours by a priest, but he said he hasn't been told who the...'

'Indeed he hasn't. This needs to be handled with discretion.'

'Sir?'

'The victim,' said Captain Bell, with a dramatic sigh, 'was one of my closest friends.'

Brennan waited for a name, his deductive powers being somewhat hampered by the unfortunate circumstance of his never having realised the good captain had *any* close friends.

Bell shook his head. 'It was Arthur Morris, Sergeant.'

Brennan flinched as the implications swarmed

round his brain like angry wasps. It couldn't have been worse. 'I see.'

'He has, according to Genesis, "returned to dust".' Bell paused, weighing his words carefully. 'He appears to have been stabbed. Apart from the tragedy for his family, you will, of course, realise what this could mean for the whole town?' His eyes reflected the note of fear in his voice. He picked up a small envelope and handed it across.

'This was found in his inside pocket. Curious, don't you think?'

Brennan looked down at the crumpled and stained envelope. It was addressed to *A. Morris*. Quickly, he took out the filthy scrap of paper that lay inside and read what was written, his frown increasing as he did so.

The writing was clumsy, spiderish, its scrawl rendered more vile by the soiled quality of the paper. *Whoever had written this,* thought Brennan, *hadn't sat at a desk armed with crown vellum note-paper and a blotter.*

'Any ideas?'

Brennan gave a shrug. 'Doesn't look like a calling card, sir, does it?'

The snarl forming around Captain Bell's mouth made him devise a less impertinent observation.

'It's quite plainly a threat, Sergeant, is it not?'

Brennan looked down at the writing:

His hand shal be agenst evryman and evryman's hand agenst him.
Strike causes hell – O Lord end suffrin
Or die

26

'Sounds familiar,' he said. 'The first line at any rate.'

'Genesis. I think the sentiment is self-evident.'

'Have you any idea what he was doing in Scholes, sir?'

'A complete mystery. Smacks somewhat of Daniel in the lions' den, does it not?'

It did indeed.

The miners' strike was now in its fifth month, and feelings around the town were running higher than ever since the rumour that Morris and his fellow colliery owners had threatened to bring in blackleg workers from south Wales. The last time that had happened, twenty or so years ago, pitched battles were fought in Standishgate between strikers, police, blacklegs and even the militia sent from Preston. It had been enough to ensure the newcomers were prevented from taking up their work, and the miners had declared it a historic victory.

A subsequent gloom had settled on the town and its inhabitants like a pall, soup kitchens a common feature now of life in the borough. The sprawling area of Scholes on the edge of town was home to many colliers who would have welcomed the opportunity to impress upon Arthur Morris – literally – how they felt with the help of their size ten clogs.

It was chiefly his intransigence that had brought about the strike in the first place – as the owner of the largest collieries in the whole of Lancashire, he was the most vociferous and influential supporter of the coal owners' insistence in imposing a national twenty-five per cent reduction in the miners' wages in an attempt to reduce costs. Now, the spectre of starvation haunted almost every home in the borough and throughout the coalfields of the North and Midlands.

'This morning,' continued Captain Bell, 'Arthur Morris was reported missing by his son, Andrew. By all accounts his father dined at home last night, then received a mysterious letter...' He threw a nod at the paper on the desk. 'And left immediately despite the bitterly cold weather. That was the sum of what he had to tell us.'

Brennan frowned. 'Perhaps he was transported to Scholes.'

'Meaning?'

'Well, sir, if he were dispatched elsewhere, then conveyed to the alleyway...'

Captain Bell leant forward. '"Transported"? "Dispatched"? *"Conveyed"*? You speak as if the man was a parcel!'

'Sir.' Brennan lowered his head respectfully.

'Besides, according to the preliminary report I have here, it was evident the brutal assault took place where he was found. A single stab wound, the man's life blood splattered around the walls of that ... loathsome place. His innards molested by vermin, for God's sake!'

He broke off, allowing the blasphemy, the silence and the venom in his eyes to conjure up what he thought of the Scholes district. 'Knowing Arthur Morris, he would never shirk a challenge. If someone sent him that note he would never rest until he hunted the man down like a wild animal.'

Brennan examined the letter and the crumpled envelope more closely. 'There's no address, sir.'

'What?'

'There's no address on the envelope, for one thing. Just the name – *A. Morris.* So I presume it was delivered by hand.'

'Is that relevant?'

Brennan shrugged. 'Possibly. But neither is there an address on the letter itself.'

'So?'

'It's curious, that's all. If Morris was in Scholes as a result of this letter, how did he know where to go?'

'The letter may have nothing whatsoever to do with his presence in that godforsaken place.'

'But he left immediately after receiving the letter. It's a fair assumption.' He read the letter's contents once more. 'And perhaps there is an address of sorts here.'

'I beg your pardon?'

'The second line, sir. *"Strike causes hell– O Lord end suffrin".*'

'What about it?'

'It makes a veiled reference to Scholes.'

'Does it? I fail to see...'

'That's because you are failing to *see*, in the true sense.' He spoke quickly, to remove any hint of accusation. 'If you were *looking* at the words, it would, of course, strike you at once. The initial letter of each word, sir. They spell out *Scholes.*'

With a flourish, Captain Bell grabbed the paper and looked at the words once more. Then he glanced at his detective sergeant with an expression of pique and admiration. 'It could be coincidence, you understand, Sergeant?'

'It could indeed, sir. But if, as you say, this letter

was delivered last night, prompting Mr Morris to leave hastily, then it's highly probable he saw it as some sort of message, or threat from Scholes. It may be that he recognised the handwriting.'

'Hardly likely, Sergeant. Scrawl like this...' he slapped the paper as if crushing lice. 'Nevertheless, it was well spotted. Well spotted.'

He placed the letter on his desk and smoothed it out with his left hand for a few seconds before speaking once more, this time in a low voice. 'And now you have a painful duty before you, Sergeant. You need to call upon his widow and break the news to her.'

'She hasn't been told?'

Captain Bell visibly blanched at the implied rebuke. 'The man was found in the early hours by a priest. It was naturally assumed the victim was from the area.'

And therefore the process of identification would have followed at a funereal pace, Brennan thought. Death, too, has its social hierarchy.

'After the report of him missing, our desk sergeant, showing an uncharacteristic talent for arithmetic, put two and two together, recalled the remains of the victim lying in the infirmary morgue, and for once got four. He saw fit to send for me. I myself had the unenviable task of viewing the remains. Gruesome, ghastly business that was.' He shook his head. 'Although as for formal identification, that melancholy duty must fall on a member of the family.'

Brennan stroked his moustache and grunted.

'Yes, Sergeant, what is it?'

'The words may give us the district, sir, but they

make no reference to a particular address, not even a name. How would he know where exactly to go? I wonder who he went there to meet – or to confront?'

Captain Bell, who had clearly grown weary of his sergeant's musings, could barely conceal his impatience. 'That is for you to discover, Sergeant. Or do you wish me to do all the work of the detective branch while you stay here and enjoy a steaming hot mug of tea?'

He heard her coming. When the back door opened, Tommy was standing by the table, his small chest thrust forward proudly.

Bridie Haggerty closed the door softly behind her.

She was in her mid-thirties, and had once been comely, her jet-black hair the envy of many, yet the careworn expression she always seemed to bear these days, and the wisps of a premature grey in her hair, aged her ten years. Thin lines stretched from the corners of her eyes, and her cheeks were sunken, seeming to depress even further the downward turn of her narrow lips. She removed her shawl and the long coat she wore, hung them with a slow deliberation behind the door, and placed her head against the rotting door frame, alarming her young son.

'Mam?'

Bridie turned round and gave him a weak smile.

'What d'you reckon, Mam?'

He nodded to the table. She moved slowly towards him, placing a hand on the table top to steady herself. For a few seconds, she stared at the dead pigeons, a joyless and stony expression on her face, before reaching down to pull him to her.

'Ee, love,' she said with a long, slow sigh. Her fingers were cold and damp against his skull.

He could feel her heart beating fast – thump-thump, thump-thump. She must be more grateful for the birds than even he'd expected.

'Mam. You're hurtin'.'

Her arm was forcing his head against her breast-bone, making him feel dizzy. When she let go, he looked up at her, and saw the tears streaming down her cheeks. 'There's enough for all three of us,' he said proudly. 'That's why I wouldn't come 'ome till I got three. One each, eh, Mam? What'll our Molly say, eh?'

He'd heard mothers, and women in general, cried when they were happy. Perhaps his sister would cry too when she saw the booty he'd brought home. It was a man's job, to provide for his womenfolk, and he was the only man in the house now.

'Aye, lad,' she sniffed. 'You've done us proud.'

Tommy smiled as she reached out and gently stroked his ruddy cheeks.

Two miles to the north of Wigan, on the edge of the small village of Standish, Arthur Morris's house lay in its own grounds overlooking – some would say overseeing – the valley where the Morris Colliery had been, until recently, the most pro-ductive pit in Wigan.

Only weeks before the dispute began, a huge block of cannel coal from the colliery had been transported across the Atlantic to become one of

Great Britain's star attractions at the Chicago World Fair, a source of wonderment to the thousands of visitors to the exhibition, whose fulsome encomiums had caused Arthur Morris's chest to swell with pride at what his company had produced. In one of the many speeches he made during the exhibition, the Americans failed to grasp his humour when he pointed out that his gigantic exhibit was being shown in Chicago, a place where the burning of coal fires had been prohibited to prevent the white façades of the exhibition palaces being stained with smoke.

'Bit late for the palaces in Wigan!' he had quipped, thus giving his American audience a quite erroneous impression of the town.

It had been therefore ironic that the subsequent article in the *Wigan Observer*, in which his Chicago speeches expounding on the dedication and resilience of his colliers were quoted at length, was followed a week later with a report of another speech, this time to the South Lancashire Coal Owners' Association calling for the same colliers to 'share in the bad times as well as the good.'

Now, that Chicago triumph was a euphoria consigned to history.

From the extensive gardens that sloped at the rear of the house, one could see plainly in the distance the two giant chimneys that stood at either end of the colliery, tall and indomitable sentinels looming over not only the head frame of the pit but also – and more symbolically – the rows of terraced houses that spread outwards from the outer edges of the pit, like the strands of a spider's web.

Strange, thought Brennan as he alighted from

the hackney carriage, *how fresh the air tastes up here,* despite the bitter cold and the fading afternoon light.

'Ten minutes,' he barked to the cab driver who had brought him from the station, a pasty-faced walrus who scowled his response by blowing into his hands.

Brennan walked along the snow-crusted drive and came to the front door, where he lifted an enormous knocker curiously shaped like a Davy lamp in heavy brass and slammed it twice against its rest. The loud echo it produced slightly unnerved him, as if its weighty announcement gave rude notice of the tidings he bore. Seconds later, a maid opened the door and gave him a small curtsy as he introduced himself.

'One moment, sir, if you please,' she said with a second curtsy before closing the door again and disappearing. He could hear firmer, heavier footsteps from beyond the door, which now swung open with a far greater sense of urgency.

A young man stood on the threshold. He was tall, mid-twenties, Brennan guessed, with dark features and a heavy set of eyebrows. The firm set of his jaw suggested a resoluteness that was tempered somewhat by the mildness in his eyes. 'I'm Andrew Morris, Sergeant. Have you found my father?'

The infinitesimal pause before the word 'found' imbued his question with a morbid prescience. He half-turned to acknowledge the presence of a tall, elegant woman behind him. Mrs Morris, Brennan presumed. She appeared to be walking with some difficulty, leaning on who he presumed was her personal maid.

'My mother's half-demented with worry. It's so unlike him to stay out all night. If he's been in an accident...' He let his voice trail off, his eyes registering the sombre but steady gaze that bore down on him. 'Please, Sergeant Brennan. This way.'

The young man led the way past his mother, who Brennan noticed was now trembling, her grip on the maid's shoulder tightening and causing the poor girl to wince. Once they were all ensconced in the small morning room beyond the stairs, Brennan wasted no time, directing his words to the one he deemed strong enough to bear the raw force of their meaning. 'It is my sad duty to inform you, Mr Morris, that your father has been the victim of a brutal assault...'

Before he could finish, he heard a muffled cough, then what sounded like a long, mournful sigh. He saw Mrs Morris grip her temples with both hands, every limb appearing to tremble with a growing lack of control.

'Mother!' Andrew Morris yelled.

She slumped forward, held steady by the alertness of her maid, who gently laid her onto a chair beside the door, her head lolling back loosely, like a rag doll torn by a child intent on mischief.

Molly Haggerty stood beneath the big lamp in Market Place. The yellow glow from the hissing gas cast a dim circle around her, affording light but no warmth. She held herself tight, pulling the flimsy shawl close to her head and burying her hands deep inside her skirt. Several beggars shuffled by, heads bowed, shoulders slumped, as

35

they made their way home, the day producing the same meagre results as the day before, and the day before that. Curses drifted skywards.

Like some bronchial behemoth, a large double-decker bogie car rattled past, shunted along by the smaller engine in front. It was barely half full, the few passengers on the lower deck giving her no more than a cursory glance. She gave the driver, standing by the throbbing engine whose belly was bursting with fiery hot steam, an envious look.

'Lucky swine!' she whispered to herself, her teeth chattering.

The driver swayed from side to side as the tram made its way towards Standishgate, and Molly diverted her gaze to the road beyond.

Where *was* he?

She would recognise that confident, jaunty gait of his anywhere. But he was nowhere to be seen.

And yet last night ... what had she done last night?

She shivered, casting the memory aside.

She glanced at the clock above the Legs of Man. Five-thirty. Half an hour late.

Molly bit her lip, a habitual action whenever she was worried, or nervous. She watched as the tram made a sudden descent, its squat chimney belching steam with a screech that made her jump, before it vanished over the brow of the hill. An agony of indecision swept through her. She needed to see him. To be reassured. A sudden fear swept through her, and she shivered once more.

What if she'd seen the last of him? There were men like that, she knew. Get what they want and then the thrill of the chase dies like a damp ember.

Was he capable of such falseness as that?

Suddenly she felt a hand rest itself on her shoulder, and warm breath on her neck. Her heart danced. Eagerly, she turned round.

But it wasn't him.

CHAPTER TWO

Brennan sat in the Crofter's Arms and stared gloomily at his frothing pint.

A few early customers were scattered around the long, narrow parlour room, but the atmosphere seemed muted, almost broody, as if the chill from outside had crept in through every crevice and settled itself on the room like a deadening frost. He knew why, of course. Normally, at this time, the place would be crowded with men, most of them miners and foundry men, who would see Sunday night as the last opportunity for a big drink before the monotony of work began again on the morrow. There would be yells, sudden bursts of chesty laughter, the occasional scuffle as a difference of opinion turned into something more physical, and he would even join in the banter himself, savouring their earthy, often lewd, humour.

Yet now the men who stood at the bar nursed half-pints and grievances, and spoke in low, conspiratorial tones, their heads bowed and ears turned to take in the whispered confidences.

They cast their eyes around the room, surveying him with a frigid courtesy. The dispute had rendered him an outsider, a representative of the forces of law, order, and capital. A row of pewter tankards hung unused on a polished wooden rack above the landlord's head, a sad reminder of their owners' absence. Empty spittoons stood at each end of the curved bar.

He thought of the sad place he had just left.

The maid had been dispatched to the kitchen for smelling salts. Young Morris had fussed around his mother, the sad news about his father being momentarily superseded by a greater concern for the living.

'Please, Mother,' he had said while stroking her head gently, 'please.'

Once the smelling salts had been successfully applied, the maid stood at a discreet distance and Mrs Morris finally opened her eyes.

'Andrew? Did he say...?' she stopped, giving her visitor a look of contempt for being the bearer of such awful news.

Brennan, who had been kneeling beside the prostrate woman in an almost reverential attitude and had felt the cold clamminess of her hands, stood up and took a deep breath. 'I'm afraid I must be the bearer of tragic news, ma'am. Your husband was found last night.'

'Found?' In spite of the frailty in her voice, her tone implied rebuke, anger and even a scintilla of hope at his unfortunate and ironic choice of word.

'The victim of an attack, ma'am. I'm afraid he is dead.'

She gave a short gasp, and held her hand to her throat.

'Where was this, Sergeant?' Andrew Morris glanced up.

'Scholes, sir.'

'Scholes?' Mrs Morris stretched the syllable to emphasise her disbelief. 'What on earth was he doing there...?'

Her son took hold of her hand, patting it gently to restore her circulation.

Brennan slowly shook his head. 'At the moment we have no idea. I thought perhaps you or your son...' He looked from one to the other, but registered only the mixture of grief and incomprehension on their faces.

'My mother is obviously in great distress, Sergeant.'

He turned to the maid, whose pallid hue betrayed both concern for her mistress and horror at the mention of death.

'Grace, stay with her. I won't be long.' Andrew Morris stood up. 'Sergeant?' He nodded to the door leading to the hallway.

'Of course,' Brennan said and turned to take his leave. 'My condolences, ma'am.'

But Mrs Morris had once more closed her eyes as Grace held her hands.

Out in the hallway, Andrew Morris gently closed the door and turned to face his visitor. 'You said an attack, Sergeant. Can you be more specific?'

Brennan held his gaze for a while before answering. 'He was stabbed, sir.'

His eyes widened in horror and disbelief. 'But ... Scholes?'

'Yes, sir. It does appear to be curious. Did he know anyone there?'

'Hardly. As far as I know he's never been to the place. It's hardly ... well, you know. We own several houses there, of course, pit houses, but my father wasn't in the habit of playing rent collector.'

Brennan nodded. 'Of course.'

He knew that many of the houses in Wigan, not only in Scholes but scattered around the entire borough, were either the property of the colliery owners or the mill owners. He'd always regarded it as a particularly convenient arrangement on their part. He paused before continuing.

'When did you last see your father, Mr Morris?'

Andrew Morris blinked, as if he realised the sad innuendo in the word 'last'. 'Yesterday evening. Before I went out. He was dining with us – that is, with myself, my mother and my uncle. Ambrose Morris. I presume you know of him.'

Brennan nodded once more. Ambrose Morris was the town's Member of Parliament.

'He returned to London this morning. He left early, not knowing my father hadn't returned.' He broke off. 'My God. He'll have to be informed.'

'Anyone else here last night?'

'The Coxes. James and Agnes. They were guests at dinner.'

'James Cox? The iron and steelworks owner?'

'Yes.'

Arthur Morris. Ambrose Morris. James Cox. *A powerful triumvirate indeed*, Brennan reflected.

'I don't suppose you have any idea who might have done such a thing?'

'It's very early in the investigation, sir.'

40

'You'll have no shortage of suspects. Not in Scholes. At a time like this.'

'No, sir.'

'So what happens now?'

'We'll need someone to identify the body, I'm afraid.'

The young man visibly shook. 'I see.'

'Shall we say eleven tomorrow morning? At the infirmary?'

'Yes. Yes, of course. It will be me, you understand, Sergeant? I couldn't possibly expect...'

He let his voice trail off, turning slightly to the closed door behind him. Both men could now hear the slow regular pulse of sobbing, the early stages of grief that would soon lead to angrier, more universal proclamations when grief turns to grievance.

'Well then, I shall intrude no longer.'

As he turned to go, Brennan paused. 'Oh, just one thing, Mr Morris. Might as well ask now.'

'Yes, Sergeant?'

'You say you all dined together last night. I gather your father received an unexpected letter.'

'So I'm told.'

'You weren't present when the letter arrived?'

Morris cast his eyes downwards. 'I had left before then.'

'Before your father?'

'I felt in need of some air. This wretched strike has set all our nerves on edge. At times the conversation around the table reached Olympian heights, and I had had rather enough ambrosia and nectar for one night.'

'Olympian heights?'

41

Andrew Morris blinked, as if he were suddenly conscious of a breach of etiquette. 'I simply wasn't in the mood for politics and business and the conflict they produce. So I left.'

'I see. What time was this?'

Morris narrowed his eyes. 'Is it important?'

'Just trying to work out a sequence of events, sir.'

'It must have been around eight-thirty.'

'Where did you go?'

'I've already told you, Sergeant. I went out.'

Brennan looked at him levelly for a few seconds, then told himself that now was not the time. 'What time did you return?'

'I really can't say. Before midnight I expect. The servants had gone to bed and I let myself in. I went straight to my room. It was this morning when I heard the commotion downstairs and my mother's raised voice that I realised something was wrong.' He swallowed hard before adding, 'Do you need to know what was served for breakfast?'

Now, as he sat alone in the Crofter's Arms and watched the frothy head of the beer break up, Michael Brennan frowned, struck by a sudden thought. *Why would someone leave a nice warm dinner to get some air, when it's snowing and freezing cold outside?*

'Waitin' for somebody, Moll?'

She gave a non-committal shrug and tried to hold his gaze. The glare from the gas lamp above them caused a tiny blue flame to flicker in his eyes, like the dance of a frenzied devil. The same intensity of passion was there, the same hunger in his eyes that was always kept at bay by some mastery of will, suffusing his features with a melancholy blend of loss and bitterness.

She had loved Frank Latchford, once upon a time.

'I am. I mean, I was.'

'Who?'

One of the qualities she had admired in him was his directness. Two years ago, before the strike and Frank's part in it, the future had seemed as structured and as linear as the Leeds–Liverpool Canal, a course leading inexorably to marriage, children and a comfortable home. 'It's what I want,' he had said with the same firmness and conviction of tone, the same underlying sense of passion, that he used when making his fiery speeches to thousands.

It had also been what Molly Haggerty had wanted, once.

She gave a furtive glance behind her, just in case even now *he* was rushing past the beggars to take her in his arms with a kiss and a panted apology.

A romantic nonsense, she knew, for that was the one thing he wouldn't or couldn't do. The beggars shuffled down the street with their hunched shoulders, but there was no biblical parting of the waves as he came rushing through their midst. She smiled, but it was a self-mocking gesture, and turned her gaze back to Frank, holding his large, rough-hewn face in focus. He had stubble below his thick, dark moustache, and his heavy-lidded eyes were rendered even darker by the rim of his cap. There was no coal dust now flecking his features. He hadn't seen coal dust in months.

43

'Just a friend,' she said, hugging herself to show that she wouldn't be waiting much longer and it wasn't of any great consequence anyway.

He was on the verge of saying something, but licked his lips instead, choosing silence over interrogation.

'How've you been keepin'?' She tried to keep her tone neutral, just in case he misinterpreted her question.

'Badly. But not as bad as some. Fished another poor sod out last week.'

No further explanation was needed. The canal or the River Douglas – both of them had cold, welcoming depths.

'Your friend,' he said, looking over her head and scanning the darkening figures behind her, 'she's late. You'll catch your bloody death out 'ere.'

Involuntarily she smiled at his presumption that her friend was a lass – perhaps an error calculated to elicit a correction. Instead, she said, 'Aye. I'd best be off.'

'I'll walk you.'

Quickly, before she could protest, he had slipped an arm through hers and she allowed herself to be escorted at least part of the way. Besides, if the one she had been waiting for were to come tearing along right now and see them both arm in arm from across the street, why, it would serve him bloody well right, wouldn't it?

'You ill, Mam?'

Tommy Haggerty's voice quivered. He had been five when his dad had died twice. The first time – the night he failed to come back from the pit – had been something that had transformed itself into the stuff of nightmares, and he often imagined, in the black quiet of the night, that he himself were down there in the dust-filled mine, although wherever he looked as he scrambled through the dust, no matter how many grinning corpses he turned over and lit with his lamp, he could never find where his dad was lying. He always had the feeling that he was just round the next corner, but when he scratched and dug his way round, more often than not the only thing he came across was the twisted body of a pit pony, its broad teeth bared wildly in a dreadful grimace of death. In the worst of the nightmares he could even hear its plaintive, pain-wracked whinnying and see the red gums clamping on black air, and blood, speckled with coal dust, slithering down its teeth.

He could still hear the whispers outside the front door on the night of the explosion, whispers that grew into voices – raised voices, angry voices and crying, sobbing voices. Then the sound of clogs, hundreds and hundreds of clogs rattling down the street with the screams of women and the cries of girls and the terrified yells from children seeing their mothers rushing out of houses with tears down their cheeks and the doors slamming and the curses and the prayers and the fear and the panic gouged onto every face as the tide of bodies poured its way out of Scholes to the gates of the Morris pit.

What was more frightening though, even than the screams of the women, was the silence as they all stood there at the pit gates, waiting, listening to the sounds of digging, digging, followed by billows of dust and the rescue men staggering through the clouds coughing and retching and cursing. A hollow shout in the dark, echoed by another. Then the whispered news, passed with agonising slowness along the lines of dark, hunched figures, the lift of the head and the wringing of hands and the constant sound of women sniffling and old men coughing, and then back the men would go, hauling their picks and their shovels once more into the rattling cage. Then the silence again, and the vigil, and the pale coming of the dawn.

Tommy remembered, too, the slow walk back, the crunch of his clogs on the cobbles, no screaming now, just small clusters of friends who muttered and urged and consoled, their voices sounding dull and heavy in the mist that swirled around their feet. Then the three of them dozing before the flames and jumping with every slam of a front door, every distant scream along the street, until he was curling up at his mam's feet the following night. Molly, his elder sister, with her arms wrapped tightly round him, her tears making his cheeks damp and cold, and whispering into his ear that everything would be all right and Dad would be with them soon.

She'd lied. They all seemed to lie back then.

He'll be back before you know it, Tommy Tin Can. Just as soon as the rescue team can dig him out.

Only they didn't.

Not then.

Later that same night, as he'd crept downstairs, he saw his mam drop to her knees in front of the statue of the Holy Virgin on the mantelpiece and lift her hands to the ceiling, mouthing silent words to heaven. For a second, as he looked up, he was sure he saw the statue darken as a shadow flitted past, and he thought it was Dad's soul flying upwards, flapping black wings against a bright full moon, just as Father Brady told them at school.

It had been a week later when they got the knock on the door to tell them his dad's body had been found and was now lying wrapped on a coal-hut table waiting for them. That was when his dad had died a second time, and the three of them started grieving all over again. They'd said it was something called *firedamp* that caused the blast and killed his dad and all the others. But what Tommy had never been able to understand was how fire – *damp* fire – could even burn properly, let alone cause a huge blast. Fire was hot, and damp was wet. Even he knew that.

He had wanted so much to wash his dad as he saw his broken, blackened remains lying there on the table, the way he always did when he came home from the pit and his mam took the tin bath from the peg behind the door. Then the solemn ceremony as his dad took off all of his clothes and Tommy was given the great task of scrubbing his back spotless, rubbing so hard to get rid of those tiny black grains that seemed to be lodged stubbornly beneath his white skin. And every time, his dad had splashed his face with the blackened water telling him it'd be his turn soon enough, and then there'd be that huge great laugh as he wiped the soap from his eyes.

Now, after she'd taken the pigeon pie out of the oven beside the fire, after she'd served up three steaming hot plates and put one back in the stove for when Molly got back from her friend's, his mam simply sat there and gazed into the dancing flames. People who didn't eat died. That's what she'd always told him. He didn't want his mam to die as well. So he repeated the question. 'Mam. You ill?'

Bridie blinked and looked at her son. 'What?'

'I said are you ill?' He pointed at her plate with a knife coated with slivers of white flesh. 'You normally werry that.'

'No. I'm just ... feelin' a bit off. Heartburn, I reckon.'

Tommy's eyes widened. *Heartburn.* He threw a quick glance at the fire, tried not to imagine his mam's heart sizzling on the coals.

Just then, the front door flew open and Molly entered. A cold blast followed her, carrying tiny flakes of snow that melted on the banister rail. Tommy felt relieved. His sister would soon make Mam's heart stop burning.

Molly scraped the untouched pigeon onto her little brother's plate and watched as he began eating. Her mother was busy at the sink, her head bowed so low that in the flickering of the coal flames she looked headless.

'You all right, Mam?' she asked. 'Only you seem a bit quiet.'

She moved over to join her mother at the sink, lowering her voice to keep their conversation from little Tommy.

'Oh I'm fine, child. You heard about the poor chap they found this morning.'

Molly looked quickly back at her brother. 'I saw

the police in the backs.'

Bridie wiped her hands on a cloth, then walked past her daughter and picked up the poker in the hearth, ramming it into the dying coals, hot mis-shapen pebbles clanging in the ash pan beneath. From the chimney breast, they could hear a howling from the bitter wind outside. Black spots that had once been snow now stained the hearth.

'They say it was Arthur Morris, child.'

Molly gave a short gasp and put her hand to her mouth.

She watched as her brother thrust the knife into the remaining piece of meat, the thickest one, saving the best until last. As he cut through, his knife caught on a shard of bone, and he sawed and sawed until the blade caused the bone to snap. Then he sucked on thick flesh.

At eleven-fifteen the next morning, Andrew Morris stood on the steps of the Royal Albert Edward Infirmary, watched the swirling snow beyond the covered entrance and inhaled the cold air deeply. He felt it catch against his throat, and imagined its cleansing properties frosting over the sad and impersonal horror of what he had just seen. The sight of his father laid out like that, so quiet, so unimportant...

Immediately he regretted the thought. *Unimportant.*

Twenty years ago, as a small child, he'd stood a few yards away from where he was now and stared in wide-eyed wonder at the Prince of Wales and Princess Alexandra as they declared the new infirmary open. He couldn't hear all of what His

Royal Highness was saying, but he did catch the words 'splendid new building' uttered in rich rounded vowels. He'd been standing beside his mother that day, holding onto her gloved hand and marvelling at the colourful array of royal blue feathers streaming from her hat. Like a wild and beautiful bird, he thought at the time. My mother, the peacock.

Standing on the steps just behind their Royal Highnesses, his father and Uncle Ambrose looked splendid in their morning dress, bowing their heads and smiling every time the prince uttered some whispered aside.

Splendid. And *important.*

He hadn't been old enough to feel pride in seeing his uncle, as the town's recently elected Member of Parliament, deliver the welcoming address to their Royal Highnesses, nor to appreciate the great honour bestowed upon his younger self by the Prince of Wales himself who, upon being presented with 'this young nephew of mine, sir' responded by leaning down and giving Andrew's chin a rub and declaring, 'What a capital little fellow!' But he had been young enough to enjoy the many festivities that followed. After the 'Grand Opening Ceremony' he'd spent much of the time watching cycle races, wrestlers, military bands and, his secret favourite, the fairy grotto where he'd even played chase with some of the children from the labouring classes: grubby, foul-mouthed and utterly fascinating urchins who had sneaked in unseen by the large police guard.

For years afterwards, he'd listened to the story of the Royal Banquet at Haigh Hall, where the

50

royal couple had stayed. Of the Prince's amazement at the gift of a plaque to their majesties carved out of black cannel coal.

'Remarkable piece of work!' the prince had declared.

'We *mined* it for you, your Royal Highness, now you must *mind* it for us!' his father announced to the amusement of all.

The Prince of Wales had held his stomach, so heartily did he laugh at the drolleries. And soon the entire banqueting hall was roaring with laughter.

'Not everybody can say they've made the heir to the throne laugh at a piece of coal!' was to be his father's climactic comment as he told and retold the historic moment.

Now, Andrew gazed out at the snow-filled courtyard, the fresh ruts of carriage wheels and the people who tried to keep their footing as they passed by with their shoulders hunched, smothered by their own private concerns. He blinked away the memories.

'Is there anything I can do, sir?'

Andrew started a little as the words broke into his thoughts. 'Sergeant Brennan. I thought you were still...'

He gave a curt nod behind the policeman in the direction of the infirmary's interior, and the small, claustrophobic room they had left.

'Few formalities, a signature,' Brennan replied. 'I apologise again for having to put you through that. It's never a pleasant duty, even when circumstances are more...'

'Natural?'

Brennan nodded.

'It's strange,' said Andrew, allowing his gaze to drift beyond the main gates of the infirmary, across Wigan Lane to the entrance of Haigh Hall, the ancestral home to the 26th Earl of Crawford and one of his late father's friends and business rivals. 'How peaceful he looked.' With a long, slow sigh, he said quietly, '"Fear no more the heat of the sun, nor the winter's furious rages."' Then he put a hand to his forehead, pressing his fingers against the temples. 'There are numerous arrangements I have to make. The undertaker, the funeral, mourning cards, and a hundred and one things I'm sure have slipped my mind. Shakespeare's words focus on the dead, and not the consequences for the living.'

Brennan looked at the bereaved son closely. It was a curious thing to say.

'It will certainly be interesting,' Andrew said with a wry smile.

'What will, Mr Morris?'

'The funeral.'

'Interesting?'

'He wasn't the most popular figure in town, was he? My father was by far the most vocal of advocates supporting the wage reduction. I realise they are suffering great privations. And with winter now upon us...' He turned and faced the detective. 'I wonder if the townsfolk will – you know – express their disapproval in some way.'

'I doubt it, sir. Whatever people feel, they have a deep sense of decency.'

'Yes. Of course. Everything bows to death, doesn't it? I just had a nightmare vision – crowds hissing, missiles flying, horses bolting – you can imagine.'

Brennan pursed his lips. It was time for pragmatism. 'You'll appreciate that it's my duty to find out who committed this heinous crime.'

'Of course.'

'And I'll therefore need to visit you, and speak not only to yourself but also your mother, your uncle – when he returns from London – and, of course, your staff.'

Andrew flinched at the prospect of his mother facing what would inevitably be questions of the most distressing nature. But he merely nodded. 'We sent word to my uncle yesterday, Sergeant. When he returns, as I'm sure he will as soon as is practicable, I'll let you know.'

'That would be kind, Mr Morris. I have already made arrangements to speak with Mr James Cox at his residence.'

'It seems rather excessive, doesn't it?'

'What does?'

Andrew cleared his throat. 'It's just, well, the fact that the Coxes dined with us two nights ago can surely have no bearing on what happened to my father after he left. Can it?'

Brennan gave him a cold smile. 'One of the things my chief constable finds annoying is what he calls my overzealousness. I would have thought that to be an admirable quality in a detective, wouldn't you say so?'

Andrew gazed into his eyes for a few seconds, then lifted his head to look up at the entrance to the infirmary. 'He made the Prince of Wales laugh, you know.' Without offering any sort of explanation for such a curious statement, he bade Brennan farewell, turned and walked away, his shoulders stooped into the bitter chill of the morning.

The snow fell heavily. Through the half-moon windows high above the machinery, the girls cast the occasional furtive glance at the thick flakes caught up in the angry wind, seeming to dance like frenzied souls leering at them before swirling their way from the leaden sky to earth.

The noise in Weaving Room Number Two at Ryland's Mill was deafening, and yet a stranger visiting the room would be amazed to see the girls working the machinery, talking to each other with apparent ease and understanding. This mythical stranger would not, of course, realise how the girls had developed their unique way of conversing that transcended the roar of the shuttles and the constant whirr of belts and overhead pulleys. Lip-reading, and responding in exaggerated mime – or *mee-mawing* as it was known locally – was second nature to the girls, and it even came in useful beyond the factory gates, where they could communicate across a crowded pub and swap the latest gossip without leaving the side of their undiscerning escorts.

Today, with ten minutes to go before their break, they took great delight in ruining the character of Mr Alfred Birch as he walked along the row upon row of weaving machines, keeping a careful and admonitory eye on every single one of the girls for what he always referred to in his monthly reports to Mr Ryland as their 'congenital idleness'. His narrow moustache did nothing to hide the sharp overhang of his nose, which led inevitably to the soubriquet 'Beaky'.

One of the girls, however, took no part in the ribaldry, keeping her head bowed low and giving her machine her fullest attention. As the over-looker walked past clasping his thin hands behind his back, a clump of soiled calico flew across and struck the girl in the chest. She looked up at the one who had thrown it, a pert, flighty little girl of fourteen who mouthed the words *'What's up?'*

Molly shook her head and bent to pick up the calico. She placed it in the waste box beside her.

'You been skrikin' Moll?' the girl's lips asked.

'Mind your own business.'

'Big Frank been botherin' you again?'

'No.'

'Well, why have you been skrikin' then?'

'I've not.'

'Tell Beaky you're ill.'

'May, just leave me alone, eh?'

Molly sighed and looked at the overlooker's straight back, his head perched aloft like a falcon sniffing warm flesh. *'I'm all right,'* she said finally, and let her gaze drift upwards at the thickening storm.

CHAPTER THREE

James Cox was the sole proprietor of the Cox Iron and Steel Company. His sprawling acreage south of Wigan was one of the most highly productive works in the country, producing not only equipment for the mining industry but also locomotives, wagons, canal boats, textile machinery, and, six months previously, had been awarded the hugely remunerative contract to provide supplementary materials for the final stages of the new Blackpool Tower which was due to open in the summer of 1894.

As Brennan stood in the small morning room waiting for Cox to arrive, he gazed out of the large window that overlooked a long, sweeping garden at the end of which two children – a girl and a boy of around the same age of six or seven – were busy constructing a snowman. They were wrapped in thick coats and mufflers and seemed to be enjoying the falling snow.

Along the small overmantel surrounding the empty grate he saw several framed photographs of these same children in studied poses, their gilt frames resting on a dull purple fabric embroidered with tiny floral swirls that ran the length of the mantel.

'To scold or not to scold, eh?'

Brennan swung round to see James Cox standing with one hand on the open door. He was tall, heading inexorably towards corpulent middle age, and sported a well-trimmed beard beneath fleshy jowls. Although Brennan had seen Cox on several occasions, this was the first time he had actually spoken with him, and he was immediately struck by the bluff friendliness of the man, who now strolled over to stand beside him at the window. There was a faint smell of toilet soap on his skin.

Cox smiled, understanding Brennan's confusion, and nodded to the innocent scene beyond the window.

'The twins. At this time of the year it's always bloody difficult being a father, eh? Tell me, Detective Sergeant ... what did Hastings say your name was?'

'Brennan, sir.'

'Aye. That's it. Now tell me, should I let 'em stay outside and get sodden to the skin in all that bloody snow, or should I wield my heavy hand and get 'em in out of harm's way, eh?'

Brennan shrugged. 'Fresh air does them good. And I can see they're well wrapped up.'

'Bloody good advice an' all. In my opinion there's far too much mollycoddlin' goes on. It's what makes children weak and sluggish, don't you think?'

Without waiting for an answer, he went back and closed the door gently, then walked over to one of the two armchairs in the room. With a lazy wave of the hand he invited his visitor to occupy the other, with only a small table between them. 'My wife conducts all her business in here, so we'd best not muck it up, eh?'

The man seemed pleasant enough, Brennan

57

thought, but the lightness in his voice was belied by the shrewd way he looked at him, rather as if he were weighing him up and considering which way to continue with the meeting – with bluffness and bonhomie, or sharpness and condescension? Of course, reflected Brennan, this was a man who had built up a powerful business with an international reputation. Such men had a strength they sometimes liked to conceal.

'Now that we're both settled, so to speak, perhaps you can get on with business, Sergeant Brennan.'

'Yes, sir. It concerns the incident in Scholes on Saturday night.'

Cox lowered his voice, glancing quickly towards the window. 'The murder of Arthur Morris.'

A plain speaker, then.

Brennan cast aside the kid gloves, but dropped his own voice to barely more than a whisper, just the same.

'He was found stabbed to death in an alleyway. Not long after he broke up the dinner party you were attending.'

Cox gave a wan smile. '"Dinner party" makes it sound grander than it was. Just old friends sharing old tales. Ambrose was going back to London on an early train. We like to meet up now and again; keep up with all the rumours from that bloody cesspit in Westminster.'

'You've known both Arthur and his brother for a long time?'

'Thirty odd years.'

'This must then be difficult for you, I know, but...'

'Not half as difficult as it must be for Prudence.'

'Mrs Morris?'

'Aye. It'll hit her hard, will this. She's not in the best of health, as you've no doubt seen for yourself.'

'I have indeed. Now, if you could tell me anything at all about that night...'

'Such as?'

'Arthur Morris. What sort of mood was he in?'

Cox laughed mirthlessly. 'Same bloody mood he was always in. Cantankerous. Unyielding. Treats advice the way a blast furnace treats coke.'

'There was a difference of opinion?'

'That suggests a discussion, Sergeant. There was no bloody discussion with Arthur, not when it came to this godawful strike. His way or no bloody way. That was Arthur Morris's negotiating stance and the devil take the hindmost.'

'You didn't agree with him?'

Cox flickered an angry glance at him before redirecting his gaze to the garden, where the squeals of his children could clearly be heard. He blinked a few times before replying. 'Neither of us did. Ambrose informed us that the president of the Board of Trade is furious with Arthur and the rest of the owners after the catastrophe of Westminster Palace Hotel.'

Brennan had read about the unproductive meeting in London between the owners and the miners' representatives, and the 'generous' offer from the owners to reduce the miners' wages not by the original figure of twenty-five per cent that they had insisted upon, but by the renewed figure

59

of fifteen per cent, an offer they considered the height of generosity and which was rejected summarily by the miners.

'So the talk around the table was of the progress of the strike?'

'*Progress!* That's a bloody good one! Ambrose told his brother in no uncertain terms that things are coming to a head in Parliament. He's heard a whisper, only a whisper, mind, that Gladstone himself intends to take charge. Imagine that, Sergeant – an industrial dispute being grabbed by the scruff of the neck by our very own prime minister. What next, eh? Holidays for the undeserving poor?'

Brennan allowed the revolutionary concept to settle between them like dust before responding. 'Were you there when Mr Morris received the letter?'

Cox's eyes narrowed. 'That awful banging, you mean?'

'Banging?'

'Young Andrew had made his excuses – I think he was either embarrassed by the forthrightness of the discussion or angry at his father for his stubbornness, I don't know, but he'd got up, made his excuses and gone. About ten minutes later – give or take – we retired to the smoking room while the ladies stayed behind. Ambrose went to bring a couple of particularly fine Cubans from his room while Arthur and I settled ourselves ready for a good smoke. No arguing in that room, wouldn't be proper, y'see? Time and a place and all that. Ambrose was halfway down the stairs clutching his box of cigars when the most awful banging was heard from the front door. Arthur and I both rushed out into the hallway just as one of the maids ran to the door and swung it open, but there was no bugger out there. Bloody ghost, eh?'

'Could whoever had been knocking there have simply run off?'

'Must have done. Ambrose says he thought he caught sight of someone skulking through the bushes at the side of the driveway, but he couldn't be sure from where he was standing on the stairs. Neither could the maid.'

'I see. What happened then?'

'The maid pointed to the letter box. They've got a sort of cage-like contraption for catching the letters. There was a letter lying there. She swore it hadn't been there before.'

'Did Arthur Morris open it?'

'He did.'

'What did he say?'

'Nothing much. Muttered something about having to go out and would I mind? I said of course not and asked him what was the matter.'

'What did he say to that?'

'Told me to mind my own bloody business while I still had one.'

Cox had spoken that last sentence with bitterness.

'What exactly did he mean by that?'

Cox shrugged. 'Some peevish reference to Blackpool, I expect.'

'Blackpool?'

A long, heavy sigh. He stood up and went to the window, at first watching the twins at play, then rattling on the glass with his knuckles. 'In!' he shouted with a backward jerk of his right hand. 'Now!' He spoke, almost to himself. 'I won't have that sort of behaviour, not to be tolerated.'

Brennan was perplexed but stood up quickly. 'Blackpool, Mr Cox?'

He shook his head and stroked his beard. Then he turned round and faced Brennan. 'If this strike continues, my foundries will be permanently damped down. I'll lose the contract for the new tower. A large part of the discussion that night was about exactly that – me, minding my own business.'

A dark gloom had settled upon his features. *A sign perhaps of the tremendous financial pressure he must be under,* Brennan reflected. There were gradations of suffering wrought by this dispute.

Then, as quickly as it descended, the gloom lifted once more as the door to the morning room burst open and the two children ran into the room, bringing with them the freshness, the chill and the exhilaration of outside. Snow clung to their outdoor coats and their faces were ruddy and glowing.

'Now, you young scamps!' Cox roared, the benign father once more. 'Can't you see I'm entertaining a guest?'

'Are you singing a song?' asked the girl.

'Or playing the piano?' asked the boy, whereupon they both giggled.

Cox beamed. 'Sometimes having a governess for their education is a bad idea, Sergeant. Gives 'em a way with words, eh?'

Brennan smiled back. The twins bowed exaggeratedly to their father's guest and scurried from the room, pleading starvation as an excuse to seek out the kitchen and the hot biscuits they had smelt earlier.

During summer and autumn, the girls had grown accustomed to leaving through the mill gate, taking a right turn and strolling, arm in arm, towards the entrance to Mesnes Park, where they would sit on the grass, uncork their billy cans of cold tea, and eat the buttered bread that constituted their lunch.

The early onset of winter had curtailed that. Today, for instance, the weather was so bad, the snow falling so heavily, that a stroll anywhere would render their clogged feet soaking wet and offer them nowhere to sit and talk. Instead, they sat in the covered entrance to the mill, or in the cloakrooms, or in the long draughty corridors that led to weaving rooms, card rooms, drawing rooms and mule rooms, anywhere, in fact, that offered any sort of shelter, if not warmth, from the snow. They were even prepared to endure the tiny motes of dust and cloth that swirled around the entire mill like some sort of internally produced snow, accepting the occasional crunch when they ate as dust settled unseen on their buttered bread.

In the chill of the corridor, May Calderbank sat beside Molly and watched her pick at the thick crust she had obviously no intention of eating.

'What's Beaky's wife like, Moll?'

Molly said nothing.

'I reckon she's big and fat and gives him hell-fire, that's what I reckon.' Her eyes glistened.

Molly gave a small laugh. 'Why?'

''Cos he hates us girls. Hates us 'cos his wife hates him. It's like gettin' his own back.'

'You're fourteen, May. Those are grown-up thoughts.'

'I've got eyes. And I think he's picked on at home. And for his wife to pick on him she'd have to be bigger than him, see? Else he'd be able to leather her.'

Molly looked at the young girl and blinked slowly. Five years separated them. But it was hard for Molly these days to remember if she had ever been fourteen.

'And I know summat's upset you an' all,' the girl went on, buoyed by her logic. 'Your eyes are red. That's not the snow.'

'No.'

'So is it Big Frank?' May shuffled closer to her. Her large brown eyes narrowed, and a frown creased her forehead in an effort to bestow a con-fidential gravitas on her next words. 'Y'know, I've heard some of the lasses talkin' about 'im. They reckon you were daft throwin' him over. They say he's got a golden tongue on 'im. They reckon when he speaks at them public meetings he...'

'It's nowt to do with Frank Latchford.'

'He didn't take it well, did he?' May went on, unable as yet to distinguish between truth and deception. 'When you ended it?'

'That was months ago.'

'My mam reckons men have long memories. Says they never forget. Says they have the memory of an elephant and the brain of a cock-roach. Or is it t'other way round?'

Molly handed her the buttered crust. 'Here.

This'll keep you quiet.'

May took the food but wasn't ready to let the subject drop just yet. 'And the appetites of pigs. My mam says the one word men don't understand is "no".' She giggled, suddenly a little girl again. 'You can hear everything, can't you? Through the walls I mean. Don't know about men being pigs, you should hear me mam grunt and snort when she gets goin'!'

At last she took off a chunk of bread and began to chew, a look of pride and maturity on her face.

Donald Monroe, MB and CM (Edin.) had been house surgeon at the Royal Albert Edward Infirmary for over fifteen years. He had seen great changes in medical practice in his time, not least of which was the development of anaesthetic and antiseptic treatment. But the concomitant rise in diseases such as tuberculosis and rickets often made him feel there was a malign presence manufacturing new diseases whenever a medical breakthrough was announced. Such thoughts stamped his sombre persona, tempered with a genuine sadness whenever he treated any poor child whose lungs were failing, or whose limbs were twisted and malformed.

His standing within the community was such that those who recognised him found it hard to stop themselves from bowing whenever he passed them in the street. Perhaps, he told his amused dinner guests on more than one occasion, unlike priests and vicars, he had the unique, ectoplasmic aura of both saving lives and exploring the secrets of death. 'A heady cocktail,' he would add with a sly wink.

At the moment he held Arthur Morris's heart in his gloved hands. Detective Sergeant Brennan, who was standing on the other side of the stone slab, was reminded of the painting that had hung above his mother's bed ever since he could remember – the *Sacred Heart of Jesus*, exposed beneath a glowing open chest with the Lord's right hand extended higher than the left as if in a gesture of protest and supplication.

'You can see the damage it caused. Right here.'

Dr Monroe held it towards him, as if it were a particularly weighty trout he'd just caught.

Brennan gazed down at the fatty object that glistened sickeningly beneath the bright glare of the star gaslight, and noted its intricate network of veins and arteries punctured at its base by a stab wound.

'Quite fortunate, in a way,' Monroe said cheerily.

'Fortunate?'

'If the wound had penetrated the apex of the heart, well then, death can take painfully longer. With each beat, you see, a little blood seeps out until it fills the chest and suffocates the victim. No, this fellow was fortunate on that score. You, on the other hand, are unfortunate. Perhaps if he had survived until the priest discovered him, he might have given a description of his assailant – even a name.'

He placed the organ gently into a bowl, and Brennan watched it settle into position, as if it still held some trace of life. He cast a quick glance to the doorway, beyond which Constable Jaggery was seated on the long wooden bench normally used by exhausted theatre staff. He had flatly refused to join his sergeant, arguing that he had no desire to see his breakfast again.

'Long-bladed knife. Narrow, tapering point. I don't suppose you have retrieved the murder weapon?'

Brennan shook his head. He held out no real hope of ever finding it.

'He's been stabbed just the once, but that was sufficient.'

'Was it a frenzied attack?'

'Not necessarily. There are no defence wounds on the victim's arms, see?' he held up two white, limp arms, 'Which suggests the attack was sudden and completely unexpected. One thrust – but a deadly one.'

'More than one attacker?'

'Impossible to say for sure. One would expect some bruising around the arms or neck where the victim might have been restrained while the blow was struck, but there are no such indications.' Dr Monroe shook his head. 'The more I see of death, Sergeant, the more I despair of life...'

He let his cheerless philosophy hang in the air.

Brennan gave a silent nod. He recognised and felt an affinity with the sentiment. 'What about the time of death?'

Monroe took hold of a length of pipe to which a section of India rubber hose had been attached. He then proceeded to wash away the waste matter that had gathered in the hollow groove that ran the length of the stone slab.

'Sometime between ten and twelve, I should say, but given the very low temperature and the

67

rapid onset of cadaveric rigidity...' His words were drowned out by the thick gurgling from the grating at the lower end of the groove that led to the waste pipe.

Once outside, Brennan gave his constable the gist of the preliminary findings of the post-mortem.

'So meladdo finds himself in an alleyway up Scholes,' Jaggery began after some period of thought. 'An' I know it's a bugger him bein' in Scholes in the first place, Sergeant, but it's one thing *bein'* there, an' another thing altogether bein' in an *alleyway* up there. Why, it's like hidin' in a bonfire just waitin' for the match an' then crawlin' right into the middle.'

Indeed it was, Brennan reflected. *Why Scholes? And why in God's name an alleyway in Scholes?*

They both pulled the collars of their greatcoats around their faces to ward off the bitter cold. The snow was coming down so thickly now it was difficult to see any great distance. Once on the main road, they steeled themselves for the trudge down Wigan Lane into town and the relative warmth of the police station.

Very few carriages were around, the conditions rendering any sort of vehicular travel a serious risk. Even the trams were now few and far between. The sky was heavy and leaden, and lamps were already lit inside every shop they passed, even though it was early afternoon.

Outside the entrance to the Griffin public house they saw a long queue of men, women and children, the children dressed in nothing much better than rags. Many of them wore their mothers' scarves and shawls around them to ward off the cold, while the mothers themselves stood as close to the pub wall as they could. Their menfolk were beside them, heads held high and defiant despite the snow sticking to their threadbare coats. One child reached down to mould a snowball and was about to hurl it at another child a few yards ahead in the queue, but a snapped command from a distinctly unamused father, quickly followed by a clip around the ear, brought about a surly quiescence.

'Poor sods,' Constable Jaggery mumbled as they passed the long queue.

'Be the only food some of them will have all day,' Brennan added.

There were several similar scenes being replayed throughout the borough: soup kitchens in pubs, church halls, temperance bars and Mission Halls. He thought of his own son, and how fortunate they were that he was employed, and earning. To imagine little Barry wracked with hunger and clutching his gut in the middle of the night.

Through a window, he caught a glimpse of the landlord standing behind the bar in the vault, ladling hot steaming soup into the row upon row of proffered bowls, and the sparkle of gratitude in the children's eyes as they pushed themselves from the serving area to enjoy their meal. It was now common knowledge throughout the borough that the publicans of the region had, by and large, provided basic food for a large proportion of the populace, and the Miners' Federation had promised their unstinting support would not be forgotten.

'Damn this bloody strike,' he said to himself, realising as he said it that it was the strike itself doing the damning.

Ambrose Morris MP sat in the first-class carriage of the LNWR Railway, and stared out of the window at the fields covered in snow. He was an imposing man, tall, broad-shouldered and be-whiskered, with a pair of steel-blue eyes that served him well in committee. Many who knew him only slightly or by reputation saw the elegantly dressed exterior and judged him a dandy, and it was true that he took great pains with his appearance. He liked the sharp cut of a well-made bespoke suit, the elegance of a dark waistcoat offsetting a fine silk shirt, and the sober formality of a frock coat. Indeed, he looked down at the coat he was now wearing and nodded his approval – it wouldn't do to arrive at the station like some holidaymaker, with his brother having suffered such a grievous end.

To think, only a few short months ago Arthur had been filled with a transatlantic optimism when he returned from the Chicago World Fair laden with gifts for himself, Andrew and Pru-dence. He gazed down at the black hessian boots his brother had bought him in Chicago.

'Hyer Boots from Kansas, Ambrose!' Arthur had boasted proudly when he unwrapped them. 'Show *them* to your fine friends in the House!'

He smiled wanly at the memory, recalling the expression on Lord Salisbury's face when he was informed of their provenance, giving Ambrose the soubriquet of Buffalo Bill, despite Ambrose's objection on the grounds that they were unembel-lished with fanciful swirls of any description and were damned comfortable, thank you very much. Still, everyone thought it was a great jape.

Thoughts of the Party Leader reminded him of the excitement, the frustration, of Westminster. In recent months he had been encouraged by the depositions of several of his constituents who hailed from the Emerald Isle and were filled with the fervour of hope that Mr Gladstone's Home Rule Bill would at last be able to breathe above the waters of denial and procrastination, and that the Lords would for once forego its drowning. He had made what he considered to be intelligent and constructive speeches during the debates, even defying his own party on the issue and relishing the fight. But once again the Bill had been defeated and Gladstone had failed in his mission to 'pacify Ireland'.

Suddenly, as the wintry countryside rattled by, clouded occasionally by billows of steam from the engine ahead, he felt a wave of guilt fill him almost with despair. To think of politics at a time like this...

His eyes, that had flashed defiance and challenge across the floor of the House and even, at heated moments, turned on declaimers seated alongside him in his own party, now looked distant, uncommunicative, an impression reinforced by the redness around the rims and the heavy lids that hung mournfully below the curved arch of his brows.

In summer, this was a pleasant journey. The gently undulating countryside, the higgledy-piggledy hedgerows and winding country lanes would fill him with a *joie de vivre* that was difficult, if not impossible, to put into words. It was, he sup-

71

posed, something akin to identity. It was the land.

Something his great friend Sir James Acland, himself professor of the Royal College of Surgeons, once said, came back to him now. They had been cycling around the new velodrome at Herne, both founding members of the Westminster Cycling Club, and the conversation had moved along metaphysical lines. 'You coal owners are explorers, Ambrose, just like us,' Acland once reasoned. 'Like surgeons, you know the land with an intimacy far from the remit of those farming the land or quarrying rock. Farmers caress the flesh and crop it like barbers, and the quarrymen, well let's say they perform minor surgery – but you, my friend, cut deep. To bring to the surface a mineral that has never seen the light of day ... why, it is surely reasonable to compare the entire process with the miracle of birth itself?'

Thus, in the reverie inspired by steam locomotion, and a tedious journey from the capital, Ambrose Morris would normally spend his hours travelling north.

Today, he thought about the brother he had lost, the brother who had been his youthful companion so long ago, in the days when they lay spreadeagled beneath their father's billiard table and played endless games of Nine Men's Morris.

Why is childhood such a fascinating and yet melancholy place to visit? he wondered. A dark cave of craggy outcrops of rock, occasionally illuminated by some phosphorescence, a sudden memory that glows and is gone.

What were your final moments like, Arthur? What thoughts flashed through your mind when the fatal blow was struck?

He bit his lower lip and tried to banish morbid speculation from his mind, but it would not leave.

Perhaps, in those last seconds of life, you left the brutality of that dreadful place and returned to childhood, to the nursery we shared, the tiny wooden figures we carved for our Noah's Ark and the songs we learnt for spellings:

'A was an apple that grew on a tree, B was a new boat that will hold you and me, C was the cat that caught all the mice, and D was a doll all dressed up so nice.'

He glanced up and realised he had been singing the old verse softly, the man opposite pretending not to notice.

Now, the snow streaked the window, flakes dissolving on impact, like the past, and he felt the beginnings of a severe headache. There was too much whiteness out there. He reached up and pulled down the blind.

'And still only November,' said the only other occupant of the first-class carriage, a huge ruddy-complexioned man who had introduced himself as the owner of a print works in Preston. He had spent a profitable few days in London examining new lithographic printing methods and it had taken half an hour of evangelising after pulling out of Euston before he realised his new-found companion, whose elegance of dress betokened a possible investor, was poor material for either conversation or conversion.

'I beg your pardon?' Ambrose Morris sat back and rested his head. Perhaps if he closed his eyes the incipient pain would subside.

'Snow, sir. In November. It makes one wonder what the rest of the winter will be like.'

'The winter will be cold and bitter,' returned Ambrose, before finally closing his eyes and allowing the rattle and sway of the carriage to give him some respite, for a while at least.

CHAPTER FOUR

'I am to meet with the family this afternoon to present my condolences and you tell me there have been no arrests?'

Captain Bell stood gazing out of the window. He had his hands clasped firmly behind his back, the tips of his fingers white with the pressure.

Beyond the frosted glass, he was watching the slow, laboured progress of a tram bearing the legend 'Minorca Grill Rooms' as it made its way through the mounds of snow along King Street. In front of the Theatre Royal, a small knot of men were huddled together, tiny steam clouds billowing from their mouths as they spoke animatedly, one man fisting the air to make a point the others evidently disagreed with. He could be a radical stirring up even more trouble, or he could simply be complaining to friends about his wife.

That was the problem these days. Public and domestic strife seemed to create a compound of unrest, the one blurred and fuelled by the other, and the only people who stood between the town and anarchy were the police, and the smattering

74

of soldiers who made infrequent appearances on the streets at sensitive times. It wasn't the most propitious time to be chief constable. Sometimes, he harboured a wish to be back commanding the troops in Limerick, or enjoying a late afternoon's sailing on the lake at Udaipur, marvelling at the beauty of its white buildings and the magnificent shrine of Jagannath.

He gave a long, meaningful sigh. He dreaded the consequences of further trouble, although there had been precious little violence so far, unlike the events across the Pennines. He had read with dismay of the way the dispute had escalated in Featherstone, where the reading of the Riot Act had preceded the horror of troops shooting indiscriminately into the crowd. Two miners had subsequently died, and the mood around Acton Hall Colliery was as volatile as a sizzling powder keg.

His sergeant's words broke into his thoughts. 'It's very early, sir. There's a lot to...'

'Early!' He swung round, reminding Brennan of a vengeful gargoyle. 'He was murdered four days ago. Four days!'

'Yes, sir.'

'And the cells down below are empty, Sergeant.'

He decided against pointing out the error of the chief constable's observation: they had several non-paying guests down below. Still, he understood the spirit, if not the accuracy, of his words.

'We are making enquiries, sir. Even as I speak my men are going from house to house in the Scholes area and asking...'

'Do you know how that place has been de-

75

scribed, Sergeant?'

'No, sir.'

'The ash-pit of human life. That's what Scholes is. Scoop your hand into an ash-pit and what do you come up with?'

Brennan deemed the question a rhetorical one.

'It would do no harm to stir the cauldron a little, Sergeant Brennan. Look at the houses nearest the scene of the crime and examine the list of dwellers. I'm sure more than one name will jump to the surface like a half-boiled toad.'

As an investigative ploy it left a lot to be desired. Feelings were already running high because of the miseries caused by the strike: hasty and unpremeditated arrests would merely serve to make a bad situation worse and divert anger from the coal owners to the police, who were already regarded as the capital's official arm.

'You may consider that an order,' said the chief constable, facing his inferior squarely now. 'I will be able to inform the family – including Ambrose Morris himself who, I hear, has arrived and is already with his bereaved sister-in-law – that an arrest is imminent. I'm sure you can find me a suitable suspect, Sergeant, if only to assuage the grief of that sainted lady.'

He gave a nod of dismissal, and Sergeant Brennan left the room in search of a suspect.

Constable Jaggery knew there was no point arguing. There had been a time when an arrest was founded on the firm and irrefutable principle of evidence. Fair enough, sometimes you had to crack a few bones in order to get to the meat of the evidence, a bit like eating rabbit, really, but it made things a damned sight easier when you stood up in court and faced the awesome glare of a magistrate or judge, or sometimes even the wheedling insinuations of a smooth-talking barrister. Evidence was something you could fall back on when you had no answer to withering accusations of incompetence from some bugger wearing a wig.

'But blow me,' he said, as if Sergeant Brennan had already been privy to his train of thought, 'this is a bit of a sod, ain't it?'

They stood outside the door of number 17, Hardybutts, on the outer edge of Scholes.

Behind them, lined up along the kerbside in their black greatcoats, five police constables, all hand-picked because of their size, stood with their hands hidden beneath their coats, not, as it appeared to be, a precaution against the bitter late afternoon chill, but in a state of readiness, clutching wooden clubs to ward off any unwanted attention. Every door along the street was open despite the cold they were letting in. Dim shadows were cast from within, flickering oil lamps catching the waft of a breeze as women stood on doorsteps, their arms folded, and their menfolk drifting with an air of disdain towards the centre of the street. The crunch of their clogged feet on the snow carried the steady rhythm of menace. Small, almost ghostly children, their faces smeared with dirt or scabs, clung to their mothers' skirts, their older siblings strolling alongside their fathers in a sort of familial display of solidarity. There was an unmistakeable mood of resentment in the growing dark.

There must be thirty of the devils, thought Jaggery. A thin, reedy voice broke the silence before Sergeant Brennan could reply. 'Have I to wait or what? Only me wick's burnin'.'

Brennan turned to see a tall, lanky individual, whose face was obscured by a thick woollen muffler and whose eyes glistened beneath a long pole that he held in his right hand. From atop the pole came a tiny glow from the already illuminated wick. The man gave a nod upwards. They were standing beneath a gas lamp.

'By all means,' said Brennan. 'Go about your business.'

Better to allow the man to light the gas, to let the locals have at least an appearance of normality before the arrest was made. With a meaningful sniff, the lamplighter stretched upwards and flipped open the glass door of the lamp, and, with a skilful twist of the wrist, he slipped open the gas valve that, with the application of the flame from the wick, immediately became a bright green light. He gave the row of policemen a lugubrious nod and went slowly on his way.

Still, throughout the process, not a word came from the crowd.

'Right then,' snapped Brennan. 'Let's have him!'

There was no knocker, so Constable Jaggery reached forward and rapped loudly on the upper panel with his huge fist. No response.

'Again!'

Brennan almost spat the word out. He knew full well the man was inside: one glance through the grimy window had shown a grate piled up with coals, and the white smoke that was billowing up the chimney as a precursor to the flames was a clear indication that the coal – probably lifted from the slag heaps near the collieries – had just been placed there, and he was probably ensconced in the bedroom, but he had to go through with the charade anyway. Under less public circumstances he would have ordered Jaggery to smash the door from its hinges, but the presence of an audience brought its own restraint.

Once more Jaggery hammered against the door, and once again there came only silence from within.

'Looks like he's out, pal!' yelled someone from the middle of the street, to a chorus of jeers.

Jaggery turned round, his face now flushed with a dangerous blend of anger and incipient humiliation. 'Som'body else'll be out in a minute!' he roared back. 'Bloody well flat out.'

More jeers.

'What's-he-called done any road?' came another anonymous query.

'Nothing to concern yourselves with!'

Brennan turned fully to face the crowd. Most of them knew him – he had been born not a hundred yards from this very spot – and although these last few months had wrought a bitter deterioration in the relationship between the townsfolk, especially the striking miners, and the forces of law and order, he knew he, at least, still commanded a residue of respect. What happened next would compel him to revise that opinion.

'No, an' it's none of thy concern either, Micky lad!' yelled one.

'We know where tha lives an' all,' yelled another. 'Happen we'll come an' pay *thee* a call, eh? Hammer on *thy* door.'

He could sense the mood shift, a dark, brooding malevolence in which even the low hiss of the gas lamp above his head seemed to be a disembodied rebuke. It seemed the silence had become something he could reach out and touch. His men shifted uncomfortably, their breath freezing in the evening air, and their eyes flickering from the crowd of people gathering around them in a semicircle to himself, searching in his face for the reassurance of command. He looked down at the clogged feet of the enemy, the studded iron trim above the soles damp with crusted snow.

'Look,' he said, attempting a conciliatory tone, 'we just want to ask him a few questions. Nothing important.'

'Why the bloody artillery then?'

A man stepped forward, a good few inches taller than the rest. His broad shoulders were tense, ready to spring into action. Brennan recognised him. He and Ellen had stood in the market square with over ten thousand others a few months ago and listened to his powerful speech in defence of the miners' right to earn a decent wage. What was it he had said that stuck in Brennan's mind? 'We are the bees that make the honey. We take the risks and they take the money.'

Frank Latchford, prominent member of the Miners' Federation, had an almighty way with words.

The others stepped back and muttered their support. This was their spokesman and their champion.

Out of the corner of his eye, Brennan caught the gradual closing of ranks, each local moving closer to his neighbour, teeth gritted, like a slovenly but bitterly determined squadron ready to attack. The children adopted the same pose, stern-faced and holding themselves rigid, the inconstant flicker of their eyes the only indicator of youth. He saw the women looking on with cold, resigned expressions on their faces.

Slowly, with both arms raised, Brennan walked over to Latchford, who now stood on the edge of the kerbstone, the row of policemen watching nervously to his left. 'We're investigating a murder, Mr Latchford. A murder that took place here in Scholes. At the rear of this house, actually. Surely it's best for everyone if we try our utmost to find who did it?'

For a second, he saw Latchford's eyes flicker.

'And making a music hall show of paying Jem Muldoon a visit will help, will it?' Latchford sneered. 'Because the body was found in the alleyway behind his house? That's a bit like blaming a lamp post for the dog piss.'

Brennan smiled and nodded. 'You're absolutely right. Perhaps if I sent the uniforms away, and perhaps if I stepped inside to have a quiet word with him, that might calm things down a bit?'

Latchford looked at him for a few seconds, a flicker of respect on his face. 'You know I spend a lot of my time negotiatin', Sergeant?'

'I do.'

'And I can tell when I'm being flannelled.'

'Of course.'

Latchford paused then finally gave an assenting

81

nod. 'You won't mind, eh, if I come with you?'

Brennan turned and whispered something to Jaggery, who gave a deep frown and appeared to protest, but who eventually gave a resigned shrug of his broad shoulders and barked out an order for the rest of the constables to make their way back to the station.

A mocking cheer went up from the gathering gloom, and the combatants gradually dispersed, taking their children and womenfolk with them.

Jem Muldoon was a small, stoop-shouldered collier, his thick neck and arms a curious contrast with the rest of his body, as if God had changed his mind halfway through. Having been re-assured by the voice of Frank Latchford calling up to his bedroom that all would be well, he came downstairs muttering curses and rubbing an unshaven chin as his only acknowledgement of a visitor and was now sitting at a small table in a tiny kitchen, his hands cupped together and continually clasping and unclasping, as if unsure whether to pray or curse. Behind him, with one arm resting reassuringly on his shoulder, stood Frank Latchford, with an expression on his face that betokened both concerned neighbour and resolute advocate.

'But I've done bugger all!'

And Detective Sergeant Brennan was bound to agree with him.

'Well, not since you got fined five shillings last week for being drunk in charge of a horse and cart.'

'That's what you get for doin' a brother-in-law

a soddin' favour.'

'I know. I was in court, Jem. Remember?'

'I paid me fine. Am I to be done twice for t'same thing? Against the law is that.'

'No. We just need to know about Saturday night.'

'What about it?'

'The night Arthur Morris was murdered. A matter of yards from where you live.'

'Nowt to do wi' me, pal.'

He spoke with the dismissive confidence of an innocent man.

'I'm not saying it is. I want to know what you know. That's all.'

The man gave a sneer, then quickly retracted it. 'I know Morris got what was comin' to 'im, that's what I know. Bastard like that.'

Latchford leant forward and said something Brennan couldn't quite catch, though he could guess at its meaning: *Don't incriminate yourself!*

Perhaps it had been a mistake to allow him to be present during the interview.

Finally Latchford said, 'Ask anyone in this street, in this district, why, in this entire town, and you'll hear exactly the same sentiments. Jem's not alone in that.'

'I agree, Mr Latchford. But nobody deserves to die like that, do they?'

'There's worse ways to die,' he snapped back. 'Slow starvation for one. Hurling yourself in the Duggie or the canal to numb the pain of seeing your children starve, that's another. A knife through the heart is quite a merciful way out, I'd have thought.'

Brennan frowned at Latchford's words, but said

nothing. He simply shook his head. He needed to put the interview back on track.

'Jem, did you see or hear anything on Saturday night, anything suspicious?'

'Bugger all. I were asleep. Too many early bloody nights these days, what with the lockout an' all. Can't remember t'last time I had a pint.'

This was hopeless. He had followed the chief constable's orders, at least in part, and come up with nothing. To drag Jem Muldoon down to the station just to fill a cell was madness. As Brennan stood up to go, Muldoon looked up at him.

'What were 'e doin', eh? Morris, I mean. What were 'e doin' up 'ere any road? No bugger's gonna make him a cup o' tea an' a bacon butty, are they?'

That was the question that lay, Brennan thought, *at the very centre of this investigation.*

What was Arthur Morris doing in Scholes at all?

As Brennan got to the door – with Latchford by his side – Muldoon spoke once more. 'Happen it were someone not from round 'ere what did for the swine. Happen it were that one-eyed little bastard, eh?'

'What?'

Before Latchford, who actually raised a hand as if it had some magical power of forestalling speech, could stop him, he went on. 'I said, happen it were that one-eyed little bastard. Him who's been askin' all sorts o' questions.'

Jem Muldoon looked at his advocate and saw only rebuke in his face. He shrugged his shoulders and held his hands steady on the table.

But Brennan's eyes had narrowed. 'What one-eyed little bastard?'

CHAPTER FIVE

Captain Alexander Bell shared a love of death with many of his fellow men.

Not that he would ever admit to it, but it was an indisputable fact that Death embraced everything he held dear about Life. It brought the best out of people, reminding them not only of the transitory nature of this life but the spiritual sanctuary of the next, affirming both the awesome force and the sublime goodness of Almighty God. It was often said that the English were a reserved, insensitive race, that they nurtured the concept of the stiff upper lip to the detriment of rather more continental displays of emotion.

Death put the lie to that.

What greater demonstration of emotion could there possibly be than the convention of mourning, with all its outward panoply of grief and bereavement that betokened an intensity of inner grieving? He recalled the outrage he had felt in India the first time he had seen a widow become a *suttee*, throwing herself on her husband's burning pyre in Allahabad, near Lucknow. It seemed to be a thorough dereliction of all that was human, and dignified, and *British*.

He noticed with approval, as he waited in the hallway at the Morris residence, the deferential lowering of eyes in the domestic staff, the pallor of their faces and the elegiac silence as they passed each other in the sombre execution of their duties. Each one had, of course, been given attire more suitable to mourning, yet another indication of the selflessness and the unanimity Death brings to a household.

'If sir will come this way?'

The butler's sudden appearance, like mist at a séance, startled him.

'Of course.'

He was led into a small sitting room that lay to the left of the main drawing room. This, it seemed, was to be the place where the family received visitors of condolence. As he entered, Captain Bell was immediately struck by the chill of the room. At the far wall, an elaborate mahogany hearth, its inner panels inlaid with hand-painted tiles, lay cold and forlorn. The splendid Queen Anne bracket clock, with its gentle chinoiserie, lay on the mantel between two silver candlesticks, both of which were symbolically lit on a bed of crape.

He tried to recall the blazing flames dancing in the grate of the drawing room on his last, much more joyful visit a few months ago, the way they created a frenetic sparkling in the tiles that framed them as he, along with other eminent guests, awaited the arrival of their host, with a pianist playing 'Nocturne' by Chopin on the splendid Steinway. The memory and the notes faded, and he rebuked himself for his selfishness and concern for his own comfort.

'Alexander?'

He turned round and saw Ambrose Morris, Member of Parliament for Wigan, standing in the doorway.

As always, he was dressed impeccably, in full mourning: dark suit, black tie and armband, with his hair groomed elegantly with Macassar oil. Yet the aura he normally gave off – of someone perfectly at ease with his own abilities and appearance – was somehow diminished, as if his brother's death had lessened him both physically and mentally. The shoulders, he noticed, had lost some of their poise, an impression reinforced by the signs of an incipient stoop and an expression on his face, mainly hidden but there beneath the confident surface, of irretrievable loss. An involuntary image flickered in his mind: Atlas, condemned by Zeus to bear the whole weight of the world on his shoulders.

The expression on his face suggested an uncertainty as to the exact nature of the visit. Personal, or official?

'My dear Ambrose,' said the chief constable, reading the expression and reaching out to grasp the great man's hand. 'I have come merely to offer my very sincerest condolences.'

'Thank you. Thank you. Please.'

He indicated a leather armchair that stood before the hearth. As his visitor sat down, he followed suit in the companion chair.

'It goes without saying, Ambrose, that we are doing our utmost to bring the ... we are doing our utmost to bring this to a speedy conclusion.'

'Of course.'

'I have my finest detective, Sergeant Brennan, on the case. He is a rather tenacious character, and if anyone can bring the guilty one to justice...' He let the encomium fade into inference, and immediately lowered his voice. 'Your brother was a fine man.'

'None finer.'

'I can see him now, regaling us all with his experiences in Chicago. How he wasn't annoyed that the Monster Cheese from Canada was bigger than the piece of cannel coal he was exhibiting because ... how did he put it?'

'"My exhibit had a far sweeter smell!"' Ambrose added, and both men laughed gently at the memory.

There was a pause then, a mournful and companionable silence, during which Alexander Bell watched the slow sway of the candle flames for a few minutes.

Finally, he said, 'Confidentially, Ambrose, it is entirely possible that we may have a suspect in custody as we speak.'

'Indeed?' Ambrose Morris's eyebrows rose up, whether to express satisfaction or incredulity it was impossible to say.

At that moment Mrs Prudence Morris entered the room, and Captain Bell immediately stood. He had known her for years, and had always been impressed by the gentle way she comported herself. He knew she suffered from a debilitating rheumatic condition, sometimes walking with a spring in her step, while at other times she could barely walk at all and required the support of a walking stick.

If Arthur were regarded as the lion of the relationship, she might well be regarded as the lamb. Indeed, where Arthur blustered and allowed his whiskers to bristle and crackle like a forest fire whenever he was crossed in debate or thwarted in some way, Prudence would lay a hand on his arm, give it a gentle squeeze, and smile at every one of her guests the way a mother would. It was to protect and to scold at the same time.

A part of Alexander Bell had always been smitten by her elegance, by the decorous beauty she must undoubtedly have once been and still retained despite the slow corrugation of time. It was a layer of regard he naturally kept hidden to observe the proprieties of social intercourse.

Ambrose immediately went to her and offered her his seat, which she accepted with a curt nod.

'Thank you for coming, Alexander,' she said in a hoarse whisper.

He wondered how many tears she had already got through. Her eyes were indeed rimmed with a redness beneath the black weeping veil. She wore a black crape dress, unadorned and without the usual fripperies found on other, more joyous occasions. On her head she wore a widow's cap.

'My condolences, ma'am,' he bowed his head.

'They say the veil should be worn back, on the head. But I prefer the old traditions.' Her voice was low and timorous. 'Are you here in ... an official capacity?'

'Merely as a friend.'

She gazed up and looked into her brother-in-law's eyes. 'Where is my son?'

When she spoke, there was, Bell thought, an asperity in her voice. It was no surprise to him. It was known among their circle that she merely tolerated her brother-in-law. Some had suggested she found his confidence altogether overpowering, while others, of whom Alexander Bell was one, thought that she felt her husband, despite his shrewd if sometimes acerbic business acumen, was somehow eclipsed by his proximity to the greatness of Westminster. Not even death had thawed the coldness she showed towards him.

'He left some time ago.'

She cast her eyes to the carpet. 'A great pity,' she said, almost to herself.

As Molly Haggerty made her way home with the others, she kept her head bowed low beneath her shawl. The others were walking arm in arm, giggling and making the occasional ribald comment to whichever youth was foolish enough to stop on the pavement and offer some injudicious comment.

'You all right, Moll?' one of them asked.

'Course,' she said, hoping the brevity of her response would forestall any further query.

'Only you look pale.'

Before she could respond, she felt a hand tug at her skirts. She wheeled round, about to give whoever dared touch her a mouthful, when she saw a small ragamuffin, no older than seven, with dirt smeared across his face and a tight curl to his pinched lips. His coat was stained and filthy, and he was shivering badly.

'This your new fella, Moll?' May Calderbank called out with a nudge and a smirk that spread across the row of girls like the rattle of a loom. Despite the child's tender years, the girls tried to outdo each other in coarseness.

'What d'you want?' Molly asked.

'Him o'er yonder s-says can you s-spare a word.'

The child swept an arm across the road and pointed a thin finger. A tram was rattling its way past, and as it moved along he came into view, standing on the opposite side of the road, framed by the doorway of a shop. It was Ranicar's Emporium. There seemed something morbidly fitting about him standing outside a funeral shop.

Michael Brennan sat in the small alcove at the furthest end of the bar, his favourite spot when he needed to converse and where he was in little danger of being overheard.

Constable Jaggery sat rubbing his hands and contemplating the thick froth of the pint before him. His glinting eyes, the ruddy glow of his flushed cheeks, were obvious signs of his pleasure.

'So,' Brennan began, 'Saturday night Mr Arthur Morris was found savagely done to death in Scholes. Our house enquiries have yielded a sum total of nothing.' He gave a wry smile. 'Strange, isn't it, Constable? Of all the Saturday nights in the year, Arthur Morris is killed on this one.'

'Why's that strange?'

'You tell me what Scholes would be like if this strike hadn't gripped its throat and choked the life out of it. On a Saturday night?'

Jaggery saw what the sergeant was getting at. He'd spent enough time on the streets in that district knocking drunken heads together and breaking up innumerable fights, Saturday night being by far the worst. The pubs were alive with singing, yelling, and all manner of cursing until the early hours. There would be public houses filled to the rafters, many with Irishmen singing their sad laments of the old country, laments that would be liberally peppered with tales of murderous excesses by the forces of the Crown, of glorious sacrifices from young revolutionaries, and the bright green hope of a country free from John Bull's yoke. The police never went there alone, and on many occasions the cells at the station were so full they had to commandeer the cellars of compliant public houses to keep some of the offenders locked up in what was in truth a most ironic incarceration.

But on the night Morris was found – and for a good few weeks before that – the public houses had served a mere trickle of customers. Money was in scarce supply, and children had to be fed. There was little singing these days.

'So,' Brennan went on, 'either the good folk of Scholes were fast asleep at the time of the assault – which, according to Doctor Monroe probably took place sometime before midnight – or they've all become victims of a rare plague that renders everyone not only blind but deaf as well.'

'They hated him, Sergeant. I reckon if the streets had been packed wi' folk dancin' on the cobbles no bugger would've seen owt. Else they'd have danced round the body like a tribe of savages.'

'Well then. Let's say no one saw or heard a thing. Unlikely, but impossible to disprove.'

He raised a finger.

'Question number one. What was the man who locally instigated the coal dispute doing in the middle of Scholes where he is hated? Two.' He raised another finger. 'How did Arthur Morris get there?'

'Cab?'

'Possibly. Or omnibus. There's no tram service into Standish, but the omnibus runs along the main road into town. From there he could have walked to Scholes. Or again, taken a cab. Ask around the hackney drivers, see if any of them took a fare up to Scholes Saturday night.'

'Yes, Sergeant.'

Jaggery took another sip, wondering which one of the constables owed him a favour. Buggered if he was going to spend a day talking to sour-faced cabbies in the freezing bloody cold.

'Three. Was he the victim of a spur of the moment attack? You know the sort of thing: "Hey, that looks like Arthur Morris, I think I'll stab him to death with this long-bladed knife I happen to have in my pocket."'

Jaggery frowned. 'I don't think that's very likely, Sergeant.'

Brennan sighed, wondering if irony could ever permeate that stubborn and unimaginative skull of his. 'Fourth question. Who had reason to kill the victim?'

Jaggery was about to say something, but stopped himself just in time.

'Other than everyone above the age of five in Scholes. Question number five. Who is the one-eyed man?'

Jaggery, who hadn't been privy to either the interview with Muldoon or its outcome, wondered if the sergeant was suffering from brain fever.

Quickly, he explained the significance of his cryptic comment. 'According to Jem Muldoon, he's been seen hanging around some of the public houses up there. Strangers, especially one-eyed ones, arouse interest.'

'Could be owt. Could be nowt,' was Jaggery's pithy response.

'I agree. Still, it's something we can pursue, isn't it?'

'Yes, Sergeant.'

'And soon I must speak with the family. Ambrose Morris is back from London. He was present at the dinner on the night his brother was killed. He may have noticed something, spoken in confidence to him. He may even be able to give us the answer to question number six.'

'Not another, Sergeant.'

The elevation of a sixth digit, from the left hand, gave him his answer.

'What, if anything, is the significance of the scribbled note found in the dead man's pocket? "Strike causes hell – O Lord end suffrin. Or die." It's obviously some kind of threat.'

'An' thousands could've written it.'

Brennan grunted. 'But why should such a scrawled threat send Arthur Morris to Scholes in such haste? And how would he know where to go to seek out the writer of such a threat? Unless...'

Jaggery slurped at his pint, knowing when to keep his mouth metaphorically shut.

'Unless he recognised the handwriting. In which case he would need no address, would he?'

'Buggered if I know,' the constable sighed, scratching his head in confusion.

'Oh, and one more thing.'

'Bloody hell. What now?'

'How did Frank Latchford know that Morris had been stabbed through the heart?'

After they had explored several possible versions of what might have happened that night – and having come up with no rational explanation for question number one, from which all other questions and answers sprang – they parted company just before closing time.

A thick fog had descended. The cloying white mist clung to every building, every lamp post, in a chilled embrace. Immediately, they both felt the cold pinch their cheeks, the pub warmth vanishing so rapidly it felt as if they'd been suddenly immersed in a vat of crushed ice. Constable Jaggery coughed and spat a mouthful of phlegm as he heaved himself aboard the last tram, while Brennan shook the haze of the smoke-filled pub from his mind and resolved to walk home, despite the freezing fog and the curious effect it had on his sense of direction.

Wallgate sloped downwards, past the railway station of the same name and beneath the bridge, so it was a relatively simple matter to find his bearings. Not even fog could cause the walls of a railway bridge to vanish.

As he got to the walls, and reached out to feel the thick coating of ice that followed the contours of the misshapen bricks like a shroud, he thought he heard something. An echo. With each step he took, he heard a corresponding echo a split second behind him, step ... *step* ... step. When he stopped, the echo stopped. A trick of the fog, perhaps?

He gave a shrug and continued to walk.

95

But so did the echo.

He turned round and faced the way he had come. 'Anyone there?' he called out.

Silence. The silence of the fog. Thick. Hovering.

He swallowed hard and resumed his journey. *Keep the pace quick,* he told himself. *It's just this damned fog.* Quick, but just the sane side of running.

Straight along, then turn left at the second street, past St Joseph's Church on Caroline Street. Then a matter of cutting through a small entry that led on to his street. He made his way along the pavement, passing the church on his left and noticing the heavy wooden doors locked shut at this hour. Fleetingly he thought of frozen statues inside, and the sanctuary of the holy ground, the peace of the altar and the wary solitude of the confessional. He turned round once more, but could see nothing in the thick swirl of mist that turned the route he had taken into a mere memory. In his haste he slipped on treacherous cobblestones, crossing the street to the entry and reaching out to steady himself in the narrow confines of its walls.

That was where they got him.

CHAPTER SIX

When she was Bridie Hanlon, back in Charlestown, County Mayo, she had spoken at great length to her parish priest, Father James Higgins, about joining the sisterhood. She had sat for many an hour in his house on Chapel Street, sharing with him her plans for the future and a life devoted to the service of Jesus in the closeted sanctuary of Carmelite prayer and the contemplative life. There seemed something safe, something sacred, in kneeling day after day clad in the brown scapular knowing that you were one among many, praying alongside others who had the same love in their hearts, and devoting your life to Jesus and the selfless devotion of the Blessed Virgin.

Then she turned fourteen and saw a rather different future for herself, as the good and wise Father Higgins had predicted.

'Sure, ye have no vocation, child. Just a yearnin' for escape, an' a yearnin' for peace. Ye *want* love, in both senses of the phrase.'

Father Higgins knew her father well.

Now, as she lay there in the dark, listening to little Tommy in the next room snoring gently, she let herself drift back to those days.

To the time she was sixteen and she met Seamus, who breezed into her life with all the force of an Atlantic gale, with his tall stories and his mischievous grin and that mop of jet-black curls.

Seamus Haggerty.

'Sure an' I'll break every bone in his body!' her da had yelled when he caught them doing what they shouldn't on a village trip to nearby Tample to visit St Attracta's Well.

He had made sure Father Higgins was informed, too: a shrine dedicated to St Attracta, and whose holy waters from the bullaun were said to cure rickets, and that sinful daughter of his sees fit to commit all manner of lewdness which was 'not only an insult to the holy saint who was converted by Saint Patrick himself, but to the hundreds of wee children whose tortured wee bones would even now be aching in shame at what she had done. D'ye think she'll burn in hell, Father?'

'Sure it was only a kiss, Da!' she had complained with a blushing nod to the good Father, whose kindly frown showed he already accepted the inappropriateness of her Carmelite pretensions.

'There's no such bloody thing as *only* a kiss!' snarled her da. 'Beggin' ye pardon, Father.'

The young Bridie had never realised a chaste kiss could cause so much agony.

She smiled now as she recalled the whispered communications from the bedroom window a few weeks after the thrashing, the wild, hasty plan to flee to England where the streets were paved with coal dust, the flight through the night vaguely reminding her of something biblical, terrified of turning round in case she became a pillar of salt, and then the landing at Liverpool, the strange confusion of accents, the foreign country that was Wigan. And Scholes, where Seamus's grandmother lived.

The bitch.

'Sure she can stay here, Seamus me boy, when she's bringin' in the money an' not before.'

And she had promptly arranged for her to begin work as a skivvying domestic.

As a kitchen maid at the grand home of Mr Arthur Morris. Where, as a live-in servant, she lasted a whole three months, seeing Seamus rarely, gradually growing more and more despondent at his inability to stand up to the ferocious harridan that was his grandmother. Then two things happened within a fortnight of each other. The first was a letter from Seamus informing her that the bitch was dead.

The second was what happened in the laundry room.

The stinking hot cigar breath. The frantic fumbling. The indescribable pain.

For years afterwards, she convinced herself that God had His reasons for allowing the molestation to take place, for He had already provided her means of escape with Seamus assuming the tenancy of the house in Scholes.

And so he became her knight in shining armour once more, and within a few months they were married.

But for a long time, the shadow of what had happened to her at the Morris residence was always trailing behind her. It darkened her dreams, and she would wake in the middle of the night in a cold, damp sweat, unable to explain to her new husband that the nightmare that lay siege to her sleeping hours had been real.

Still, the mind is a resilient and determined citadel, and gradually the shadows began to fade, the horrors of the night grew fewer and fewer. She sighed as the better memories came back, of conversations, of nights of passion, of her pregnancy and the scream of a fragile baby girl whose life had hung in the balance for weeks.

And now Molly, that fragile baby girl, was hale and strong, her arms curled around her impish brother, and tonight she had come home with something close to a smile on her face for the first time in days.

It's strange, death. It changes so many things, and what seemed inevitable and cast in stone had now drifted into the air like a dandelion clock blown to the four winds.

So, as her eyes grew heavy, Bridie allowed herself the rare luxury of a smile. If Father Higgins had been there, he'd have said she was doing it all over again: yearning for escape, yearning for peace. Only this time, she told herself with a somnolent sigh, there was no Seamus any more to turn wish into reality.

But what had happened last Saturday night had changed things, hadn't it? For her and for her daughter.

She saw the dull white of the fog against her window, and the frosted swirls of ice on the glass that reminded her of madness. Then she slept.

It was a curious thing that a thief's breath brought him back to consciousness.

Thinking that a barge stranded in the canal ice might yield something of interest, a wizened old felon known locally as Rat-Yed (on account of his habit of biting off the heads of live rats for an appreciative and suitably drunken audience) had crept from his lodging house in the hour before dawn and made his way to the barge. Although the fog had largely vanished, there was still a thick layer of mist clinging to the canal bank, and he had to step carefully to avoid dropping onto the ice below.

Unfortunately, the boat contained nothing more than scattered lumps of cannel coal, too few even to gather together and sell for fuel. As he walked back in a cold and miserable mood, he saw what at first he thought was a pair of boots sticking out of the communal lavatory at the end of an entry near Caroline Street. His immediate instinct being to run off with them, he was in the process of simply lifting them and running when he dropped them. They were far too heavy for empty boots.

On closer inspection he saw that the boots had feet inside them. On closer inspection still, he saw whom the feet belonged to.

'Bloody 'ell! Micky Brennan!'

The proximity of his face to Brennan's had the wondrous effect normally associated with smelling salts. The prostrate detective regained consciousness momentarily with a fit of coughing and retching, and within an hour, he was lying in Wigan Infirmary, wrapped warmly in a thick layer of blankets to raise his temperature and ward off the cold that had nearly killed him. Ellen and Barry had stayed with him, Barry unable to reconcile the image of his father as a bold and daring knight with the bruised and battered figure lying on the bed before him.

Ellen had said little. But there had been a sharp expression of dread in her eyes, a silent acknowledgement that she had nearly lost the man she loved. Accusation, too. How dare he put himself at risk.

His family only left when he assured them both he was going to be fine.

He slept again, and when he awoke it was to the unedifying sight of Constable Jaggery sitting at his bedside with an expression on his face that would have made the Grim Reaper seem like the Archangel Gabriel.

'You look a sight, Sergeant,' he said with a lugubrious shake of the head. 'Seen healthier stiffs.'

Brennan winced as he attempted to sit upright. He felt a burning along his ribs. Gingerly, he reached down and touched the swathes of bandage wrapped around him.

'They reckon you've been lucky.'

Brennan tried to smile, to show he could still appreciate the odd ironic jibe, but the swelling around his lips gave him second thoughts.

'Who was it, Sergeant?'

He winced when he tried to shake his head. 'It was pitch-black. Foggy. But it had a lot to do with our little visit to Scholes.'

'How do you know?'

'The last thing I heard before passing out was a whispered warning, hot breath on my ear, telling me to "stay well away from where I'm not welcome".'

'I'll Scholes 'em. We'll take the whole bloody force up there and scour the place clean!'

'You'll do nothing of the sort. Do you hear me, Constable?' He clenched his teeth as an alternative to raising his voice, which would have caused his head to throb even more.

'But if they think...'

'Nothing of the sort! I have an idea who organised the attack, but there's no way of proving it.'

'Who?'

But the sergeant had already closed his eyes, and his mind drifted back into a deep, untroubled sleep.

During Detective Sergeant Brennan's enforced residence in Wigan Infirmary, the borough coroner had held the inquest into Arthur Morris's death. Captain Bell had given evidence on behalf of the police, and the inevitable verdict of 'Wilful murder' was returned.

Captain Bell had also taken a more active role in his detective sergeant's absence. Several occupants of Scholes were removed from their homes and questioned in the station cells, thus increasing the resentment towards the police. It was unfortunate, the chief constable was heard to remark within strategic earshot of the row of subterranean cells, that the previous year had seen the abolition of the cat-o'-nine-tails.

'That would have given them a judicious scratching, and no mistake!'

But there were no confessions, no sly hints of anyone being involved.

'Either they're scared beyond measure to open their mouths,' Captain Bell was forced to conclude, 'or there is some other explanation as yet unexplored.'

Constable Jaggery, who was one of the recipients of this startling concession, gave a momentary smirk of satisfaction. When he duly reported back, Sergeant Brennan would have smiled too, if it hadn't been too painful.

For two days, Brennan remained an unhappy and impatient patient.

His mouth still ached, but the pain had dulled now, and he was relieved to discover that his ribs had suffered terrible bruising – which in itself

103

was painful – but there had been no extensive fractures, and he could at least walk unaided from his bed. Much against his doctor's advice.

'We might have a sightin' of Arthur Morris, Sergeant. Last Saturday night.'

Jaggery was helping Brennan into a hackney carriage outside the infirmary.

'Where?'

'There's a cabbie says he took a well-dressed fare from the centre of town to Scholes. Dropped him off outside the Vulcan.'

Brennan slumped in his seat and pondered that for a while.

The Vulcan Inn, on Hardybutts, was one of over seventy public houses in the district of Scholes. If it had been a balmy evening in summer, and all the men had been fully in work, it would have been quite a risky venture for Arthur Morris to clamber down from a carriage in full view of its clientele, many of whom would have been standing outside the bar room. It cleared up one question – how he got there. But it still didn't answer the more fundamental one: what was he doing in Scholes in the first place?

'It's Morris's funeral tomorrow, Sergeant.'

Brennan's eyes widened. 'I see. Then we'd better get a move on, hadn't we?'

At that same moment, the occupants of a much more comfortable carriage were enjoying the warmth of an intimacy long denied them.

For Molly, it felt good, his fingers through her hair.

'I wish we were far away.'

'Where would we go then?'

'Oh, somewhere we can just, you know, be anyone. No one.'

'There'll be time for that.'

'When?' Molly lifted herself from his chest. Although there was still light outside, here, in the shadows of the carriage interior, she could hardly make out his face, let alone the expression it carried. Was he sincere? she asked herself. After all that had happened, was he as sincere and as purposeful as she was?

'Soon. I promise. And when I tell you about it, you'll be speechless.'

'Tell me now!' she said with an urgency of tone diluted somewhat by a girlish giggle.

'Absolutely not!'

'"*Absolutely not!*"' she echoed, mimicking his more rounded vowels. Then she snuggled back, pulling the carriage wrap tight around them both. She could feel the warmth of his body through their clothes.

Here, atop Parbold Hill, six miles from Wigan and despite the smattering of collieries that marked the outer fringe of the south Lancashire coalfields, it did indeed seem that the town and all its miseries, all the despondency of poverty, starvation, angry and unasked for indolence, were a thousand miles away. The view across the Douglas Valley, the broad sweep of land that still retained much of the recent snow, made the warmth she felt more perfect, heavenly. Even the bare branches of the trees, their harsh and twisted lines stark against the whiteness of the fields beyond, made her feel safe here, where nothing and no one could touch them.

'If you could be somewhere, right now, where would it be?'

Her voice was low, the tones soft and inconsequential, and the query the sort of trivia people always ask in circumstances such as this.

Andrew Morris sighed. 'Remember Blackpool?'

She smiled and kissed his chest through the black of his mourning coat. 'Aye. I do.'

She breathed out the words, seeing the splendid expanse of sea and sand, and hearing again the cacophony of noise that had surrounded them, especially around Central Promenade, where the frenzied comings and goings of those working on the new tower were a source of ribald commentary from amused onlookers.

There was renewed animation in her voice now. 'I remember the waves of the sea best. The sound they made crashing onto the beach. I'd never heard anything like that before. I mean, to wake up to that sound every day of your life!'

'And the wind through your hair.'

'And the band on the pier!'

'And the boat trip to Southport!'

'And the colours of the fish in the aquarium!'

'And that awful tower they'll never finish!'

She giggled into his chest. 'Remember the time gun exploding!'

Andrew gave a deep-throated chuckle as he recalled what could have been a tragedy. 'I remember the blast, and the sight of bits of metal blowing through the air like black hail! I mean, connecting a gun to the tramway current! The wonder is it lasted so long!'

She lowered her voice. 'I remember best the kiss on the platform. Remember that, Andrew?'

'What kiss?' he asked playfully. 'Oh, you mean the little peck on the cheek? I thought it was a seagull after a crumb!'

She dug him in the ribs and he laughed.

Yes, he remembered the kiss all right. That was when he knew. Even though they'd had to separate – he into first class, Molly into third – that journey home seemed something momentous as he reflected on that embrace. An *epiphany*. He had made several sketches that day, but they remained merely that, locked away in his drawer waiting for the flush of watercolour, the embellishment of his art. He could never have shown them to his father.

His father.

Guilt gnawed at him, and he tried to keep the pain away.

He gazed out of the window of his carriage now, at the panorama that swept majestically down from their vantage point at the top of the hill. If only he could see some green, creeping through the grey-white of the snow.

Wouldn't that make a perfect background? Molly perhaps leaning against the trunk of a skeletal tree with the snow still clinging to the bare branches, but melting into ever so tiny droplets of water, symbolising a coming thaw, with the resurgent green forcing its way through the shrouding snow. She would be portrayed in all her beauty, but it would be a beauty tempered with a pre-Raphaelite clarity, a realism and a symbolism that would carry their own force. He would have a cotton mill faintly suggested in the distance, rendered dim and fading by low-lying clouds, a contrast to the raw energy of her personality. He wondered if she would agree to pose for him.

But the wordless sigh from Molly ruined the image.

He felt the carriage move slightly at the subtle tug of the horse. It seemed that both of them at the same time had registered once more the black of his mourning dress, and suddenly the mood grew more sombre.

'The funeral tomorrow.' She spoke softly, and looked into his eyes.

'Yes?'

'Will you be all right?'

'I'll be as well as can be expected.'

He stroked her hair once more, realising how fragile she really was.

The assembly room was filled with cigar smoke. In the centre of the room, the large billiard table had been covered with heavy cloth, and several of the most prominent figures in town were standing around it, some of them leaning idly against its thick wooden frame and engaging in desultory conversation, their long frock coats negligently swept open at the rear vent as they placed a hand in one pocket while smoking with the other.

Despite the casualness of their demeanour, there was an air of expectancy in the room.

Suddenly the double doors opened and James Cox walked in. Beside him was Ambrose Morris.

There was a general expression of condolence, a studied wave of sympathy towards the bereaved

Member of Parliament that was reinforced by a smattering of gentle applause. Ambrose raised a hand in acknowledgement and strode purposefully to the small raised dais at the front of the room, James Cox by his side. Everyone now stood erect, and, apart from the occasional chesty cough, silence filled the assembly room of the Wigan and District Conservative Club.

'Gentlemen,' Ambrose began. 'May I thank you for your very kind words and expressions of sympathy. The tragedy that has befallen my family, the dastardly violence that has taken away my dear brother's life, has cast a shadow over our lives that will remain there for ever. But I cannot dwell on this most personal of events. Life, as they say, must go on. And although I spoke to you all several days ago before the ... dreadfulness of what happened, I have expressed a desire to speak once more with you all, and to give everyone here my assurances that I will do my utmost to assist you in this most difficult of times.'

At this point he looked at James Cox, who was staring at him intensely.

'I realise that for some of you the strike – and yes, that is what it is, despite the Miners' Federation insisting on alluding to it as a *lockout*, as if the fault were confined to the owners and no one else – I realise that this has caused great hardship and subsequent loss of income, with *profit* being consigned to fond memory. But I wish to assure you all that moves are afoot in Westminster to grab the vicious bull by the horns, so to speak. I wish to assure you all that I will do my utmost, as the one now reluctantly handed the reins by my dear departed brother, to help bring this dispute to its inevitable conclusion – before your businesses incur any greater losses. And I wish to assure you that any settlement will be a lasting tribute to the steadfastness and the humanity of a man who has created such wealth and prosperity for the people of this town – my late brother, Arthur Morris.'

There was a loud chorus of 'hear, hear' and spontaneous applause. At the front of the room, James Cox stood with a suitably sombre expression on his face. But his emotions were anything but sombre.

The interior of any church had a strange, paradoxical effect on Bridie Haggerty. Sure, she felt closer to God here. Wasn't it His home on earth after all? But she also felt a detachment from Him, a feeling that this vaulted grandeur was far beyond her, belonged to others far more worthy. She came every Sunday, sat and knelt in the same place, bestowed upon her fellow parishioners the same benevolent smile, responded to Father Brady's blessing *'Dominus vobiscum'* along with the rest of the congregation, and at the end of Mass she stood outside and swapped the small courtesies, the trite irrelevancies of gossip that only the pure of heart and soul can derive particular pleasure from.

When Seamus and the others were buried five years ago, there had been large crowds lined up all the way to Gidlow Cemetery. The explosion in the pit had touched many families – almost everyone in the town knew at least one person affected by the tragedy, not counting those who had lost their loved ones in such a brutal and sudden way, and even those whose menfolk had been uninvolved in the disaster, working the mines in different collieries, had felt the deaths deeply, wondering if they would one day be standing in the shoes of the bereaved. And so the slow procession of hearses had a particular resonance with everyone, and everyone had turned out to demonstrate their respect and, yes, their gratitude. Bridie had recognised both emotions in their eyes as she had looked out from the family carriage.

Now, as she sat in the pew beside the confessional, waiting for the door to open and the penitent to leave, she tried to concentrate, to dismiss thoughts of Seamus and the past from her mind, and focus on why she had come tonight.

The candles beside the altar flickered and seemed to have a special aura around them, though she knew that was only a trick of her tired eyes. She looked to her right, gazed into the stone eyes of Saint Patrick, who appeared to be looking directly into her soul. It was the good saint's simple description of the Holy Trinity with the help of the humble shamrock that had helped her feel there were three gods watching over her in those dark days back in Charlestown, when her da let the devil take over. *He was one snake Saint Patrick hadn't chased out of Ireland,* she thought to herself. Before the sad smile could come, the penitent, a pinch-faced old crone clutching a glistening loop of rosary beads, was tapping her on the shoulder and telling her that Father Brady was ready for her now.

'Thanks,' Bridie whispered.

She crossed herself and stood up. As she stepped

111

into the aisle and looked at the open door, she heard the wheezing cough from the old priest and, in her mind's eye, she could see the sliver of spittle on his chin that always followed his consumption of the communion bread and wine every Sunday.

It had been Father Brady who found the body in the dark alleyway. He'd spent the next few days telling all and sundry what he'd found in gruesome detail.

The ould gossip.

She wondered if God knew her deepest thoughts, if Saint Patrick's spirit had somehow read her thoughts and whispered them in His ear, the thought that, in some macabre way, she and Father Brady shared a common bond. A bond of blood.

Quickly, she shook her head, turned away from the open confessional and walked past the startled old woman who was about to kneel and begin her first Hail Mary. She pushed open the heavy wooden door at the back of the church and emerged into the starry night, unshriven.

Arthur Morris had been washed and cleaned. Now, in the parlour, he had been laid out in his open coffin, the expression on his face a testament more to the undertaker's sublime skill than to any sign of peace in death. His eyes were closed, and his lips gently pressed together. There was an uncharacteristic smoothness that swept down from his cheeks and traced the contours of his cheekbones with the coldness and detachment of a statue. Nevertheless, the immediate impression was one of contentment and reconciliation, the ideal that all undertakers aspire to.

His widow, Prudence Morris, forced her eyes away from his face and gazed instead at the two tall candles, one at either side of the coffin where the small, makeshift altar had been thoughtfully and tastefully erected by the undertaker.

'We must make a point of thanking Mr Pendlebury,' she said slowly, as if her words were adopting a prematurely funereal pace.

'We will.'

Ambrose Morris stood beside her, lost in his own thoughts.

'This is very good. Very good. Arthur would have been content.'

They remained there paying their respects for a long time. Nothing more was said. Each, in their own way, was reliving past scenes.

Ambrose saw a young boy climbing a tree, yelling down to him that he could see hundreds and hundreds of chestnuts and he was going to reach out and eat as many as he could before Ambrose could taste even one. Ambrose at first ignored his older brother, for he was too preoccupied with the splendid gift from their father, a tricycle that he wheeled round and round the garden until he was forced to pause to catch his breath.

'No!' he shouted upwards into the foliage. 'Don't eat any.'

'Why not?'

'Because they're horse chestnuts, you ninny fool. They'll rot your gut.'

'You're lying! Just because I've got them and you haven't! You look silly on that thing. You're not a horse, you know.'

'*And you look silly up that tree. You're not a bird,* *you know. It's sweet chestnuts we ate last week, Artie.* *They're not the bloody same. Now get down here at* *once or I'll tell Father.*'

Ambrose closed his eyes, trying to keep the memory fresh. Such a simple memory from so long ago, but the insidious thought slithered into his mind, the sort of gruesome but casual logic that the presence of death seems to bring with it: *what would have happened that day if I'd let him eat* *the damned things? Would he have died then and* *there? Should we therefore regard the intervening* *years as a kind of bonus?*

He shook his head and, without a word to his sister-in-law, he left the room. Prudence Morris remained where she was, gazing down at her late husband's hands, clasped lightly together in peace.

She saw a much older, more worldly-wise Arthur of only two years ago, standing on the stage in the public hall in King Street and speaking to the audience of the marvels they were about to see. The place was packed with miners – most of them from his own pits – sitting proudly, their chests thrust forward as if they were the star attraction – with their wives and their children beside them, an excited air of curiosity and amusement filling their expressions as they waited for the show to begin.

'These lantern slides,' Arthur had begun, 'are the very first in the world to show what life is like for your husbands and your sons and your brothers and your fathers. Our colliers are the finest working men on this land – and beneath it!' He had paused while the audience clapped his

114

humour. He had seemed the beneficent owner, benign and caring, the antithesis of the Beelzebub he had since become. He had even invited the families left devastated by the explosion of a few years previously, given them a special meal in the committee room at the back of the hall, making sure that he gave each and every one of the bereaved his special attention.

The door opened and Andrew came in. Neither of them acknowledged the other as he came to stand facing his mother, the coffin between them. He looked down at his late father, at the closed lips, and he too heard echoes from the past.

Had those words, those terrible words, come out of those lips? Surely, at moments like this, you were supposed to recall the good times between you. He shook his head, and was surprised to find a tear falling down, landing on the velvet edging that ran around the coffin. Prudence looked at him and closed her eyes for a few seconds to show both understanding and consolation. But her son was far away, deafened by the roar of his father's voice...

'Don't think for one moment that I won't! Do you hear me? There's Lydia Merkham, for instance. Look at the wealth she'd bring with her!'

'Lydia Merkham? With the buck teeth and the squint? I've met her once! That was enough. I don't feel anything for her at all. Nothing!'

'Keep the other, by all means keep her! But as a side dish, not the main bloody course!'

'I love her!'

'Love! Don't be bloody ridiculous! You sound like something out of a damned romance. Besides, this

115

paragon of beauty, this bitch from Hades, might not be around for much longer.'
'What do you mean?'
'Nothing at all.'
'You won't do anything to...?'
'End this silliness, Andrew. Now.'
'I refuse.'
'You will marry that slattern over my dead body! Do you hear? Over my dead body!'

CHAPTER SEVEN

The funeral of Arthur Morris, colliery owner and president of both the South Lancashire Coal Owners' Association and the Royal Antediluvian Order of Buffaloes, was a suitably grand affair. The family had listened to advice from those who argued that a display of sombre pageantry might be unsuitable in the present climate; many of the people were badly affected by the strike; children were looking pale and emaciated despite the many soup kitchens in the borough; and some of the more hot-headed of the strikers might take the opportunity to voice some sort of protest not only at the way Arthur Morris conducted himself in life but at the ostentatious way he was leaving it.

But others had argued differently.

Arthur had done much to enrich the town; his collieries were the most profitable in the whole of Lancashire and the cannel coal they produced was internationally acknowledged as the best coal in the world. He had personally granted a local vicar and amateur photographer unlimited access to his mines in order to capture his men at work despite fears that the indiscriminate use of flash powder underground would cause explosions, thus ensuring that the back-breaking labours in the bowels of the earth were preserved for future generations. Furthermore, the floral tribute from the Miners' Federation – a magnanimous gesture, given the circumstances – had touched them greatly.

Besides, he was a father and a husband and deserved the splendid journey to the family tomb.

At Captain Bell's instigation, however, police constables were strategically placed along the route, two men outside every public house where the trouble, if it came, would doubtless originate. A detachment of soldiers from the East Lancashire Regiment had been put on alert and given a temporary billet in the drill hall on Powell Street, where they sat around playing cards and waiting for the series of whistles that would signify serious disorder and ensure their immediate response.

Yet the whistles would remain silent that day.

And so the procession set off from Standish, the snow thick and stubborn beneath skies grey and heavy with the threat of yet more snow. The hearse was a magnificent carriage with glass walls and tasteful purple fittings drawn by four horses decked in black ostrich feather plumes and preceded by an attendant attired in black silk. The lead-lined coffin could be clearly seen beyond the black silk curtains that lay open, its elm veneer glistening dully in the half-light that caught also the silver trim of the handles and the nameplate.

Behind came the family in the mourning coach, velvet drapes drawn closed with the merest slip of a gap to indicate the presence of those inside.

Many people lined the route down Wigan Lane, past the Royal Albert Edward Infirmary and the gates to Haigh Hall, which were suitably decked in black cloth on the personal orders of Lord Crawford himself, who travelled with the cortege behind the family, along with the countless other dignitaries. Here, outside the gates to the magnificent ancestral home, the cortege paused for a while. The air was filled with the whispered asides of the crowd and the impatient snorting of the horses which sent small billows of cloud into the bitterly cold air. The labouring classes thought the pause was merely a mark of respect to the living as well as the dead – Lord Crawford, after all, was a very important figure in the town yet those closer to the family knew the real reason the procession stopped in this place: Arthur Morris had become, for a brief exhilarating moment, the man who made the Prince of Wales laugh. It was one of his fondest memories, and it had been at the express suggestion of Lord Crawford himself that the deceased should be allowed to savour his moment of royal triumph one last time. The family had readily and gratefully agreed.

As the sombre procession moved slowly down past Mab's Cross – that sad little monument to a woman's unknowing betrayal in the early fourteenth century – Michael Brennan stood and watched the proceedings. Ellen and Barry were with him, listening to the creak and groan of the carriage wheels and the crunching sound they made whenever they reached unbroken snow.

Funerals were a part of life, and if his son were to grow into the sort of man he wanted him to be then it was necessary to show him how to conduct himself in the common decencies of life. Ellen had agreed, reluctantly, although she would much rather have the boy safe and warm in front of the fire on a day like this, and she held Barry's hand while her husband held the other.

Brennan looked at the people, thousands of them stretching back towards Standish and forwards into the centre of town, the incline that took Standishgate towards Market Place and Wallgate beyond that. Every shop window, every vantage point along the way was filled with the curious and the respectful. It seemed, too, that every shop had been sombrely dressed in mourning, swathes of black crape tastefully twined around display windows, and those shops with blinds had brought them halfway down.

And not one murmur of dissent, of abuse.

The people bowed their heads and removed their caps and their bowlers and many of them made the sign of the cross as the late Arthur Morris passed them by. Brennan was suddenly struck by an emotion he found hard to put into words. There was a lump in his throat – these people around him, how badly they had suffered, and were still suffering, and indeed many of them blamed the man in the coffin a few yards from where they stood. Yet they showed him respect and made sure that his family could perform their sombre duties unhindered by any external indignities. Sometimes, when his job showed him the

119

worst that people can do to each other, it was a comfort to catch a glimpse of the best they can do as well.

The cortege had passed them by now and was beginning the laborious climb towards Standishgate, when he saw Constable Jaggery making his way through the crowds as people began to disperse.

'What is it, Constable?' he asked, catching the glint in his eye.

Jaggery registered the young boy still clasping his father's hand, touched his helmet to acknowledge the presence of Mrs Brennan, then whispered breathlessly into his sergeant's ear.

'I beg your pardon?' said Brennan, unsure if he had heard correctly.

'I said *"cocks"*, Sergeant,' he said, this time rather more loudly than he had intended.

Constable Jaggery was aided in the recovery of his breath by a pint of porter in the Royal Oak. They had been fortunate to find a table; the place was filled with men who had been watching the funeral procession with their womenfolk, the latter having subsequently been despatched home with the children while the men 'had a livener'. Many were reliant upon the budgetary generosity of the landlord, a man of business and foresight who allowed them a slate of credit each.

'Now then,' said Brennan. 'What's this about cocks?'

'Last night, Billy Platt got word there was going to be a cockfight.'

Brennan knew Constable Platt, a bright, alert

young lad who was handy both with his fists and his brain, an unusual combination among the lower ranks.

'Down in Taylor Pit Woods. So he took a few of the lads and went skulking in the trees waiting for the game to start. They even kept out of the way of the pipers.'

It was common practice among the cockfighting brethren to stage lookouts around the widened perimeter of the fight in case the police showed an interest. Pipers – a local distortion of *peepers* – were well paid for their alertness. A huge amount of betting took place at such occasions, and during the present difficult times such gambling had increased markedly.

Brennan took a sip of his ale, an impatient expression on his face.

'Any road,' Jaggery went on quickly, 'it was only a two-cocker but there was big money on the fight. Billy reckoned there were over a hundred stood round waiting for the action.'

'And?'

'Well, he's not daft is Billy. There he was in the trees with five other constables and there were the speckies down in the hollow: hundred of them, five of us.'

'So what did he do?'

'Waited. No point in rushing down swinging their clubs when all they'd meet would be a gang of pitmen ready for a scrap. So he let the cocks fight – said you should've seen the spurs on one of 'em, all silver and long and thin as your mam's needle. That little bugger won, wagers were paid out and the men went off in all directions. Then he sent three of the lads after the loser and two of 'em sought out the winner. Guess who it was?'

The glare he gave told its own tale.

'Eddie Cowap.'

Brennan smiled. Eddie was a notorious gamer, involved in everything from cockfights to dog-scraps.

'And that's not the good news either,' said Constable Jaggery, taking another annoying sip of porter before delivering his 'good news'. 'Eddie asked to see the one dealing with the murder. That's you, Sergeant.'

'I know.'

'Says he has summat to say.'

'What's that?'

'Well,' said Jaggery, a little crestfallen. 'I don't know.'

Brennan looked at him for a while until Jaggery could stand the glare no longer.

'Well, Sergeant, he wouldn't tell *me*, now would he? I asked him an' he just laughed. Said he would only speak to the one in charge, the one he could do a deal with.'

'A deal?'

'Reckons what he has to say is worth us turning a *blind* eye. Seemed to think that was funny, but I couldn't see the humour in it meself.'

While the two policemen were deep in conversation, Bridie Haggerty walked along the path that led to the railway track. It dropped steeply, only a few footholds showing through the snow to the coarse grass that ran alongside the metal track. She could hear a bird warbling high above her head, and, as she looked up beyond the brickwork of the tunnel some fifty yards away, she thought she could see a small flock of starlings flittering around the inner curve of the tunnel. As she stumbled her way to the foot of the embankment, she made her way towards the gaping mouth of the tunnel, where the darkness seemed so inviting.

Had it come to this? A matter of twenty minutes ago she'd been standing outside the Royal Hotel with hundreds of others and watching in silence as his hearse trundled by.

But she wasn't like the hundreds of others, was she?

Every time the carriage swayed and lurched as it negotiated the steep incline towards Market Place, Bridie felt the pain deep inside. Every loose cobblestone, every rut in the uneven surface of the road, was a fresh thorn piercing her flesh. She had felt feverish, the splendid array of mourning seeming to swim before her eyes, black merging into black, and all the while in a firm, harsh focus, the cold light glinted on the glass of the hearse. The distorted images of buildings, stretched impossibly tall, were reflected back as if even in death Arthur Morris had the power to change, to warp. She had had to lean a hand against the pillared entrance to the hotel, wave away the concerns of people she didn't know.

Suddenly, before she could reach the entrance to the tunnel, she saw one of the birds swoop low to land on a raised wooden ledge beside the track. It stared at her, its eyes blinking and unafraid, a single piece of straw in its beak. Bridie saw its breast. What at first she'd thought was black was really dark green. She stood absolutely still, for some reason unwilling to disturb the moment, reluctant to see the bird flap its wings and fly away.

Then, as if in a dream, she heard the low, heavy whistle from the deep innards of the tunnel. A train was coming. She felt the damp grass around her feet, looked down at her skirts, scuffed and smeared with dirt. She stepped onto the track, turned to the black void of the tunnel, and thought of her da, and her mammy, and Father Higgins and Seamus and the kiss at a holy shrine. She thought of another kiss and how through the brute force of it she couldn't breathe until the muffled scream burst forth and she fled from the laundry room, and she thought of the screams of childbirth, the tenderness of her babies at the breast. And then she heard, as the train rattled its way closer and closer, the sing-song voice of a wee girl and the simple words of the poem she had so loved as a child:

And 'somebody's mother' bowed low her head,
In her home that night and the prayer she said,
'Was God be kind to the noble boy,
Who is somebody's son and pride and joy.'

The train was inside the tunnel now, its whistling becoming a roar that filled its cavernous depths with a wild and frenzied crescendo as the steam blasted the underside of the tunnel with nowhere to go. The starling blinked, gave Bridie one last glance, and soared upwards to be with its family high on the rim of the bridge.

She thought of a man whose blood slowly froze

as it oozed from his chest.

And then she felt the iron track rattle beneath her feet.

'Holy Mother of God!' Bridie exclaimed as the train came hurtling from the tunnel's mouth, steam belching and flames howling like a demon expelled.

Eddie Cowap was a small, thin man with a permanent scowl on his face. Whenever he spoke, his eyes darted from left to right, never looking people straight in the eye. This gave the impression of shiftiness, of mendacity, although the habit came more from a brutalised childhood and a father whose temper was violently unpredictable. In spite of this, Eddie had grown up, a man with a strong instinct for living off his wits, and with a powerful sense of self-preservation.

Which was why he had made the offer to speak to Sergeant Brennan. He trusted him, and knew that if anyone could keep him out of the courts, Micky Brennan could.

He sat in the interview room, nervously folding and unfolding his thin, bony hands and occasionally flicking a glance at the fresh-faced constable standing by the door.

'Now then, Eddie,' said Brennan in a sombre tone. 'Not the first time this, is it?'

'No.'

'Be a fine, costs, might even get hard labour, eh? Then how'll the wife manage?'

Eddie pressed both hands together in a parody of prayer.

'And how many children?'

'Six.'

'That's a lot of empty mouths, Eddie, what with you in prison an' all.'

Eddie gave a rueful smile. 'Last time I was in Strangeways, I got a good hidin'.'

'What for?'

'Bloody flies.'

'Flies?' Brennan watched his hands spread open in a declaration of honesty.

'I bet 'em they couldn't guess how many dead flies was in a glass jar. They could see 'em through t'glass. So they reckoned it was easy money. "Daft Wiganer," they said. Smart-arses from Salford. So I took their ha'pennies and their farthings and lifted the jar up. Thing is, they couldn't see the little bugger I had squashed under the top of the jar lid. That made 'em all one out. Reckoned I'd rogued 'em.'

'Well you had rogued them, Eddie.'

'Fair enough, but they knocked me all round yon chapel.'

'You gambled in a chapel?'

''Course.'

Brennan shook his head. 'So. What have you got to tell me?'

'You'll see your way to lettin' me go?'

'Depends.'

Brennan saw the young constable shift his stance. Perhaps he'd been one of those making the arrests last night and resented the idea that the one they spent half of the night in a frozen wood trying to catch should now be offered the luxury of exoneration. But the constable didn't have Captain Bell breathing down his neck and demanding a rapid conclusion to the murder of his friend.

'Right.' Eddie looked anxiously down at his hands. Giving the police any sort of information was not the way people from Eddie's background worked. 'It's about Morris. His murder.'

'Go on.'

Eyes right, eyes left, then down to inspect his fingers.

'I seen him.'

'Who?'

'Chap that has one eye, black patch over t'other.'

Brennan recalled what Jem Muldoon had said about a one-eyed man asking questions.

'I don't see how this is relevant, Eddie. I should imagine lots of people saw this man.'

Eddie bent his head low, and appeared to be inspecting the grain of the wooden table. 'This one-eyed chap's been doin' some business.'

'What kind of business?'

'Dunno.'

Brennan gave an exasperated sigh.

Eddie looked up quickly. 'But I do know it's summat to do with Arthur Morris.'

'How?'

'I heard 'im. One night, I happened to find me-self in Little London.'

Brennan knew exactly why Eddie Cowap would be there – it was an area of ramshackle housing and narrow alleys to the north of the town, per-fect locations for the interminable games of pitch and toss that blighted the borough, with access to the housing by a very narrow entry that expanded into open space before closing in on itself once more.

'The one-eyed chap, 'e's talkin' low-like as they walk past the entry. Keeps askin' about Arthur Morris an' says 'e'll pay well if the other one tells 'im what he wants to know.'

'Who was he talking to, Eddie?'

Eddie Cowap sat back. It was time for Sergeant Brennan to place his bet.

'There'll be no charges this time, Eddie. But there'll be a next time.'

'Wanna bet, Sergeant?' he smiled and leant forward once more. 'It was Golden Gob himself who the one-eyed bugger was talkin' to. Him whose arse they all think the sun shines out of – Frank Latchford.'

CHAPTER EIGHT

There was something different about the house, Andrew felt, as the funeral cortege pulled into the driveway. Not physically, of course. Everything was in its place and the edifice still stood strong and resolute in its dominant and domineering position, a firm reminder of his father and the indomitability of his spirit. But no, he mused, not of the spirit, because that very spirit had now been vanquished. Perhaps the indomitability of the *living* spirit his father had possessed, unlike the eternal spirit that was even now finding its way to its resting place.

Why was he behaving like the leader in a varsity debate? Swooping like a vulture on the semantics of another's argument, gnawing at the inaccuracy with a stubbornness that brought applause and censure at the same time. What did it matter if his father's spirit were defeated by his murder? And was it heresy to talk about a difference between the living spirit and the eternal one?

He slowly shook his head. And yet he couldn't get out of his mind the firm conviction that the place *was* changed. The closed curtains, with their black drapes all around, seemed to suggest a difference now. A hollowness. His father was gone. He would never return. Strange, too, that he would never hear his voice again, never listen to his words of scorn, of anger, of obstruction. Soon, the curtains would be open again, and the visitors would become more frequent and less hesitant as bereavement drifted its way into history. Even the clothes he wore would, after the requisite period of mourning, for him, at least, be less sombre, indicating a desire to lay the ghosts of the past and move forward. For his mother, her period of mourning was customarily much longer.

Sitting across from him in the family carriage, she had her head held high beneath the black veil, and Uncle Ambrose was whispering condolences to her, giving the support he, Andrew, should be giving. He was her only child, he was twenty-three years old, and he was leaving it to his father's brother, a man she tolerated rather than welcomed, to provide the support she so badly needed. Perhaps the one good thing to come from his father's demise might be a rapprochement between the two of them – certainly Uncle Ambrose was showing her the necessary courtesies, at least.

He thought of Molly, and for a few seconds allowed her image to float with ethereal grace before his eyes. But, with the inevitability of fate, her face was almost immediately supplanted by that of his father, red-faced and eyes bulbous with rage. He closed his eyes, and when he opened them again his father had gone.

'Mam, did you see me? Got him straight in his middle button I did. That's what we was all aimin' for, their middle buttons. Got six runs for that.'

Tommy Haggerty sat in front of the faintly glowing fire with a proud smile on his face. It had been a good day, what with the fun of running alongside the funeral in town and weaving in and out of all those folk playing Catch Me. Four of them had gone down to watch it, and Tommy was under strict orders not to do anything to disturb the solemnity of the procession. He had given his firm promise that he would not, but chasing each other through the thick crowds had nothing to do with the procession, he argued, and so, suffering the anger of many of those watching, and even, on occasion, getting a thick ear for their mischief, they had had such a good time at the funeral. And then coming back and throwing snowballs at those policemen! He'd scored three direct hits, and his mam hadn't even been there, not at the beginning anyway.

He'd seen her come up the street walking slowly, her headscarf flapping loosely around her shoulders and her head bowed low, as if she'd lost something and was searching hard to find it, and she'd gone straight inside, ignoring all the noise and the cheering of the children in the street, and closed the door slowly behind her. He'd left the game to persuade her to come and watch the fun like all the other mams, and, after a full five minutes of arm-tugging and wheedling kisses, she'd finally got up out of her chair and stood in their doorway, and every time he looked after that she was clapping him and talking with Mrs Carter next door and she didn't have that dark look on her face any more. He liked to see her talk. For the last few days she hadn't done much of that. She'd been crying a lot and he wondered once more if her heart was still burning.

'Aye you little devil, I saw ye.'

Bridie sat in her chair, stroking his hair with her fingers the way her own ma had done before the turf fire all those years ago. She wondered if her ma, too, had felt such dour thoughts. Although living with Da must have been very hard for her, especially when he'd been drinking, had she ever contemplated doing what Bridie had that day?

The very thought made her shudder, and she comforted herself by answering, *No, no of course she wouldn't. Not my ma.*

Did Molly and Tommy have such simple faith in her? Did they have this image of her as some kind of Blessed Virgin come to earth, incapable of anything but the holiest of acts, the purest of actions, the way she thought of her own mother?

If they did, it was another shame to be added to the ones already blackening her soul. She thanked God then, with a silent prayer, that she had stepped aside from that train and spurned the oblivion it offered. Deep down, she knew there was little chance she would have gone through with it anyway. Not with little Tommy and Molly to care for. It was just ... reassuring ... that was it ... to know that an escape from everything was always to hand.

Molly was in the kitchen, sitting at the table and peeling the potatoes for their tea tomorrow. A simple potato broth that would be cooked on the range beside the hearth tonight and ready for heating up tomorrow, if the little coal they had could last that long.

Molly. In a way, she had been the start of it all, the reason Bridie was feeling the way she felt now. But then, she reasoned, Molly wasn't the start of it. In another way Molly was the end of it.

'Can you tell us about me grandma, Mam? The one about me grandma and the goat that ran away, eh!'

Tommy's voice broke her thoughts, and she was grateful. She could hear Molly humming happily to herself in the kitchen. It was 'Faith of Our Fathers'. As her daughter hummed the melody, Bridie mouthed the words until Tommy turned to look up at her in encouragement.

'Go on, Mam. I like that one. Then a story, eh?'

And so Bridie sang, a slow, haunting melody that brought the old country back, and she could smell once more the early morning mist, the dampness of clothing, as they passed the Stations of the Cross on their ascent of Croagh Patrick, where Saint Patrick fasted for forty days, her school friends blessing themselves with a shy

132

giggle hidden from the sisters; an image of herself standing before the statue of Saint Patrick himself, gazing into his eyes as he stood sublime on that holy mountain, the drizzle of Atlantic rain staining the white of his face and the pallor of her cheeks. A holy sharing. And all the while the gentle singing of the pilgrims as they made their slow progress up the mountain:

Faith of our fathers, we will love
Both friend and foe in all our strife.
And preach thee, too, as love knows how,
By kindly words and virtuous life.

When she stopped singing, she saw Molly framed in the door to the kitchen, using the knife in her hand to conduct the next verse.

When he was twelve, Frank Latchford had begun working down the mines, and for the first few years he worked as a drawer alongside his father in one of the Morris Collieries at Hindley, a few miles from Wigan. His work then involved heaving the loaded coal tubs along the underground roads to the cage where they would be taken to the surface for weighing and unloading. He would then push an empty tub back to begin the process all over again.

It was in 1891 that his father died, and it had been sheer luck that Frank hadn't died with him. The cage to take the men down was full and Frank watched his dad and the others go down. Thirty seconds later, they heard a terrible screeching sound as, it was discovered later, the cage had

133

slipped from its slides and remained stuck halfway down while the ropes above continued to drop. Somehow the cage realigned itself with the slides, but by that time the rope had descended so much that it lay coiled on the cage roof. Once the cage was freed, it plummeted to the bottom, killing four of the men, including Frank's father who suffered a fractured skull.

The investigation by the Inspector of Mines ruled negligence against the owner, Arthur Morris, who had repeatedly ignored reports all making reference to the insecurity of the descent apparatus.

Within a year, Frank Latchford's mother had died, her melancholy degenerating into a prolonged and inescapable insanity.

Both deaths affected him profoundly, and the wave of sympathy, along with his new job as checkweighman – whose duties involved weighing and recording all tubs brought to the surface, a position of trust and respect – and his natural eloquence, helped to win him election as lodge representative.

Once he and Molly began their courtship, the sadness of the last few years had seemed to ease like the healing of a deep scar, and to Frank at least the future began to appear rosy.

The first taste he had had of politics on the grand scale came in March, a few months before the pay dispute began. As a consequence of his growing reputation as a powerful orator and a man in whom the miners could place their trust, he was invited by the Miners' Federation of Great Britain, along with thirty-three other district representatives, to form part of the deputation to present their case for the Eight Hours Bill to the prime minister himself, the Right Honourable William Gladstone MP, at 10 Downing Street. There he met not only the prime minister, but the Secretary of State for the Home Department, the Right Honourable Herbert Asquith MP, and eighteen other Members of Parliament.

It was heady stuff for a twenty-four-year-old.

He was therefore disappointed when the prime minister expressed his reluctance to involve himself in what he referred to as *adult labour concerns*, and his distinguished colleagues all murmured their agreement. They also murmured their agreement when the grand old man went on to say that he did not rule out any future involvement, a statement Frank Latchford found contradictory at best and hypocritical at worst.

Nevertheless, he had enjoyed the experience in London and the camaraderie that developed among the members of the deputation.

It also helped him cope with the open wound that had pained him since Molly Haggerty had told him their courtship was at an end.

But such thoughts were far from his mind as he walked along Greenhough Street pushing a small, but evidently laden, handcart through the thick snow.

He reflected on the events of the morning with the satisfaction of a commander reviewing a well-executed sortie.

It had been like a scene from hell.

From a distance, it had seemed that the waste tips stretched almost to the foot of the pit head frame itself. At his urging, men, women and children with their carts and their buckets and their frayed old sacks, every last one of them, knelt on all fours bending low over the rubble of waste coal and scrabbling large lumps and small lumps into their means of conveyance. In the early morning air, with the pale sun barely visible on the horizon, curses had drifted upwards like demonic prayers as fingers were cut and knuckles bruised in the desperate search for something to light the cold hearths for the next few nights. Children, some of them too drawn and malnourished to run around and play, had sat beside their mothers and fathers, their sisters and brothers, listlessly dropping whatever lumps of cannel coal they could find beneath the dusty mounds of waste into iron buckets. Black dust had brought a pallid shadow to their faces, and eyes that had once sparkled were now dulled and misted, like the wasted wick of a dying candle.

And standing atop the largest mound, Frank Latchford had overseen the action with all the pride of a general surveying the aftermath of a successful charge.

It had indeed been a productive morning.

The funeral yesterday had provided many folk with a diversion, but watching such a man on his final journey wasn't calculated to put bread on your table or warmth in your grate, so he had urged everyone he could to join him before morning light.

He had organised the dawn raid on the Morris Colliery, taking with him over a hundred fellow miners, their wives and their children, every one of them bearing some kind of transportation from horse-drawn wagons to flimsily built trolleys on misshapen wheels, all taking the same circuitous route, and they had spread across the slag heaps, known locally as the Alps, picking coal and loading as much as they could gather for the benefit not only of themselves but also of those older and much more likely to die from the bitter cold of winter.

It was heart-warmingly ironic, he reflected, to take coal from the man who had shown such contempt for them all. 'His legacy is to turn us into thieves!' Latchford had yelled to them as he stood silhouetted against the lightening sky. 'Let's not insult his memory by spurning his benefaction!'

And they had responded eagerly, driven on by the bitter cold and a growing despair.

He had been home five minutes when there was a sharp knock at the door. Neighbours didn't knock like that – in fact, on Birkett Street where he lived neighbours didn't knock at all, they just breezed straight in, so he knew immediately this was no friendly visitor. When he opened the door and saw Detective Sergeant Brennan and that broad-chested lackey of a constable, he gave a most unwelcoming frown.

'A few words, Frank?' Brennan had spoken with a friendly reasonableness that put Latchford on his guard at once.

He stepped aside and waved an arm at them. 'You'd best come in then.'

James and Agnes Cox were the first to pay a call

of condolence the day after the funeral.

Andrew had sat there dutifully throughout the morning, listening to his father's friend deliver eulogies to a man whose wisdom, companionship, bonhomie and steadfastness had known no equal since the beginning of recorded time. His Uncle Ambrose sat there and made suitably grateful noises, all the while maintaining a sombre and respectful expression, and his mother, her features partly hidden behind her black veil, had accepted the assurances from Mrs Cox with a silent equanimity.

Nevertheless, the longer he listened to such drivel, the further away his father seemed to go. It was like watching an artist work in reverse – the more animated their visitors became with the picture they painted, the more colourful their praises of his innumerable qualities, the fainter the portrait grew until all that was left was a blank and futile canvas.

This was not the man he had known all his life.

He could bear no more. Pleading a terrible headache brought about by the compressed grief of the last few days, he made his excuses, ran the gauntlet of handshakes and trite utterances of sympathy, and left the parlour where his father had lain only two nights ago. When he closed the bedroom door he breathed a huge sigh of relief. For the next few hours he tried vainly to allow sleep to take away some of the agonies he felt.

Now, as he stood with the curtains parted half an inch and looked idly at the rear gardens with their patches of frozen snow reflecting the dying light above them, then at the row upon row of terraced houses in the far distance shadowed by the pit, he thought of Molly. Immediately, he felt a wave of guilt wash over him. To think of her on the day after his father's funeral when he should be attending to other matters...

And yet, in the window's reflection, he saw not his own image, but the contorted face that stared up at him last Saturday night...

There was a gentle knock on his door.

'Yes?'

Grace, his mother's personal maid, entered and gave an elaborate curtsy. 'Begging pardon, sir, only it's madam. She'd like to see you in the drawing room.'

'I'll be there at once,' he said.

Grace gave another curtsy and seemed to breathe a sigh of relief.

He closed the small gap in the curtains, and braced himself. Then, suitably composed, he walked quickly from the room.

The small front room was surprisingly well ordered. A polished dresser, with two windows latticed in lead, contained an array of silver-framed photographs. In one, a small, wiry individual was standing proud and erect against a studio background of a glistening waterfall, and in another, a middle-aged woman was seated on what appeared to be a bed of roses, a half-formed smile on her face. Beneath these lay a small collection of books, some of which were novels by authors Brennan – who considered himself quite well-read – had never heard of: *The Prophet's Mantle* by Fabian Bland, and *Workers in the Dawn* by George Gissing.

Latchford, who had sat in the room's only armchair and hadn't invited his visitors to sit, noticed Brennan's interest. 'My mam and dad,' he said with a nod at the two photographs. 'Both gone now.'

'I'm sorry,' Brennan said. Then, after a pause, 'You like reading?'

'Some things, yes.'

He was staring at Brennan intently. From beyond the window, children's screams could be heard as they played some sort of game.

Brennan decided to go straight to the point. 'You remember the one-eyed man Jem Muldoon talked about?'

'I do.'

'You didn't actually tell me you'd met him, did you?'

'You didn't ask me. If I remember right, you were asking Jem all the questions.'

'Well, Frank, I'm asking now.'

Latchford smiled, transforming his usually humourless features into something quite engaging. Brennan wondered how often he used such a trick to win over a surly or hostile audience.

'There's really nothing to report, Sergeant, not in an incriminatory sense anyhow. The man you're looking for came up to me after a meeting in the public hall. Said he'd enjoyed my speech and wondered if he could stand me a drink.'

'Just like that?'

Latchford frowned. 'We're the victims of a lockout, Sergeant. We get no pay. So if a one-eyed man offers to buy me a drink I don't send him packing.

140

If he'd had three eyes and a turnip growing out of his neck I'd still have taken him up on the offer.'

'Go on.'

'We went to the Black Horse and he bought me several drinks.'

'Because he was fired by your eloquence?'

'I'm not a naïve man, Sergeant. If someone's paying for my ale then he's after summat. The knack is to get as many drinks out of him as you can before giving him what he's after.'

'What was his name?'

'He didn't tell me. And I didn't ask.'

'Where was he from?'

'No idea. Not Wigan, I can tell you that.'

'What was he after?'

At this point, Latchford stood up and walked to the window, where Constable Jaggery had been idly watching a group of children chasing each other down the street. Jaggery stood aside to allow him access to the scene, and the young miner gazed out for a while. Then he turned round and said, quite unexpectedly, 'You have children, Sergeant?'

Brennan blinked before responding. 'A son.'

'I bet you and your wife spoke for months, making such plans for him, eh?'

'Yes.'

Jaggery, from beside the window, gave his sergeant a perplexed shrug.

'Until February this year I had such hopes, too.'

'What happened?'

'Oh, life happened. The girl I was planning to marry, she decided it wasn't a future she wanted. Not with me, anyway.'

141

'I fail to see…'

He raised a hand, a gesture that asked for patience. Clarification was on its way. 'The girl had met someone else. She didn't tell me that. She just said she couldn't see us together any more and that I should concentrate on my work for the Federation. Noble of her. But I knew there was something else. Some*one* else. I took to following her. Strange what you do when… Any road, one day I saw her being picked up by a carriage. It's not the sort of thing that happens to someone like Molly Haggerty. A mill girl. And I recognised the man who'd stopped for her.'

'Who was it?'

'Andrew Morris.'

Brennan's eyes opened wider. He assimilated the information but remained focused on what he had come for. 'What has this to do with the one-eyed man?'

'He said he'd heard me and Molly had been walking out. Began to ask me questions about her. Said he'd heard whispers about her and her new chap. Wanted to find out as much as he could about Molly. Her family. Her background.'

'Why?'

Latchford shrugged. 'He didn't say. But it's fairly bloody obvious, isn't it? Any road, I told him nowt much. But I'd had a few drinks by this time and I may have given him more information than I should've done. But I was still full of…'

He turned his gaze back to the children outside.

Brennan thought. *Now why would this stranger be asking questions about a young woman who worked in the mill? The only reason, of course, would be her*

142

liaison with young Andrew Morris. And what, then, was the connection with Arthur Morris, and his murder? Had Morris, as Latchford hinted, paid the one-eyed man to make such enquiries?

'Met the bugger once more,' Latchford went on. 'But I was sober on that occasion and told him to sod off.'

'Does your dislike of the son extend to the father?'

Latchford smiled once more, but this time it was a controlled gesture, designed to conceal darker emotions than pleasure. He glanced to his right at the photographs behind the leaded glass and the volumes below.

'You know, my dad said the worst part of working down the mines was the absence of thought. Though he didn't express it quite like that. But I know that's what he meant. You work down there for ten, twelve hours at a stretch. And the biggest curse to a miner isn't the coal dust – though that, as they say, is a bugger. No, it's an imagination. If you have a capacity for vivid imagination, then the minutes become hours and the hours become days. Far better the chap who can swing a pick and hammer a drill with nowt on his mind but the tang of the next pint. It's not a place for thinkers down there and yet the place is ideal for thinking. Hell's irony, that.'

Brennan looked at Jaggery, whose eyes had now glazed over with boredom.

'So yes, Sergeant, I disliked the father almost as much as I disliked the son. But if you're asking me if I killed Arthur Morris, the answer is no.'

'Where were you Saturday night?'

'I was here, alone, reading. You must read *The Prophet's Mantle*, Sergeant. Written by two people, actually, despite the name "Fabian Bland". That's a giveaway anyway. You've heard of the Fabian Society?'

Brennan nodded. 'Socialists.'

'Correct. Fabian Bland is Edith Nesbit and her husband. They helped create the Fabians. And the novel recounts the life of Peter Kropotkin.'

'Who was he?'

'He was an anarchist, Sergeant Brennan. You'd find it interesting and disturbing in equal measure.'

Brennan turned to go. 'Just one more question, Frank. The girl who you were courting. Molly Haggerty. Where does she live?'

'Scholefield Lane. Number 7. Give her my regards when you see her. And her mother, of course.'

They got nothing more from him. Once they were outside, Jaggery watched the children pull faces at him and one or two of them used words they had heard their parents use whenever a uniform appeared.

'Anarchy, Sergeant? Shouldn't we arrest the bugger for reading such stuff?'

'It's a free country, Constable.'

But Brennan's thoughts were far from anarchy. If, as Latchford said, the one-eyed man wasn't from Wigan, then it would be highly unlikely he would be staying anywhere other than a hotel or a lodging house. It was something he would have to look into.

'What now, then?' Jaggery asked, giving one of

144

the boys who had run too close to him a swift clatter round his ear.

'No point going to see the girl at this time, not if she's working in the mill. No, I think it's time for the Morrises, Constable. I can't put off any longer what will doubtless be a most difficult set of interviews. Still, it has to be done. I have several questions I need answering. Then we need to speak with this young woman, Molly. It's a strange liaison, is that. Mill girl and a wealthy young chap like that.'

First, though, he had to report to Captain Bell.

CHAPTER NINE

The three of them sat there around the hearth, but said nothing while the maid built up the fire. She couldn't help glancing round furtively, as if she was aware of being observed, and that made her job harder. She therefore took her time placing each lump of coal on the pile with great care, using the metal tongs with delicacy and precision. Finally, when she had finished and the flames had been subdued, waiting to rise again through the newly introduced coals, she withdrew, keeping her eyes cast down as befitted a domestic in a house of mourning.

'You wished to see me?' Andrew looked at his mother.

She was gazing at the flames striving to break through. As usual, she sat with an erectness that betrayed the pain of her rheumatic condition. Often he could detect the faintly unpleasant aroma of the tincture of arnica she applied to alleviate her pain, and he knew that often, whenever she moved suddenly, a spasm of pain would jolt her alarmingly. Yet she bore all with stoicism, never once complaining. In the other armchair – his father's favoured one – his uncle Ambrose sat with a stern expression on his face.

He knew that the relationship between his mother and his uncle was a fragile, often distant one: the reason for such a coldness between them was lost in the mists of time, but Andrew had never known them to speak to each other with anything but cold courtesy. On one occasion he had heard his mother refer to him as 'that pompous man', a rare slip of the veil behind which she normally kept her feelings hidden. His father had mumbled something in retort about his brother being 'infected with Londonitis', but it had been said in a largely jocular tone, with fraternal grace, pride even – a contrast to the animosity that always seemed to swim just beneath the surface of his mother's tranquillity, like a deadly shark.

It was Ambrose Morris who spoke. 'Your mother wants to know of your plans.'

'Plans?' His heart beat fast. 'About what?'

His mother lifted her gaze heavily and cleared her throat. 'The future. Now that your father has gone.'

'In what particular sense?'

Her voice was soft and low. 'This ruinous dispute with the colliers, for one thing. Naturally, you will be expected to take charge of the coalfields now your father is...' She glanced down at her clasped hands and took a deep breath before continuing. 'Your uncle informs me that he is to return to London very soon. He wishes to know the line you will take.'

Ambrose coughed. To Andrew, it looked as though he resented having his sister-in-law speak on his behalf. 'What your mother says is true. I have assured many of our business acquaintances that there will be – shall we say – a change of direction as far as the Morris Collieries are concerned? The future course of this dispute is our responsibility now, Andrew.'

'Isn't this a bit ... heartless?'

'Heartless?'

'My father – your brother – is very recently interred and you wish to discuss strategy?'

Ambrose gave a deep sigh. 'I have to return to Westminster. I need to know that you and I have the same design – to do all we can to bring this dispute to an end. It would help me greatly if I could make certain assurances to the right people that the wind is changing direction. The Morris name still holds immense sway throughout the industry.' He stood up to face his nephew. 'My brother's death is but one of many this town has suffered. In my opinion, the suffering has gone on long enough. To wait for a suitable period of mourning and then make decisions would be unthinkable.'

He knew his uncle was right, of course. Perhaps he had allowed his love for Molly to ignore such weighty considerations.

'As the one who will be responsible for whatever happens in the family coalfields,' his mother went on, 'you will be called upon to take some action. Or not.'

Ambrose took up the reins. 'We both know how ... persuasive your father could be. When the coal owners began this ruinous dispute, it was largely due to his influence that they dug in their collective heels. "Now is not the time for faint hearts," he said. "Now is the time to show reason with strength". He liked the idea of that phrase: "reason with strength". Well, soon the owners are meeting once more, and from what I hear in Westminster, they are determined to give every appearance of flexibility and conciliation while moving not a jot from their recently revised figure of fifteen per cent. Some are threatening to withdraw even that concession and go back to the original twenty-five per cent reduction. I have also heard a rumour, from a benign member on the government benches, that there are secret moves afoot to bring the dispute to an end. Mr Gladstone will not allow this cancer to fester much longer, Andrew.' He looked his nephew straight in the eye, as if to underpin the gravity of his next words. 'The owners need someone there who can provide the voice of common sense, the voice of pragmatism in the face of stubborn principle.'

Andrew nodded. 'I know. And I will. The dispute should never have happened. We should have learnt the lessons of 1888, but telling my father that was...' he broke off, looked at the flames and the underglow of the coals. 'It just seems a little ... callous.'

Ambrose leant forward in his armchair. 'In a few more days I shall have to return to London.

I will be here to offer you whatever advice and support you need.'

'Thank you, Uncle Ambrose.'

His mother rested her head back against the rim of the chair. 'And, of course, there is the other thing.'

'What other thing?'

She gave a weak smile and looked across at her brother-in-law, as if she expected him to say something in return. But instead he pursed his lips and uttered nothing more than a surly grunt and a muttered comment about this being an inappropriate time for such things. Then he stood up, leaving the room without another word. Andrew looked at his mother for an explanation, but she had closed her eyes with a pained expression on her face.

Now what was all that about? Andrew wondered.

It took him ten minutes to regain control of his temper. He was, after all, a detective sergeant, and soon he hoped his work would be sufficiently recognised by elevating him to the hitherto non-existent status of detective inspector. It would indeed be an acknowledgement of the work carried out by the detective branch of the Wigan Borough Police, work that involved something rather more subtle than the application of a truncheon and a size ten boot. Yet how could he gain such recognition when the chief constable himself insisted on being present at his next series of interviews, like Banquo's ghost? He had sprung his surprise as soon as Brennan had told him about the curious case of the one-eyed man.

'*The Morrises are a family bereaved, Sergeant. It is only right and proper that any such questioning should take place with dignity and compassion. The presence of an old family friend will help alleviate the anguish your interrogation will cause.*'

'*Interrogation is hardly the...*'

'*Besides, I have already made one call of condolence, as a family friend, and therefore a subsequent visit can be seen as rather more official.*'

'*Indeed, sir, but...*'

'*Do you know that Prudence Morris is a saintly woman, Sergeant?*'

'*No, I didn't, sir.*'

'*A saintly woman. And it is the melancholy fate of sainthood to suffer.*'

'*You mean the murder of her...*'

'*I mean her rheumatic condition that renders even the smallest of movements excruciating. Any but the tenderest of interviews will cause her great distress. I shall be there to act as guardian angel, Sergeant.*'

He's carrying a torch for the widow, thought Brennan wryly. *And he's wrapping it up in altruism.*

He stormed out of the office with a deep sense of grievance. As was the way on such occasions, he transferred much of his unhappiness to Constable Jaggery, whose second bite at a meat pie was forestalled by Sergeant Brennan's order for him to stop gorging his overfed self and make enquiries *with all possible haste* at the various hotels and lodging houses in the town concerning a one-eyed guest.

'But Sergeant, do you have any idea how many of them places there are?'

'No!' Brennan snapped back. 'But you must be

sure to count them and let me know.'

Brennan made the journey with the chief constable in uncompanionable silence, preferring to make his point with muteness where voluble protest had had little effect. When they arrived at the Morris mansion, the cold wind blasted their exposed faces as they stepped from the relative comfort of the carriage. It was Captain Bell who broke the silence between them as he raised the heavy brass door knocker.

'A fine specimen, Sergeant.'

'What is, sir?'

'This!' He held the knocker aloft before letting it crash down. 'A Davy lamp, eh? What finer symbol of Arthur Morris's commitment to his colliers? A symbol of his absolute insistence on safety and the welfare of those who worked for him.'

'It's certainly heavy enough. And loud enough to wake the...'

Fortunately his image was curtailed by the door swinging open, and the butler offering them a sombre and dignified welcome.

Despite their squat, ungainly appearance, the five hundred beehive ovens possessed a strange sort of beauty for James Cox. They stood in a long row quite separate from the eight open-topped blast furnaces that formed the backbone of his iron and steel works, and they had come to represent a visual fusion of nature and the ingenuity of man. The hundreds of tons of coke they regularly produced were an essential factor in the production of iron, and provided the intense heat necessary for the furnaces.

He was standing in the open doorway of the furnace manager's office, despite the bitter wind that was blowing from the east, and turned his gaze from the ovens to the range of blast furnaces to his left. Each of them stood fifty-five feet high, mighty symbols of power in both senses of the word, symbols that made the pithead winding wheels look puny and insignificant. And yet he relied on the coal they produced, for without the coal there was no coke, and the thousand tons a day of fine slack they received from the Morris Collieries was fed into the coke ovens and the coke transferred to the furnaces. The quality of haematite, Spiegel and ferromanganese they produced brought a wealth of contracts throughout the country and, more lucratively, in America.

But without coke the furnaces might as well have been igloos. And the contracts, especially the one with the Blackpool Tower Company, were fast becoming more like threatening letters than agreements of sale.

Was it only three months ago that he was boasting to all at the Club who would listen that one of his furnaces had produced over nine hundred tons of Bessemer pig iron in a single week? That his yearly output was well over a hundred and twenty-five thousand tons of iron of all kinds? Of course the buggers were envious, that went without saying, but their envy was cocooned in admiration. But now, such figures seemed a distant dream, and against the iron-grey darkness of a wintry sky, the furnaces lay silent, an army of Goliaths brought low by the slings of stubbornness.

'Won't be settled in days, Mr Cox. You can put

money on that.'

Nat Walsh, furnace manager, was sitting behind his desk, trying to read the thoughts of the great man.

'No, Nat.' Cox remained where he was, with his back to the office, addressing his remarks to the furnaces.

'How was the funeral?'

The smile that began to form on the owner's face, in acknowledgement of his manager's less than subtle attempt to draw an optimistic link between his last two statements, was quickly transformed into a suitably sombre expression of melancholy.

'Oh it was what he deserved, Nat. Only what he deserved.'

They had been shown into the drawing room.

Brennan silently acknowledged the outward signs of wealth: a large, upright piano, a polished Davenport desk, an elegantly scrolled gasolier overhanging a small table, and along the wall facing the door a series of landscapes, four in all, depicting the same scene transformed by seasonal variations: a small stream frozen in winter wound its way through bare, stark trees with a gently sloping hill, frosted with snow, in the distance. In the following paintings the scene came alive with the fresh colours of a burgeoning spring, growing into the green and blue elegance of a bright summer's day that turned into the lowering light of a leaf-strewn evening, catching the rich browns and russets of autumn. Yet Brennan noticed it was only in the winter scene that a human figure could be seen, a young man sitting by the frozen stream, his hand pressed flat against the unyielding ice. Somehow the figure was vaguely familiar.

Black crepe hung around the frame of each painting, a reminder that even the enjoyment of art must of necessity be placed in mournful abeyance.

Neither of them had been presumptuous enough to sit down. Captain Bell noticed his sergeant's absorption in the landscapes.

'You appreciate the delicacy of the brushwork, Sergeant?'

Brennan shook his head. 'I was thinking more about what the paintings convey. Or don't convey.'

'And what is that supposed to mean?'

'Just idle musings, sir. If winter is the season we associate with death, why then is that scene the only one with any sign of human life in it?'

His superior gave an elaborate and patronising sigh. 'I see the appreciation of art has taken second place to your natural querulousness.'

'Natural curiosity perhaps. It would be interesting to ask the artist what he meant by it.'

'A philistine observation, Sergeant! That is the one thing that is never done. And I trust you will observe that dictum when you have the opportunity to speak with him.'

'Who, sir?'

'Why, the artist, of course. This is Andrew Morris's work.'

Brennan was genuinely surprised. He was no art critic, but there was a haunting, almost wretched quality about the winter landscape that invested the other three seasons with a wistful, rather than joyous, air. He scrutinised the solitary figure once more, and realised why he had seemed familiar.

'Just remember, Sergeant – this is a bereaved house, not an art gallery.'

At that the double doors to the drawing room opened and Ambrose Morris, preceded by his sister-in-law, entered the room.

Mrs Morris moved with a deliberate slowness, and Brennan watched her take a seat by the marble fireplace, letting herself down slowly, as if every care was taken to avoid unnecessary pain. He noticed, too, that Ambrose Morris stood by without offering her the superficial assistance one would expect. Was there a distance between them?

After the preliminary handshakes hastily followed by an apology for the intrusion, both policemen sat down facing their hosts.

Mrs Morris's face was barely discernible through the black veil that hung from a white widow's cap. On her breast she bore a single stone of black jet, its surface dulled and smooth, blending discreetly with the silk dress fringed with crepe.

'It must be immensely distressing for you both,' Captain Bell began with an expression of deep sympathy creasing his brow. 'But my sergeant here has his melancholy duties to perform, and there are one or two questions he must ask. But if you wish to terminate the interview at any time you merely need to ask.'

Not your common or garden prelude to police interrogation, thought Brennan wryly, recalling some of the more forthright interviews he'd seen the chief constable carry out back at the station. He kept his expression neutral as he began.

'I can only echo Captain Bell's words, and assure you of our determination to bring the perpetrator of this wickedness to justice. Where is your son, Mrs Morris?'

He felt his superior bristle beside him, and realised at once the unfortunate inference that his words could cause.

Ambrose Morris narrowed his eyes, as if he were trying to fathom out if there were any trace of irony or flippancy in the policeman's question. 'My nephew is not at home, Sergeant Brennan.'

'I will need to speak with him.'

'And we will let him know.'

Brennan paused before continuing. He had the distinct impression that the Member of Parliament for Wigan was rather abrupt in his manner. Was this a trait of his personality? Or was he reluctant to engage in any productive conversation with the one whose duty it was to investigate the murder of his brother? If so, it was rather a curious way of showing devotion.

He took out a notebook and pencil, and flipped it open at a fresh page. He could sense Mrs Morris's eyes watching him keenly behind that dark veil. 'I wish to make clear the sequence of events last Saturday night. When you were all dining here.'

'Is this relevant?' Ambrose asked.

'Yes, sir.'

Ambrose waited for him to elaborate, but Brennan just looked at him with equanimity. 'Very well.'

'When I spoke with Mister Andrew Morris, he

told me there were six of you for dinner.'

'That is correct.'

'Can you tell me how your brother was that night?'

'How he *was?*'

'Did he seem quite himself?'

Prudence Morris spoke up, her voice thin and clear through the veil. 'My husband was as much himself as he could be, considering the damaging effect the strike was having on his health.'

That's a bloody rich one! Brennan thought, keeping the ironic observation to himself. Instead he looked at Captain Bell, who was gazing at the widow with a wealth of compassion on his face. 'Your husband was ill?'

She shook her head. 'As strong as an ox. No, Sergeant, perhaps I should have used the phrase "state of mind". Forgive me. But he was very agitated, despite his public utterances to the contrary. And poor James didn't help.'

'James Cox?

'He broke a cardinal rule of dinner, Sergeant. Business should be discussed over port and cigars, not over a haunch of mutton.'

Ambrose gave a heavy sigh and took up the story. 'James Cox is suffering, like many others in the town. The danger of losing a quite lucrative contract. It tends to sour the most savoury of dishes.'

Here he gave his sister-in-law a peevish glance before continuing.

'So he and Arthur had, shall we say, an exchange of views? The whole thing was blown over of course – I threw onto the table a few scandalous little titbits from Westminster. Guaranteed to monopolise any conversation when you discover the many and various peccadilloes of the high and the mighty. It's amazing how people seem to find such tittle-tattle of interest. Any rancour was quickly forgotten.'

Prudence Morris coughed primly.

'And at what stage did your nephew leave the dinner table, Mr Morris?'

'After the Cabinet pudding, and before the Stilton, if you want exactitude.'

'Was there a reason he left before the meal was finished?'

Prudence Morris lifted a hand gently. 'Andrew had found the conversation not to his taste. He was not in total agreement with his father over the unpleasantness in the mines, and he had some sympathy for James and his position. I suppose he could not in truth take sides. So he made his excuses and left.'

'Did he say where he was going?'

'"To clear his head", I think was the phrase he used.'

'Despite the bitter cold, the snow?'

'He is a grown man, Sergeant,' Ambrose stated with ill humour.

'I understand, sir. So, and then there was someone at the front door?'

'We had finished our dinner and I went upstairs to select some fine Cubans. A rather splendid box of cigars I had purchased in London. Lewis's, in St James Street.'

'Admirable specimens!' Captain Bell interjected. 'I can vouch for 'em myself.'

Brennan ignored the inconsequentiality of the comment. 'Not a place I'm familiar with, sir.'

'No? Sorry. Well, then there was that awful knocking at the door. I was halfway down the stairs and nearly dropped the whole box, it was so loud. Angry, you might say. I saw something flutter into the postal basket. It was an envelope. Grace – that's the maid, Sergeant – came running out of the kitchen and immediately opened the door – the knocking had been quite excessive and I was about to give the perpetrator a piece of my mind. But when she swung the door open, there was no one there. I thought I saw someone, rather a large figure, crouching low and diving behind the bushes, but that could have been a shadow cast by the open door. Not something I could swear to.'

'A large figure, you say?'

'I couldn't swear to it, Sergeant. The maid swore she saw it too. Perhaps she could give a better description than I can.'

'That could well be your mysterious Cyclops!' said the chief constable with a meaningful frown at his sergeant.

'Cyclops?' Ambrose Morris looked perplexed.

Before Brennan could prevent him, Captain Bell went on. 'We have a highly suspicious suspect, Ambrose. Highly suspicious, and a person we are actively seeking as we speak. Many of my men are scouring the town looking for him.'

'*Cyclops?*' said Prudence Morris, unconsciously putting a hand on her neck.

Captain Bell had the decency to flush a rather deep scarlet. 'I do apologise, ma'am,' he said with a bowing of the head towards the bereaved widow. 'A flippancy that was thoughtless. I was merely referring to a suspect who, we are reliably informed, is bereft of binocular normality.'

'What?'

'He's one-eyed,' Brennan explained.

Ambrose Morris's mouth gaped open. 'Is this a joke?'

'No, sir,' said Brennan, inwardly cursing his superior.

With a caustic glance at Captain Bell, Ambrose continued with his narrative. 'Whoever delivered it must have moved quickly. I immediately sent one of the servants out to scour the bushes. These days it could have been anyone with a grudge against my brother. But there was no one. It was most puzzling. By that time, Arthur and James had come running from the smoking room, and Prudence and Agnes Cox had rushed from the dining room.'

'I will need to speak with your servants, Mrs Morris.'

She declined her head slightly. 'Of course. Isaacs, our butler, will assist you.'

'Thank you.'

'Our cook is Mrs Venner. Then Jane, our kitchen maid. A couple of scullery maids fresh from the workhouse. It is a very small domestic arrangement, Sergeant, but we value privacy over ostentation.'

Brennan thought about the funeral. Hardly private and unostentatious. Through the veil, he thought he saw her eyes narrow, as if she had suddenly experienced a sharp stab of pain, and her hands gripped the sides of the armchair tightly.

Ambrose, who had also noticed the spasm, coughed with impatience. 'My sister-in-law is not well, as you can see.'

Captain Bell made to stand up, but sat down again when Brennan spoke once more.

'I do apologise once more, ma'am. Just a few more questions and then we'll be gone.'

'Please,' she said in a low whisper. 'Continue.'

'Tell me about the letter that dropped into the postal basket.'

Ambrose thought for a while. 'Nothing to tell, really. It was white, it had Arthur's name on the front with no address. He opened it quickly and read the contents – a single sheet of paper. Naturally, I asked him what it said and he replied that it was a reminder of a meeting he had completely forgotten about.'

'Hardly surprising,' Prudence Morris added. 'Considering.'

Brennan turned to Mrs Morris. 'Did you see the letter, ma'am?'

'No. Not the contents at any rate.'

'The envelope, then? Were you able to make out who it was addressed to?'

'I may be infirm, Sergeant, but I am capable of recognising my own husband's name.'

He nodded and addressed Ambrose Morris once more. 'So what happened next?'

'My brother made hasty preparations to leave, and James and Agnes Cox decided it was best they should leave also. An unsatisfactory end to the evening.'

'An unsatisfactory end to Arthur's life,' Prudence added with bitterness and, thought Brennan, more than a slight hint of displeasure at her brother-in-law's insensitive comment.

'Quite,' Ambrose said curtly. Then something seemed to occur to him. 'You say you found the letter?'

'Yes, sir.'

'Well, then you know exactly what it said?'

'Yes, sir.'

'Are you going to enlighten us?'

'Perhaps later, sir. When we have someone in custody.'

Prudence Morris looked up and gave Captain Bell a sharp look. 'I thought you had someone in custody?'

'It's a fluid investigation, ma'am,' he said weakly.

Ambrose, however, was not to be thwarted. 'Is there any reason why we shouldn't know what the letter said?'

Brennan shook his head but gave Prudence Morris a quick glance. Ambrose gave a slight nod of understanding and let the matter drop.

'What happened when Mr Morris had left?' Brennan asked.

'I went to bed, Sergeant,' the widow said. 'And my brother-in-law ensconced himself in the smoking room with one of those vile objects.'

'She refers to my finest Cubans,' Ambrose added with a touch of humour. 'I stayed there until Isaacs roused me – I had fallen asleep. And I had an early train the following day.'

'I see. Perhaps you would be good enough to summon the butler, Mr Morris. Now is as good a time as any to have a few words with the servants.'

'Of course.' Ambrose Morris stood up and, as

he pulled the cord beside the fireplace, turned to Captain Bell. 'Alexander, you are more than welcome to remain here while your sergeant makes his way below stairs.'

The chief constable beamed and accepted the invitation with gratitude.

Brennan, too, for different reasons, was grateful for the offer.

'What's this?' Brennan asked.

He pointed to something that looked like a cupboard – two heavy wooden doors on short, squat legs – yet there was a metal strip that ran all the way around the door frame.

'We store food in it. Keep it cold with ice.'

Grace sat at the kitchen table watching the policeman swing the door open and close with almost a child's curiosity.

'This is not where I normally work,' she added with a note of hurt pride in her voice. 'I'm not a kitchen maid, y'know.'

She was, Brennan guessed, fast approaching thirty, and there were traces of the young pretty girl she had once been in the smoothness of her skin and the youthful defiance that still lingered in her eyes like a half-guttered candle. She wore a plain black cotton dress, and he guessed this was the customary mourning apparel of the servants.

Brennan smiled at her and joined her at the table, placing his hands flat down in a conciliatory gesture. Grace seemed fidgety, almost afraid. Perhaps her experience of policemen had not been a happy one. He then leant back in his chair. 'That's a curious accent, Grace. Where are you from?'

'Wolverhampton.'

'Ah. Then you must find the local accent a bit ... difficult.'

'I get by. Don't have much to do with 'em. Don't get the time.' She'd pronounced it *toime,* with a rise on the mysterious second syllable that caused him to smile. She caught the expression and glared at him, but said nothing.

'I suspect they work you hard.'

Grace shrugged. 'It isn't too bad. Mistress helps.'

Brennan frowned. 'What do you mean?'

'I've been a lady's maid before. Got the highest testimonials,' she added with a defiant lift of the chin. 'But the woman I worked for previous couldn't do a thing for herself. They're all like that. Why dress yourself when ye've a maid to do it for you? But missus, she does all that sort of stuff herself. I reckon she's shy. As if I ain't seen it all before. Got the right name, Prudence.'

'Do you like her?'

'I'm paid twenty-four pounds a year to like her.'

She softened slightly and added, 'But yes, I do. Suffers something awful with her rheumaticals. Like I say, independent. Can't say I like the smell of that stuff she rubs on. Arnica. Sickly stuff.'

Ironic, he thought. *The maid complains of former employers who had her doing everything and when she has a mistress who helps herself she is equally indignant. Women,* he reflected wryly.

'And Mr Morris?' he went on. 'The late Mr Morris, I mean.'

'Oh him.' She looked down at her hands again. 'It's bad luck to speak ill of the dead.'

'Not to the police,' Brennan interjected, imbu-

164

ing the interview with a superstitious untruth.

'Well, there was him and his son. Master Andrew.'

'Go on.'

'Hammer and tongs these last few weeks. Warmer in that thing.' She indicated the cold safe that had taken his fancy.

'Have you any idea why they argued?'

Another fumble with her hands. 'No, sir.'

She was a typical servant, relishing the above stairs gossip but going only so far in disseminating it. You never knew where it would end up.

'Was it to do with the coal strike?'

'Well, yes and no,' she said. 'I did hear a few scraps, as it happens, *loike*. The strike, yes, but also somethin' about a girl. But that's all. Honest.'

Molly Haggerty, thought Brennan.

'Remember anything they said about this girl?'

She thought for a few seconds. 'Master didn't approve. And Master Andrew, well, I reckon I heard him cryin' once.'

'Crying?'

She nodded. 'Sobbin' then. Wasn't a nice sound, whatever it was.'

'Was anyone with them?'

'Oh no, sir.'

'Yet they were shouting?'

'Well, when I say shoutin', it was more like whisperin' loud.'

And a damned nuisance when your ear's pressed flat against the door, he mused. 'Tell me about Saturday night. The night Mr Arthur Morris left the house.'

She took a deep breath. 'Jane and I had cleared the dinner things and left mistress and Mrs Cox in the dining room. The gentlemen had gone into the smoking room.' She sniffed her disapproval. 'Stinks to high heaven, that place, 'specially in the mornin'. I'm just glad it's not me has to disinfect the room. They spend hours burnin' trays of charcoal to get rid of the pong.'

Brennan raised a hand to stop her before she ran the whole gamut of domestic chores. 'Jane? She's the kitchen maid?'

'Timid as a mouse, she is. She's walking round this place now as though the master's goin' to jump out an' take her with 'im. The dead are dead, I keep tellin' her, but you should see her run past a mirror!'

'Saturday night?'

'Yes, well, I was sitting in 'ere when I heard the front door.'

'Heard it?'

'Someone thumping on it. Loud. I reckon they bruised their hand they thumped that loud.'

'What then?'

'I rushed along the corridor, got to the hallway and saw Mr Ambrose coming downstairs with a box of somethin'. He goes to the door and looks out, an' I think he saw someone in the bushes. Anyway, then he shuts the door and Mr Arthur tells me to get some letter in the post box. Then when he reads it he says somethin' about havin' to see someone he'd forgot about and says he's goin' out.' She shrugged. 'By this time Isaacs was there, too. He's the butler. And he'd been with Mrs Venner. He's always with Mrs Venner, if you get my meanin'. They share a glass of sherry.' She imbued the phrase with all the wickedness of

Sodom and Gomorrah.

'You saw no one outside?'

'Not sure. Might've seen someone in the bushes, but it was dark over there.'

'What about Master Andrew?'

'He'd left earlier. Lookin' not best pleased. Besides, leavin' at that time, with 'em just havin' dined an' all. That's how you get indigestion.'

'I see. Did you see what was written on the letter?'

The maid again raised her chin. 'I don't read private mail. No matter who it's from.'

Brennan looked at her for a few seconds. 'Can you describe the envelope then?'

'What?'

'The envelope.'

She gave a careless shrug. 'An envelope's an envelope.'

'Was it clean? Dirty? Smudged, wet, damp, crumpled, torn?'

'It was an envelope, a nice white envelope. That's all I can tell you.'

'And written on the front?'

'Master's name.'

'*Arthur* Morris?'

'That's his name, I reckon.'

'What happened then?'

'Then? Nothin' happened. Once Mr Morris had gone mistress said we should finish our duties and then retire for the night. She asked me to escort her upstairs an' she went to bed. I think she was goin' to read for a while.'

'And Mr Ambrose?'

'He went into the smoking room for one of

those awful cigars. Why, he might as well stand in the middle of a thick fog an' take long deep breaths. Never seen the sense in it, myself.'

Before she could launch into a general attack on the filthy habits of those above stairs, he smiled and stood up to indicate the interview was at an end.

The girl Jane had done nothing but look at him like a startled deer just before the hunt begins, and could add little to what Grace had told him. She, too, heard the hammering on the front door, and said she thought they were all going to be attacked by a gang of drunken bloodthirsty miners wielding shovels and pickaxes.

'I got their coats an' that was that.'

'Whose coats? Ah, you mean Mr and Mrs Cox?'

Her face darkened. 'Aye.'

'You don't like them?'

'Not my place, is it? Likin's not expected.'

Brennan's curiosity was piqued. He said, in his most solicitous tone, 'What is it, Jane?'

'Nothin', sir.'

'You can tell me.'

The kitchen maid held his gaze for a few seconds then said, 'Oh she's all right. It's *him*.'

'James Cox?'

'Aye.'

'He treats you with disdain? Is that it?'

She shook her head. 'Takes liberties.'

She looked him fully in the eye as if to challenge him to pursue the obvious.

'I see.'

Inwardly he grimaced. *With some of these people,*

168

you would think we were still living in the eighteenth century and not seven years short of the twentieth. But there was nothing he could do unless the girl made a complaint.

'So they left?'

She nodded. 'I heard *him* say he was goin' to his club. But Mister Ambrose lifted his cigar by way of an excuse. I got the impression the mistress would have been delighted if he'd gone an' all.'

'Why?'

'Not much love lost between Mister Ambrose and the mistress, if you ask me.'

It merely confirmed what Brennan had suspected from the briefest of interviews with them. He wondered what the reason was?

When he sought out Isaacs, he found him standing at the table in the butler's pantry, leaning over an array of silver ornaments, all spread out on a white cloth. He was busy polishing a two-handled silver cup, its scroll handles ending with a flourish of heart motifs. Brennan could see himself reflected on its curved surface and was captivated by the grossly rotund figure he presented.

'Yes, sir,' said the butler, maintaining the regular rhythm of his work. 'I did indeed hear the knocking. I was quite alarmed by it.'

'Alarmed?'

'Well, when someone thumps so hard on the door like that, it's bound to be bad news, isn't it, sir?'

Brennan considered that for a moment. 'Whoever it was didn't avail themselves of the brass door knocker then?'

The butler sneered. 'Using a door knocker – in moderation – is a sign of good breeding, Sergeant. The *person* who hammered on the door probably had no conception of its use. Probably thought it was a real lamp and not an ornamental one.'

Brennan thought of the myriad of houses throughout the poorer areas of the town whose doors contained nothing but a panel of hard wood to knock on. He lowered his voice for his next question. 'What was your master like, Isaacs?'

'I don't understand.'

'Was he a good employer?'

Curiously, he stopped his polishing and placed the silver cup carefully on the cloth, a smile almost making its way to his lips. 'Do you know he had a sense of humour, sir?'

'Really?'

'On the first day of the coal strike, do you know what he did?'

'Tell me.'

'He called me into the drawing room and said he was going to raise my salary by twenty-five per cent. "That'll show them, Isaacs," he said, and burst out laughing. So yes, sir, I reckon he was a good employer.'

Mrs Venner, the cook, was a small, petite individual in her forties, Brennan guessed, with red hair neatly tied up in a bun. She was putting the finishing touches to a shoulder of lamb, placing it carefully onto a roasting tray.

Brennan watched her with fascination. She was meticulous, wiping away any salt or fat that had caught the rim of the tray before stooping to place it into the large oven. All around the room, neatly hung with handles all facing the same direction, copper pans caught the reflection of the large fire burning in the grate near the oven. There was a tempting aroma of freshly baked bread, the yeast almost overpowering in its intensity. He was instantly hurled back in time, when he would sit before the blazing fire, playing with his toy soldiers and yelling at his two brothers who always insisted on wrecking his military stratagems by pinching his favourite pieces. When they scampered off with their prisoners, he would sit and watch the dough rise between swathes of steaming clothes on the wooden maiden, cursing them. He smiled sadly at the memory of Rory and Ciaran, killed down the pit when he was only twelve.

Smells, he reflected. *They carry their own history.*

'There's days when she doesn't eat enough to keep a sparrow alive.' The cook's words broke into his reverie.

'I beg your pardon?'

'Mistress. She doesn't eat. Not when the pain's bad.'

'The rheumatism?'

Mrs Venner walked over to a large cupboard and opened one of its doors. He was amazed to see how well stocked it was with all manner of jars filled with preserves and pickles, and bottles of exotic-looking cordials. She extracted a jar of what looked like strawberry preserve and closed the door.

'Aye. The rheumatism. Sometimes she can hardly walk. Poor woman.'

'What was Mr Morris like?'

She placed the jar on a side table and looked into Brennan's eyes. She had piercing blue eyes, and he thought it little wonder that the butler was rumoured to be stricken. 'My sister lives in Kendal, Sergeant. A great reader. She wrote to me about a short novel she read, written by Mr Stevenson. About a man who is kind and gentle one minute and a brute the next.'

Cleverly done, he thought. She gave her opinion of her late employer while speaking no ill of the dead.

'On the Saturday night, you heard the knocking on the door?'

'Fit to wake the dead it was,' she said, then coughed at the impropriety.

'Where were you?'

'Me an' Isaacs were discussin' household matters in his pantry,' she said, almost succeeding in not blushing.

'What then?'

'Nothin'. Isaacs went out to see what the commotion was, came back an' said we were to go to bed.' This time she did blush. 'I mean, to our separate rooms, of course.'

'Of course.'

'I gather Mr Arthur and Mr Andrew had been having a difference of opinion recently?'

She sniffed and began to unscrew the lid of the preserve. 'Strange sort of phrase for Jane to use, Sergeant.'

'It wasn't Jane, actually...'

He stopped suddenly and blushed, inwardly cursing himself for falling for one of his own interrogative ploys. Mrs Venner was clearly no fool.

172

'Grace then. Thought as much. Thinks herself a cut above, just because she's a lady's maid and doesn't come from round here. Let's see her prepare a Nesselrode pudding, shall we?'

'I asked you a question.' He decided the abrupt approach was the only way he could reassert his authority with this woman.

She sniffed. 'They were father and son. Fathers and sons fall out. It's to be expected.'

'About what?'

'That boy is a sensitive soul, Sergeant.'

He thought of the series of landscapes upstairs. 'I'm beginning to see that.'

'And his father had this notion he should be getting married. To someone of his choosing, you understand?'

'And Andrew Morris objected?'

'He's his mother's son, not his father's,' she said cryptically, waving a knife at him laden thick with strawberry preserve.

Inside Ryland's Cotton Mill, the deafening roar of the shuttles and the looms and the mule spinning concealed a deepening gloom. Many of the girls knew their families depended upon their wages to keep the food on the table and the rent collector at bay. Their fathers and their husbands sat around the house or lounged on street corners during the day, and the only thing the girls were greeted with when they returned from a full day in the mill was a grunt or a hard word.

They worked the machinery with a shared sinking feeling in their gut, and hid that feeling with laughter that was just a little too raucous. And all

173

the while that afternoon, the wind blasted its way round the building, carrying with it flurries of snow that flew past the windows set high in the walls.

Alfred Birch, the overlooker, walked along the aisle separating the rows of shuttles keeping a careful eye out for the shirkers. He saw Molly Haggerty standing by her machine, staring into the distance. He gave her a sharp rap on the shoulder and mouthed the words *'Get on with it!'* before moving on.

Molly blinked, looked across at May Calderbank, and mouthed an obscenity. May gave a thin smile and resumed her work. In only a few days the young girl had lost some of the perkiness, some of the bounce in her walk. Her younger brother had developed a rash, and had complained of deafness. May had heard her mother whisper the word 'typhus'.

Molly returned to her work, her mind in as much turmoil as the flurries outside.

There was Andrew, of course. The funeral had been a very hard time for him and something she was only too familiar with: seeing your own father laid to rest is the darkest of days, and she remembered the long, drawn-out process the three of them had had to go through – the explosion, the agonising wait, the discovery, the inquest – before they could finally lay Father in his grave. Now there was a plaque at the Morris colliery with his name on. His and the others. It was as if he hadn't left the pit after all.

She knew there had to be a time of separation. How bad would it be if she ran after Andrew like some foolish young thing? And yet she felt a pain in her gut. A real, physical pain of longing. Selfish. Of course. She should be – what was the word? – *patient*. But there was a part of her, hidden beneath all her thoughts, that gnawed away with the fear that he would never return to her.

Had last Saturday night been for nothing, then?

But when she turned away from such miseries she found her mind blown dizzily to the thought of her mother, and the strangeness that had recently wrapped itself around her like a black cloak.

She was fretting about something. It could be the worry of all mothers in the town: the spectre of starvation haunted every household, and poor wee Tommy was looking thinner by the day – but somehow she felt that wasn't the cause. She herself was still earning a wage, and her mother's cousin in Liverpool always seemed to make some contribution to the family purse whenever Bridie went over there to see her.

They were luckier than some. Luckier than most.

Yet ever since the murder in Scholes not fifty yards from their back door, her mother had been different.

Still, she told herself with a sad shake of the head, the same could be said of her: Saturday night with Andrew had changed everything.

Which naturally took her thoughts swirling back to him.

It was with some relief that she heard the whistle that signalled the end of the shift. At least on the chilly walk back up to Scholes she would be able to link arms with the other girls and laugh at nothing in particular.

As she got through the iron gates, her head covered in a thick scarf and her hands stuck deep in her coat pockets, she fell into step with May and a couple of others and began the walk into Wigan town centre, quite unaware that a dark figure had detached itself from the doorway of a shop across the street and was following the same route back into town.

CHAPTER TEN

'Not like his lordship to get his bloody hands dirty,' said Constable Jaggery as he walked alongside Sergeant Brennan.

True, he wasn't in the best of moods, and it had seemed to him that the chief constable accompanying Micky Brennan on a murder investigation was an insult both to himself and to the sergeant. Besides, his search for the one-eyed man had so far proved fruitless, and he had been forced to endure the worst of responses from uppish reception clerks and pugnacious landlords:

Eye, eye, Captain!

You can rely on me, pal – I'll keep an eye out for 'im!

Never turn a blind eye to the truth, Constable. That's my motto.

What compounded his surliness was the unwelcome invitation to resume his working relationship with Brennan by making the long trek back up to

Scholes when he had half an hour before his shift ended, and already the late afternoon gloom was bringing with it a sharp lowering of temperature. It would be a bloody cold night. Ding-Dong Bloody Bell hadn't insisted on accompanying his sergeant this time, had he? The bastard.

'Captain Bell is a conscientious officer and I will hear no more mutinous observations on his desire to seek out the truth. Is that clear, Constable?'

But Brennan tempered his admonition with a mischievous wink.

At last they stood outside number 7, Scholefield Lane. The home of the Haggerty family. The curtains were drawn, but they could see shadows moving beyond the flimsy fabric. A few seconds after Brennan's imperious knock, the front door opened and a young boy of around ten years old swung the door fully open, then just as swiftly moved to close it again as his eyes registered the uniform of Constable Jaggery. It was the latter's boot that prevented the door from closing.

'Mam!' the boy yelled. 'Mam!'

Bridie Haggerty appeared at the doorway, took one glimpse at the uniform and reversed her son's attempts at exclusion by slowly opening the door. 'Stand there much longer,' she said with a throw of her head in the general direction of the street, 'an' they'll have enough to natter about for a week. In with youse.'

Brennan saw the signs all around the room: beside the front door, a tiny bowl hanging from the wall by a nail containing holy water; the small statue of the Blessed Virgin on the mantelpiece, and a crucifix at the foot of the stairs. Even the mahogany longcase clock standing in the far corner of the room had a set of rosary beads hanging from the small round door handle. He noticed the way the clock's polished surface gleamed far brighter than anything else in the room, and its glass panels had a sparkle that was missing on other, far cheaper ornaments. On a small table beside the clock, a red votive light was flickering. A feeble fire was burning in the grate – lumps of coal supplemented by jagged slivers of wood that occasionally gave off sparks and a belch of smoke that filled the room.

The woman, he guessed, was Molly Haggerty's mother, and her brown eyes, the gentle sweep of her brow, the boneline of her jaw, were all indicative of a once beautiful young girl. The thin wisps of grey already flecking her hair, the pinch in her narrowing cheeks and the creased lines around her eyes told a sadder tale.

The young boy now stood beside his mother, keeping a wary eye on their visitors. Both his small fists were tightly clenched and ready to spring into action at any moment to defend his mother's honour.

'Well?' She stood with hands on hips, challenging, but with more than a hint of apprehension in her voice.

'We're looking for Molly Haggerty. I presume you're her mother?'

'I am. Bridie Haggerty's the name.'

'Is Molly at home?'

'Out.'

'Where out?'

'At work.'

'And where is that?'

'Ryland's.'

Bridie sat down in a small armchair by the fire. Her son remained standing, now with an arm resting protectively on her shoulder.

'And when will she be back? The mills turned out a while ago now.'

She looked up at the longcase clock in the corner.

'She's a bit late. I'm sure she won't be long.'

'I see. That's a splendid clock, Mrs Haggerty.'

'Yes, it is.'

'Is that real mahogany?'

'It is. My late husband bought it a year after we were married. Took him that long to save the money but he managed it.' She lifted her chest, showing some irritation at having let slip something so personal. 'Why do you want to speak with my Molly?'

'Just a few questions. They concern the events of last Saturday night.'

Both men noticed the change in complexion, the rapid whitening of her face. She said nothing but looked at the grate, and the ashes, some of them still glowing, in the pan beneath.

Brennan went on. 'That was the night they found the body of Mister Arthur Morris. Just round the corner from here, as it happens. He'd been stabbed.'

A puzzled expression now creased her forehead. 'An' what in the name of all the saints has that got to do with my Molly?'

Brennan saw the boy staring wide-eyed at him now. He cursed himself. There had been no need

179

to mention the stabbing. 'I'd rather ask your daughter, Mrs Haggerty.'

Slowly, deliberately, she stood up and went over to the clock. She reached out and detached the rosary beads from the handle. Then, again with a slowness that seemed almost ethereal, she sat back down and held the first bead between finger and thumb, and her lips began to move as if she were starting to pray, her gaze never leaving the glow of the ashes.

Brennan, who was standing beside her right shoulder, looked across at Jaggery, who stood at the other side. 'Mrs Haggerty. Can you tell us where your daughter was last Saturday night?'

'"...the Lord is with thee. Blessed art thou amongst women, and blessed is the fruit of thy womb, Jesus. Holy Mary, Mother or God, pray for us sinners..."'

Jaggery shifted his weight from foot to foot. The look he gave his sergeant was distinctly uncomfortable. This was intrusive, standing here like this. While the woman was praying.

But Brennan ignored the glance. He leant down and placed a hand on hers. Gently, he took the beads from her grasp and placed them on the arm of her chair. 'It's just a question, Mrs Haggerty. Where was she?'

'Here. In bed. With her little brother.'

'Yes, I mean earlier. Say, around eleven, twelve o'clock.'

'Here. In bed. With her little brother.'

He breathed in. 'She go to bed early?'

'Saves on coal. An' Tommy couldn't sleep. On account of the pigeon shoot the next mornin'.

180

Promised me faithful he'd bring me a panful of pigeons,' she reached up and placed a hand beneath her son's chin. 'Loves pigeon pie, my Tommy.'

'Can you tell me if you've ever seen a stranger, a one-eyed man, hanging about the area?'

At that, the boy shifted his stance and moved ever closer to his mother. He had a nervous pallor about his face now.

Bridie brought her son close to her bosom, shielding his head with her hands. 'Is it your intention to scare my son witless, Sergeant? Don't you think he's had enough nightmares to fill a lifetime after his poor da died?'

'I'm sorry. Was it recent?'

She shook her head. 'Blast down the pit. Five years ago.'

Brennan remembered the disaster as if it were yesterday. It had been twenty-three years since Rory and Ciaran had been killed, but time made no difference: pit blasts would always be with them. He saw the pain in her eyes and felt a dark fellowship. 'The Morris Pit Disaster?'

'Aye.'

He watched her stroke the back of the boy's head. 'If you could tell me one way or another – about the gentleman I described.'

'Sure I'd remember a devil like that, now, wouldn't I?'

He stared at her for a second or two then decided not to pursue the matter. She hadn't actually said she *hadn't* seen the fellow, but maybe it was her circuitous way of answering a policeman's question, or perhaps she didn't want to tell a lie in front of her son.

He was about to suggest to Constable Jaggery that they should wait outside at the end of the street to waylay young Molly Haggerty when the front door opened and Molly entered quickly. When she saw the two visitors she slammed the door shut and removed her outer coat and headscarf with a hostile sniff.

'Molly, love, these men...' her mother began, but Molly cut her off.

'I know who they are and why they're here.'

'Miss Haggerty,' Brennan said with an air of authority. 'If we could have a few moments of your time?' He inclined his head towards the small kitchen beyond the front room, but immediately Bridie placed both hands on the arms of the chair in a defiant gesture.

'Anythin' you've got to say to me daughter ye can say in front of meself. There's no secrets in this house.'

Molly, however, nodded to Brennan and raised a hand to invite him through to the kitchen. Then, just as her mother was about to protest, she pointed to little Tommy, whose head was still hidden from view, and said, 'I won't be long, Mam. No point upsetting everyone now, is there?'

Bridie looked up at her daughter and then gave a feeble nod. Brennan knew that whatever passed between himself and Molly would later be revealed to her mother, and he got a strong impression of closeness between the two women. Still, for the moment he was glad to be able to speak to the girl without hindrance.

She leant back against the white slopstone below the back window. The tiny yard was now bathed in darkness, though Brennan could see once more the swirls of snowflakes that were gaining in strength. They were in for another heavy fall of snow, he mused, and wondered if Ellen had built up a roaring fire, with Barry sitting before it, one side of his face a bright red from the heat of the coal as he played, undisturbed, with his soldiers. He thought of the young boy in the next room.

'Well?' said Molly, breaking into his thoughts. 'I've just done a day's work and I'm fair beat, so can we get this over with?'

Brennan coughed. Jaggery gave him an amused smirk.

'We've had information that you are seeing Andrew Morris. The son of...'

'Yes, I know full well who he is. And I know full well who gave you this *information.*'

'Oh?'

'Frank Latchford needs to mind his own business.' Her voice contained an element of scorn.

'But you have been seeing Andrew Morris?'

'Yes.' A defiant lift of the chin.

'And how did his father respond to the news that his son was seeing a mill girl?' Brennan knew there was no need to handle this one with kid gloves.

Molly shrugged. 'I dunno.'

'Had Andrew told his father about you?'

A faint smile creased her lips. 'You mun ask him yourself.'

'I will. But for the moment I'm asking you.'

She pushed herself away from the stone sink

183

and turned her back on the two policemen.

Over her shoulder, Brennan could just make out the reflection of her features in the window. She was biting her lip and gazing downwards. An attempt to control her emotions?

Finally, she said, 'Whatever passed between 'em, he didn't share it with me. Only that ... he said his dad was like a sea wall. Said it needs a constant pounding before...'

She whirled round, conscious of how her words could be misconstrued. 'I mean...'

Brennan nodded quickly by way of reassurance. 'I think I understand the symbol, Molly.'

She seemed to relax a little, and licked her lips.

'We've also been informed that someone has been asking questions. About you and your family. A man with only one eye.'

Was there a flicker of recognition on her face?

'Not easy to forget,' he added.

'No.' She paused before saying, 'but you might like to know I was followed after work tonight, Sergeant, only this one had two eyes.'

He frowned at the unexpected statement. 'Followed by who?'

'Your informant. Frank Latchford.'

'And why on earth would he follow you?'

'Oh, he soon caught up with me. Said he needed to warn me. About you comin' to see me. He told me what he'd told you.'

'About the one-eyed man?'

'Yes. An' I told him the same as I'm telling you now. I've never met the man. And, as you say, he wouldn't be easy to forget. So as to why he's been askin' questions about me and my family, I'm as much in the dark as you. Now if that's all, Sergeant?'

'Just one more question, Molly. Then you can get your feet up.'

She gave a heavy sigh. 'Go on.'

'What were you doing last Saturday night?'

There was another flicker now on her face, but it was one generated by fear.

'I was here.'

'All night?'

'Yes. Ask me mam. It was a bad night, as I recall.'

'Oh it was certainly that, Molly. You didn't step out at any time?'

'Aye, I had a game of hopscotch about midnight.'

Jaggery, whose sense of irony was still in its embryo stage, looked astounded at this new piece of evidence. It was only later that Brennan told him they could take that part of her statement with a pinch of salt.

The walk from Scholes back to the police station in King Street takes ten minutes. But as the two of them made their way down the steep hill, flanked on either side by a huddled collection of shops and public houses, Brennan was put in mind of a story he had once read as a child, where the cowboy hero was forced to run the gauntlet through a double line of savage, tomahawk-wielding Apaches. Constable Jaggery's uniform, a reminder of the numerous arrests recently carried out under Captain Bell's orders, seemed to inspire the slouchers in every public house doorway to spit out some vile obscenity, daring them to respond. But they both knew that any response would be met with casual brutality, so Brennan advised extreme caution, a course of action alien to his seething companion. Luckily for them, the bitterly cold weather and the heavier fall of snow kept most of them inside, where they would nurse a half pint for an hour in memory of happier drinking times.

To take Jaggery's mind away from the insults – *Come round t'back wi' me, ye fat bastard, an' I'll shove that truncheon up thi arse!* being by far the mildest of the threats – Brennan urged him to ponder the problems they were faced with in hunting down the murderer of Arthur Morris.

'It all stems from the letter that he received,' he said, ignoring the louring brute outside the Rose and Crown.

'It's a puzzler, is that,' Jaggery, gritting his teeth, shook his head. 'I mean, it's one thing workin' out it come from this bloody place. What with them letters spellin' it out an' all, but it doesn't give us any idea who sent the bloody thing, does it?'

'There was no name, certainly.'

Two children, sitting on the steps of the Harp Inn, picked up some loose stones and hurled them at the two policemen, one narrowly missing Brennan's right ear.

'Unless Arthur Morris recognised the writing.'

'Bloody unlikely, that, Sergeant.' Jaggery consigned the faces of their two young assailants to memory. They'd be feeling his fist soon enough.

'I don't know. It's the nature of the letter that troubles me. How many people here in Scholes would have the education to write an acrostic?'

'I thought it were a letter?'

At the Oddfellows Arms, the door swung open and the contents of a large brass spittoon were emptied over their boots, which glistened with a thick, heavy mucus. Brennan, alerted by the guttural roar from Constable Jaggery, grabbed his arm and guided him ever onwards and townwards.

'So let's say the letter contained something that gave Morris a good idea where to go in Scholes. And the only way it could have done that was if he recognised who had sent it.'

'So where does that leave us?'

Brennan saw the meagre light burning in The Shamrock. It was a place he himself had occasionally visited with his father many years ago, a happy time when those pale, hollowed cheeks would expand in delight as soon as the old songs rang out through the singing room and he would stand at the piano and belt forth:

Though the last glimpse of Erin with sorrow I see,
Yet wherever thou art shall seem Erin to me.

He could still see the tears sparkle their way down his sunken cheeks as he recalled an Ireland he'd left years earlier, fleeing the Great Famine for a better life in Wigan.

The windows of The Shamrock were misted, and he could hear the slow, melancholy strains of 'My Lodging is on the Cold Ground' and he wondered whether the pianist was drunk or merely expressing the mood of the place. They

187

passed by, and he caught sight of a man's face watching them. He registered the pale, almost skeletal cheeks, and urged Jaggery to walk faster.

'It leaves us the envelope, Constable.'

'What about it?'

He brought his coat collars closer to ward off the snow. Ahead, he saw the dim lights of the street lamps fighting a losing battle against the thickening snow. 'The maid, Grace, told me it was a white envelope. A *clean* white envelope.'

'So?'

'So, when it was found on Morris's body, it was in a filthy state.'

Jaggery pondered this for a while. By the time they'd reached the Weavers Arms he had a solution. 'Morris must've took it out and looked at it. Remember it was snowin', Sergeant.'

'Possibly. And that might account for the letter itself being in a filthy state, which doesn't seem to be the case when he received it. Still, it's a curious thing.'

Jaggery, noticing the door to the public house opening slowly, said simply, 'It is indeed, Sergeant. It is...'

Suddenly he launched himself forward and grabbed the empty bottle of brown ale that had appeared miraculously to raise itself in the air, twisting the neck of the bottle so that it fell with a smash on the icy stone steps of the entrance and dragging their would-be assailant from the doorway, hurling him face down into the snow. Brennan, acting with admirable speed, grabbed the handle of the door and held on tightly in case an accomplice from inside should seek retribution. When he turned round, Constable Jaggery had the man pinned to the pavement with a heavy knee pressing hard against his back.

'Tha breakin' me fuckin' back!' yelled the man, a thick-set individual whose words were muffled somewhat by the amount of snow filling his mouth.

Brennan looked up and saw several faces at the side window. There was an amused curiosity, rather than a lust for vengeance, on their faces. Perhaps they were considering the desirability of allowing their faces to be recognised and filed away for future reference if they made any attempt at rescue.

Slowly, Jaggery eased the pressure on the man's back, and there came a sudden gasp of relief as his victim slumped forward, spreading his arms by his side as if that were the most comfortable position he could find.

'Count to fifty; *if* you can, then get up. But if I see you lift so much as a soddin' eyebrow before fifty I'll bloody well come back an' snap you like a twig. Understand?'

The man muttered a resentful 'Aye' and began to count.

By the time they got to the Free Trade Inn, Jaggery turned and watched the man stand up, helped by a clutch of new-found allies who were busy brushing the melted snow from his damp coat.

'Something else about that envelope,' Brennan went on as though they had been interrupted by nothing more irritating than a wasp. 'It said "A. Morris" on the front.'

189

'Arthur Morris,' Jaggery said with patience. 'But it could equally have been "Andrew" or "Ambrose".'

'I s'pose. His house, though. Perhaps he presumed...'

Brennan shook his head. 'No. I think he recognised the handwriting immediately. And if he did, then he would know exactly where to go in Scholes, whatever the message said.' Brennan stopped and let his gaze drift down the steep incline towards town. Suddenly he said, 'There *is* another explanation, though.'

'What?'

But Brennan merely bit his lower lip and said, 'But that would mean... Never mind, Constable.'

Jaggery, who was by now accustomed to the sergeant's frustrating habit of dropping heavy hints then catching them before they could smash open, merely grunted.

They walked on for a while, then Jaggery said, 'Summat I don't get, Sergeant.'

'What is that?'

'If somebody from round 'ere sent it, wantin' Morris to come an' see em, well then, who delivered it? I mean, they'd hardly deliver it themselves an' then rush back to Scholes. It's hell of a way, ain't it?'

Brennan looked at his constable with a renewed respect. 'A shaft of illumination, Constable. Well done!'

It took until they reached the Douglas Tavern on Millgate before the smile left Constable Jaggery's face.

Bridie Haggerty had closed her eyes and was back on Achill Island.

Her mother had relatives there, an ageing cousin whose husband worked away for most of the year and whose tiny, beehive-shaped hut was home to herself and five daughters of varying and indeterminate age. She was twelve again, one minute sitting before the blazing turf fire and watching the smoke curl its way through the hole in the roof, and, as is the way with dreams, the next minute standing on the sandy beach catching the spray from the huge breakers that washed over the craggy rocks and made herself and her cousins screech with laughter. Then, she was leading the family donkey over the mountain paths, listening to its wheezing complaints at the burden of turf strapped to its back in creels, all of her cousins rushing away from the hazardous route to clamber to the summit of some small mound and declaim to the entire island the name of the boy they were madly in love with.

Back once more to turf fire, and her ma's cousin singing the praises of turf over coal: *'Sure the turf doesn't spit at ye the way coal does. Give me a turf fire any day. D'ye ever see hot cinders crash to your floor wi' a turf fire? Sure ye don't. An' at least ye don't go violatin' the land for it. Turf's all ready an' waitin', so it is. Like a woman willin' to be told she's ready an' needin' only the tug of a hard hand!'*

The wrinkled smile and the wink of a mischievous eye, and her own ma giving her that scolding glance that wasn't a scolding glance at all.

And then someone knocked on the door of the hut and all the girls screamed as the smoke bil-

191

lowed inwards, and Bridie could no longer see her ma, or the ageing cousin. What she could see, dimly through the thick white smoke, was a figure moving towards her, a figure that stood a few inches away and leant down, grabbing her shoulder and squeezing it tightly with one hand.

She opened her eyes and looked dully at the dead ashes in the grate. Achill Island was gone. Instead, Molly stood there, gently touching her shoulder.

'Mam? You awake?'

'I am now,' she said with a residual sense of resentment.

'Can I tell you summat?'

Bridie sat upright in the armchair and rubbed the sleep from her eyes. By the expression on her daughter's face she could tell that this was important to her, and although she guessed what was ailing her, she said nothing until the tale was done.

She had known for a while, in the way that mothers always seem to know, that Molly was harbouring a secret. She had sensed from the beginning that her relationship with Frank Latchford was doomed, not through any serious defect in the young man's character, more a feeling that he was a man with a burning sense of injustice and ambition, a powerful combination that suggests he would never be happy coming home night after night to a house and a wife and a collection of troublesome children. Frank was a thinker, a powerful thinker, and she imagined he would sit brooding for hours, and that would soon transmute itself into a smouldering indignation towards the woman who kept him trapped in a domestic prison when he could be roaming the land righting wrongs and urging the workers to rise up.

When they broke off the courtship, Bridie was relieved, but it was to last just a few weeks. The problem with the secret new man in Molly's life was the fact that Molly denied any such person existed. And such a denial told Bridie one thing: there was something shameful about it. At first she thought he might be married, and her daughter guilty of the grossest of transgressions. But when she came tripping home one day and had such a smile on her face, Bridie had come straight out and asked her who the new fellow was.

'Well,' she had said. 'He's not from round here.'

'Where's he from then?'

'Outside town.'

Bridie had taken a deep breath before asking her next question. 'Ye're not doin' anythin' foolish, child?'

'Foolish?'

'Is he married?'

Molly had thrown her head back and laughed. 'Oh Mam, you're a funny beggar! No. I swear on all the saints he's not married.'

'So who is he?'

'That's my secret for the time bein', Mam. But I'll tell you, soon enough.'

And she had promised Molly there and then she would ask no further questions. *Let the girl have her mystery,* she had thought. *Sure I've enough of my own.*

But it was only a week later that the one-eyed messenger came, asking her to meet someone interested in her welfare, and when she met that someone in Mesnes Park, she found out exactly who Molly was seeing. Things were made very clear to her that sunny day by the pond. And she had kept silent ever since.

'Mam?'

Bridie blinked away the memories. 'What is it, child?'

Molly came and knelt at her mother's feet, gazing up at her with eyes that were beginning to fill with tears. 'The man I've been seeing. It's Andrew Morris.'

She waited for her mother's response, but when it came it wasn't what she expected.

'I know.'

'You *know*?'

'Sure, I've known for a while.'

'How?'

'Ah, now that would be tellin'.'

'Then why didn't you say anything?'

'Would it have made a difference?'

'I don't suppose. I wouldn't have given him up, if that's what you'd have tried for.'

'So why bring him up now?'

'Because I'm frightened.'

'Why?'

'I saw Frank Latchford tonight. He followed me from Ryland's.'

At the mention of Latchford's name, a cloud passed across Bridie's face.

'Pesterin' you?'

'No, Mam. Not that. But he said some things that ... scared me.'

'What things?'

Molly gripped her mother's hands. 'He told me

about the police askin' him questions. But he said summat else as well.'

Before her daughter could say anything more, Bridie's hand flew to her mouth and an expression of shock filled her eyes. She muttered something incomprehensible in Gaelic and made the sign of the cross.

Molly reached forward and held her mother's hand. It felt cold, and clammy.

'Mam? What on earth's the matter?'

'Nothin', child. Nothin'.'

Molly was afraid. Whatever she had said had somehow brought such a look of terror to her mother's eyes that she thought she might faint at any moment. But what *had* she said? It had only been about her meeting earlier with Frank. Perhaps she thought he had molested her in some way?

Quickly, she went on. 'He said he wanted me to arrange a meetin' between him and Andrew.'

Bridie let out a long sigh of relief. Whatever she had feared had passed over, like the Angel of Death, and she attempted a weak, curious smile. 'An' why would he want to do that?'

'That's just it, Mam. He wouldn't tell me. But he said if I didn't make the arrangements, he'd see to it that everyone in Scholes would find out just who I'd been seein'. What would that do to us, eh, Mam? To you and little Tommy, eh? What should I do, Mam?'

'You do what Frank Latchford says, child. He's a man you can trust.'

195

CHAPTER ELEVEN

Josiah Sweet's father had once run a thriving business, transporting all manner of goods along the canal waterways of south-west Lancashire on his narrow boat drawn by their horse Pegasus, Josiah's particular favourite. In those halcyon days – or so they seemed to the infant Josiah – they had lived in a small cottage built not a stone's throw from the Top Lock near Aspull, and it was always a treat to leave the boat, *Wellington,* moored nearby and run into the cottage to smell the bread baking in the oven by the hearth and see the look of playful disgust on his mother's face as she scolded him for the mess he had made of his shirt.

But then the railways spread like smallpox, and as the years went by, Josiah saw the change in his father, the way the lines on his forehead became deeper, more permanent with every trading order that was withdrawn. A late attempt to offer summertime passenger trips down the length of the canal had failed to halt the slide, and when they had to leave the cottage to live permanently on the boat – the three of them in such a cramped space – it was as if something died in both his parents: his mother had lost her home, the place she saw as her domain, a spick and span refuge she kept for her menfolk at the end of a burdensome day, and his father had lost his calling. And when a man loses his calling, he becomes a husk, hollow and useless. The makeshift cabin he had built was sturdy enough, but then the canal boat inspector had taken him to task for the way the boat was beginning to smell. Bilge water had been building up beneath the cabin floor, causing a loathsome stench.

The inspector had ordered it to be pumped out but his father, stubborn as the day is long, had refused. It was against the law, he'd pointed out, to pump bilge water into the canal. When the by now furious inspector had told him it was also against the law to let the bilge water gather like that, the summons was issued and his father taken to court.

The magistrates, flummoxed by the apparent legal stalemate of the situation, dismissed the case and his father was victorious. But the case took its toll, and he lived precious few weeks after that to savour the moment.

When he was fourteen, Josiah reached down into the canal with a long boat hook and fished out his father's lifeless body. He could still, in darker moments, smell the foul dampness of the cord trousers, see the dull sheen of the brass buckles below his knees, and hear the gurgling of the filthy water as it drained from his bloated mouth. Within a year, his mother had been admitted into the idiot ward at the Wigan Infirmary, and it was there she died of consumption brought on by a 'morbid listlessness', or so the official report said.

Josiah, whom everyone regarded as simple-minded, lived on in the boat, and in time he transported goods once more, only these were now illicit goods, stolen from one civic borough to be resold in another. He risked the wrath of the canal boat inspector, but he had little idea of any other kind of life and he became adept at concealing any contraband he was transporting. Josiah's only crime – if indeed it were a crime – was to provide transport, at a price. He himself was no thief, but he reckoned somebody somewhere owed him something.

Which is how he came to meet Bragg.

Months ago, Josiah had been carrying the results of a housebreaking. One of the large houses at the top end of Wigan Lane, where doctors and lawyers lived in semi-rural splendour, had been emptied of its treasure trove of contents while the owners were away in France and the spoils transported to his boat by covered wagon. The brains behind the operation – a local ne'er-do-well – had assured Josiah he had merely to negotiate the locks between Wigan and Blackburn, where he could unload free from the prying eyes of the law.

But he hadn't reckoned on the prying eye of Bragg, a private inquiry agent who had been following the nefarious activities of the gang for weeks. He boarded the barge one night and almost caused Josiah's heart to stop when he leant over his bunk and stared at him with dark eyes that seemed to glow in the glimmer of moonlight reflected on the water.

Bragg, it appeared, wanted not only the reward for the stolen goods, but also had designs on a couple of the gilt-edged paintings that, as he put it, 'would simply be seen as unfortunate victims lost in the theft.' He arranged for Josiah to find a suitable hiding place for the paintings while the rest of the goods were placed on the waiting wagons, and all that was left was for Bragg, along with several hired hands, to waylay the wagons before they could reach the Prince of Wales yard on King William Street in Blackburn.

It went as planned, and Josiah was suitably rewarded.

He'd thought that was the last he'd see of Mr Bragg. But he came back, and now Josiah would rather their acquaintance were brought to an end.

For one thing, Bragg had been staying on the *Wellington* for well over a fortnight and company was something Josiah had never got used to. He was far happier when the boat was sailing leisurely down the canal and the route he followed was assured.

For another thing, the last week had seen the waters of the canal freeze, leaving his boat stuck in a solid mass of ice. To someone who thrived on motion, stillness was a sort of hell on earth.

And worst of all, Bragg had a disconcerting habit of vanishing for hours on end and re-appearing at the ungodliest of times without saying a word about where he'd been.

He flipped open the curtain and looked outside. The brickwork of the canal banks was invisible, thanks to the still-falling snow and the ice clinging to it. Beyond the right-hand bank, a small towpath led off towards the small tunnel that lay in the distance, and across the bridge overhead he caught sight of the dim lights of a tram as it shuttled across, capturing the thick flakes in each window before grunting its way back into Wigan. He looked down at the silver pocket watch that had been his father's proudest possession and read the time: 9:15.

It was an hour later when he heard the heavy clang of boots on the narrow deck. The door flew open and Bragg stood there, his dark hat pulled low over his face to deter inquisitive passers-by. He said nothing until he had divested himself of his outer clothing and sat on the low bench before the small paraffin heater.

'Tomorrow,' he said.

Josiah sat opposite him and waited for more. Eventually it came.

'Tomorrow night. Five o'clock.'

'What about it, Mr Bragg?'

'You won't be here.'

The look of surprise on Josiah's face made Bragg smile.

'But I won't be nowhere else. This bloody ice, see, Mr Bragg? Boat can't move backerds or forrards.'

'I'm not talking about the boat, you imbecile.'

This was a great puzzle to Josiah, who saw the *Wellington* as an extension of himself.

'I don't get you.'

'Tomorrow night at five o'clock, you'll be in town having a drink.'

'Oh no, Mr Bragg, I'd rather not.'

'Well in that case go for a walk through the woods at Hindley.'

'That'd be daft, that would. In this weather? Folk'd call me mad.'

He tried to smile in order to convey the ludicrousness of such a suggestion.

'Fine. Take a stroll on the moon then.'

200

'What?' Josiah stared upwards at the ceiling of the boat.

Bragg gave a long, impatient sigh. 'Tomorrow night at five o'clock. I need to be alone here, Josiah.'

'Why?'

'Because I shall be entertaining a guest and it will be a very confidential meeting.'

At the word 'guest' Josiah flinched. Even in his befuddled brain he knew that guests could only be invited by himself. And he'd invited no bugger.

'Can't be doin' with havin' guests on *my* boat, Mr Bragg. Why, he might be...'

Before Josiah could say any more, Bragg flung himself at his throat. Slowly, with his green eyes wide and fierce, he began to squeeze his thick fingers round the slender throat until his victim's eyelids started to flicker, oblivion a matter of seconds away. Only then did he let go.

'Tomorrow night at five o'clock,' he rasped, some of his spittle dribbling onto the terrified face. 'Imbecile.'

'All ... right,' came the hoarse reply.

It was almost as if a bridge had been crossed.

For the first time, Bridie spoke to Molly not as her daughter but as an equal, another woman for whom feelings weren't confined to vague reflections on life and love but to the hard, sometimes painful realities that mark a woman's entrance into the world. Bridie spoke of Molly's father now, not as a saint or a hero to be lionised in her daughter's eyes, but as a man of flesh and blood, and the normal fallibilities all men are guilty of. She even

201

spoke of their first kiss, the way Seamus and herself had decided that they had a future and that no matter how dire the threats were from her father they were filled with a romantic determination to face the future together. She spoke also, and with careful frankness, of the troubles they'd encountered once they crossed the Irish Sea.

Yet even in this new spirit of openness, she couldn't tell Molly of the few months she spent as a maid working for the Morrises, nor of the attack she'd been forced to endure in the laundry room. Why upset the girl? She hadn't told a living soul about the way that man treated her like some rag doll. Better, far better, to let the truth lie stinking in its grave.

Then Molly, having listened with the solemnity of someone realising the significance of the moment, told Bridie of Andrew, of the way she felt whenever she so much as saw him from a distance, of their first encounter by the canal and the way she giggled at his striped flannel jacket. She spoke of the dark times, too, when he had explained to her that in order to keep seeing each other they needed to become very careful, secretive, for his father had plans for him marrying, in due course, the very eligible daughter of a wealthy landowner, a girl Andrew once described as having the teeth of a horse and eyes that looked both ways.

Bridie had smiled, recognising in Molly's urge to speak now that some valve had been tapped, as if she finally wanted to share him after all this time. Then there had come a silence between them. Molly had spoken of their deep, abiding passion for each other and how she knew him the way she had known no other man and that she could see no parting of the ways. Not ever. Especially since the main obstacle to their love had been removed.

At that, Bridie had coughed to clear her throat and said carefully, 'You need to speak with him, child. If Frank Latchford wants to speak to him then you should give Andrew Morris the chance to decide. He's a great thinker, is Frank. He'll have something very clever up his sleeve, just you see.'

'I dunno. He worries me. What if they fight?'

Bridie smiled. 'D'ye think Frankie boy'll do such a thing? Sure he'd never work at a colliery again, attackin' the new owner!' She lowered her voice. 'Besides, whatever Frank's up to, I'm sure it'll be for the good of all. You'll see.'

Molly looked confused but remained silent. It seemed that her mother had revised her opinion of Frank Latchford, for it hadn't been too long ago that she could barely utter his name without an accompanying sneer.

What had happened to change her mind?

'Damn this snow!'

James Cox stood in the billiard room of the Wigan Conservative and Unionist Club and glared out of the imposing bay windows that overlooked the bowling green. Green, of course, was a misnomer, as the overnight fall of snow had submerged even its outer boundaries beneath a thick covering of white. A solitary robin landed on the railing below the window and surveyed the wintry scene with far more equanimity than its human counterpart.

'Oh, I don't know,' Ambrose Morris remarked.

He was sitting on the other side of the billiard table reading a newspaper.

'What do you mean?' Cox asked, whirling round with little grace.

'Well, the foul weather is regrettable, of course, but it tends to crystallise one's situation, does it not?'

Cox frowned. He wasn't in the mood this morning for cryptic observations. The only reason he had come to the damned club this bitterly cold morning was to bid farewell to Ambrose Morris, who was returning to the capital and his parliamentary duties at Westminster later that day; it was a gesture compounded not so much out of a genuine fondness for the man – though he did feel that – but rather out of a burning eagerness to urge his friend to do everything he could to bring the stoppage in the coalfields to an end. If the rumours were true, and there was an atmosphere of conciliation in the air now that Arthur Morris, the chief obstacle to concession in any form, had been removed from the picture, then he needed to do all he could to ensure everything was done to expedite matters. He had a contract with the Blackpool Tower Company that was fast in danger of becoming a historical curio.

'How so?' he asked, picking up a cue from the rack by the wall.

'There's precious little coal left. The poor souls are forced to scrabble on slag heaps or work the outcrops in the dark.'

'You should get the law on them. It's stealing is that,' Cox fumed.

'What good would that do? The last thing we

want is to be held responsible for sending half-starved miners to Strangeways and leaving their wives and children helpless.'

'You're too bloody soft. Horsewhipping's too good for the bastards.'

'What I mean is, the bitter cold of the last few weeks has shown all of us the edge of the precipice. We can't go over that edge. That's why I'm convinced a more sensible, rational approach will now prevail.'

'Bloody better do, Ambrose. I stand to lose everything.'

Ambrose carefully folded his newspaper and watched as Cox took aim at the spotted white, pushed the cue forward forcefully so that the white ball slammed the red into the far pocket, a collision that slowed it down and sent it rolling smoothly towards his opponent's white and just kissing it.

Perhaps billiards can teach us a thing or two, thought Cox, but he kept the thought to himself.

CHAPTER TWELVE

Prudence Morris had no intention of seeing her brother-in-law catch the London train. She was in mourning, after all, and besides, the journey by carriage down to the Wigan North Western Station would have caused her untold agonies in her painful condition. So she allowed him to kiss her on the cheek, but Andrew, standing on the steps and shivering in the falling snow, saw, as always, that any such casual intimacies between them were perfunctory at best.

He had heard his father mutter once that she felt Ambrose guilty of hubris, with overweening political ambitions that she was convinced would lead to the inevitable fall from grace. *Then the family name becomes besmirched*, she had said within Andrew's hearing. Yet to her credit she maintained a civility between them, mainly, Andrew reflected, for his father's peace of mind. Still, there had been the faintest glimmerings of a thaw between them over the past few days, and he prayed it would continue.

As the two of them journeyed towards Wigan, Ambrose spoke of the challenges facing the country and his desire to serve in government should Gladstone decide to resign and call an election.

'He's looking older, more careworn, every day, Andrew. Spent all last Christmas in Biarritz for all the good it did him.'

'You say he may intervene in the strike?'

Ambrose slowly shook his head. 'Oh, I think he will, right enough. But he's a crushed man. The defeat of the Home Rule Bill in the Lords was a bitter blow to him. I saw him the day after they threw it out – he was in a dreadful state.'

'This can't go on, Uncle Ambrose.'

He looked at his nephew, saw the growing signs of anguish in his face. 'Oh, it won't. Never underestimate the power of public opinion, Andrew. Many of the London newspapers are firmly on the side of the miners. I know of one editor, Fletcher of the *Daily Chronicle*, whose paper is in receipt not only of large sums of money for the strikers, but also bundles and bundles of clothing. Men's, women's, children's. You would be amazed at the strength of support the miners have from Londoners. They filled Hyde Park last month. When the tide turns, it makes sense to set your sail accordingly.'

'Let's hope it's a fair wind.'

There was silence for a while.

Outside, the stark beauty of the fields swept smooth with a uniform whiteness soon gave way to the houses of the wealthy on Wigan Lane, their gardens fringed, almost guarded by tall bushes. Soon, these buildings gave way to meaner, less imposing structures the closer they got to the brow of Standishgate and the steep decline into the town centre.

Andrew, sensing the desire in his uncle to remain silent for a while, cast his mind back to a time when he had sat beside him in rather grander surroundings.

The journey from Euston Station to his uncle's residence near Regent Street had taken in Leicester Square, and the undergraduate Andrew, even then filled with the artistic fervour of youth, had been fascinated when Uncle Ambrose set him down outside number 47, and told him that this was where Sir Joshua Reynolds had lived, and these were the very steps where Sir Joshua found the child whom he would later immortalise in his painting, *Puck*.

He recalled, too, the earnest way Ambrose had told him, on those visits, of the history of the capital, its places of interest and the sights he should see; how they stood beneath a small gas lamp in the middle of Charing Cross and watched the sea upon sea of faces and carriages and all manner of dress, and how he felt the hand on his shoulder and the voice in his ear telling him that this was the place from which all distances in London are measured.

Ambrose's voice broke into his reverie. He spoke in low, confidential tones.

'This detective. Brennan. He will be speaking with you.'

'I expect so.'

'Be careful, Andrew.'

'Careful?'

'I'm no mean judge of character. Westminster is a place filled to the rafters with every sort of vice, virtue, weakness and strength. I meet with them every day, and I've learnt to gauge what they're capable of. Sergeant Brennan is no fool.'

'Why are you telling me this?'

'Because he will be asking you about last Saturday night.'

Andrew shifted his position, looking out of the carriage window at the falling snow, and the white fields beyond. 'Why should that disturb me?'

There was a moment of doubt on his uncle's face, a small creasing of the forehead, that soon vanished. 'No reason.' He glanced down at his watch. 'I hope the damned train is on time. I have a party meeting at seven tonight.'

Later, after the train – mercifully on time – had steamed its way from the icy platform of the station and Andrew had returned to the waiting carriage, Ambrose Morris sat in his first-class compartment and watched the Lancashire countryside flash by.

He tried, with little success, to turn his mind to lighter things. His first victory, for instance, those heady days in the capital when he could put the initials MP at the end of his name. He remembered standing on Victoria Embankment watching a steamer sail by, its large central funnel belching smoke skywards, and many of the women at the stern half-hidden beneath their parasols yet flirtatiously giving him a wave. He smiled as he recalled his first visit to the Bank of England where he was shocked to learn of salaries in excess of a thousand pounds. 'For counting money?' he had declared open-mouthed, to the amusement of his hosts, who had countered by asking him if he, like another Morris, had elaborate 'designs' with 'socialist leanings'. It was only later that he learnt what they had been referring to.

But these were glimpses of a happier time, attempts by the brain to divert his thoughts from the melancholy of the present. A sort of mournful ritual in reverse.

His mind kept returning to Andrew, and the veil of secrecy that had shrouded his face when he mentioned the night of Arthur's murder. Whatever he had been doing – and he didn't suspect for one second that the boy could have had anything to do with Arthur's death – he hoped he had enough steel in him to ward off the redoubtable Sergeant Brennan.

He felt the train slow down. As he looked through the window, he saw the familiar approach to Warrington Bank Quay Station. With a long sigh, he realised that he still had a very long way to go.

Andrew had been home barely five minutes when Isaacs told him Sergeant Brennan was in the hallway and wished to speak with him.

'Show him into the drawing room,' he said and watched the butler back out of the room, closing the doors behind him. Suddenly, the bravado he had shown to Uncle Ambrose quite deserted him, and he spent a full five minutes composing himself before making his way to the drawing room.

'I really do apologise for this intrusion, sir,' said Brennan, accepting the offer to sit down. 'But you will appreciate any information you can give me may help in building a fuller picture of what happened on Saturday night.'

'Of course.'

Brennan produced a notebook and consulted its pages before continuing. 'You say you left the dinner at around eight-thirty?'

'That is correct.'

'And you left the house to – what was it? "Get some air".'

'Also correct.'

'And yet the weather would hardly be conducive to fresh air, would it, sir?'

'You may be unaware, Sergeant, that I am an artist.'

'I've seen the landscapes. Impressive scenes.'

'Well then. I wanted to see how the snow affected the fields and the houses down in the town. You can see them from here. Something almost mystical about the long rows of houses, and the gloom of the gaslight through curtained windows. The slightest hint of misery within. The faintest of shadows. But from a distance there's a beauty to them. A deceptive beauty, though.'

'You stood outside looking down the valley?'

'Not quite. I took one of the carriages and rode for a while. I like solitude. It helps me reflect.'

'I see. But there must have been a destination.'

'Does there have to be one, Sergeant? Sometimes I feel the world revolves around journeys and destinations. Not enough time for the stops in between.'

Brennan saw the look in his eyes. It was contemplative, but there was something else. An anxiety, perhaps even a sense of fear. He decided there was only one way he could get through to this young man. 'You didn't, for instance, see Molly Haggerty last Saturday night?'

It was as if he had been struck a blow across the face.

'What did you say?'

'Did you see Molly Haggerty last Saturday night?'

There was a moment when he looked like denying any knowledge of such a person, but it soon passed.

'My uncle said you were not to be trifled with.'

'Quite so.'

Andrew walked over to the window and gazed out. 'I presume you have already spoken with Molly?'

'I have.'

'And she told you?'

Brennan gave a gentle cough to conceal the

deceit in his voice. 'She told me.'

'Then why ask me?'

'Simply to confirm that what she says is true. It helps to place people.'

'I see.'

Brennan saw his shoulders sag.

'Well, I did take the carriage to Wigan. Not to Scholes, you understand.'

Brennan nodded. It wouldn't have been wise to take a carriage through the streets of Scholes. 'So you had arranged to meet her?'

'Yes. She was waiting at the gates to Mesnes Park. Poor girl was freezing.'

'And where did you go?'

Again there was a hesitation in his voice. 'That is of no concern. She sat inside, I held the reins. Then we sought shelter.'

'Where?' Brennan's voice was firm, insistent.

Finally, Andrew said, 'The colliery.'

'What?'

'We went to the manager's office at the colliery. Took shelter from the snow. There's something quite cosy about that.'

'I see,' said Brennan, who did indeed see.

'My mother knows nothing of Molly. Yet.'

'But your father did, didn't he?'

A slow nod. He turned round and faced the policeman. 'Somehow he'd found out about us. He had always had his mind set on a union between myself and the daughter of a friend of his. Lydia Merkham. It was almost medieval and I told him so. But yes, he was against the match.'

'And this was a source of friction between you?'

'Yes.'

Brennan held his gaze for a while. 'What time did you leave the colliery?'

Andrew licked his lips. 'I can't recall.'

'I'm sure you can.'

He thought for a moment. 'It must have been eleven. Eleven-thirty.'

'And you took Molly all the way home?'

'Yes. A risk, I know, but it was late and I didn't want her walking those streets at that late hour. So I went to the end of her street and she alighted there.'

'Then what?'

'Then I went home.'

'And you saw nothing? No one? Your father, for instance?'

'The streets were deserted. The snow was still falling. To think, even then he might have been...' His voice faded.

'I see. Have you any idea what he was doing in Scholes?'

'None.'

'Not, for instance, paying a visit to the Haggerty home? He was found not far away from there.'

'Why on earth would he want to do that?'

'To put a stop to your relationship.'

Andrew swallowed hard and turned his gaze on one of his paintings, the wintry scene, where a solitary figure sat by a stream with his hand pressed hard against its icy and unyielding surface.

'It's possible,' he said finally. 'He was a resolute man. Obdurate to the point of...' He broke off and smiled. 'If he were bound for Molly's home, Sergeant, why did he choose that night of all nights? A companionable dinner? Heavy snow? Surely he would have the sense to choose a more convenient time to confront the girl he regarded as his enemy?'

'You would have thought so, wouldn't you?' said Brennan, non-committally.

'Now we'll never know, will we?'

'Oh, perhaps an answer will present itself, sir.'

Andrew looked at him long and hard, as if he sensed the detective knew far more than he was willing to express. At last, he sighed and said, 'Will that be all?'

'For the moment, sir.'

A few minutes later, as Brennan stood on the steps and gazed across to the bushes, he thought again of what Ambrose Morris had seen – a large figure skulking in the undergrowth having delivered his mysterious letter. He wondered who that had been. If, indeed, it had been the murderer, he must have moved pretty quickly to make the journey down into Wigan and then up the hill to Scholes in this inclement weather. Not an impossible task, but an awkward one, given the conditions that night.

He sighed and glanced backwards at the closed door and the heavy brass knocker in the shape of a Davy lamp. 'If only you could talk,' he said, and immediately felt foolish.

Two minutes later, he had an idea, unaware that young eyes were watching him.

Tommy Haggerty saw it as a great adventure. Whatever the letter contained, he would never dream of opening it. Molly had made him swear on his mam's deathbed, and there was no more sacrosanct oath than that. He had jumped on the rear bar of the tram that went as far as the Boar's Head, then trudged his way through the snow until he came to the grand house itself. He then had to wait among the bushes until he was sure no one could see him. The presence of the policeman standing on the steps had shocked him, and for a moment he wondered how on earth he'd known Tommy was there. But then he walked off, looking deep in thought. Tommy was sure he'd heard him mutter *'The bloody knocker!'*, just before he disappeared from view. Then when the coast was clear, he rushed to the front door and posted the letter. But the most important part of the mission, Molly had told him, was to knock hard on the door to make sure someone came. That way, they would be sure that the letter would be discovered and passed on to Andrew Morris himself.

'Why?' he had asked.

'Why what?'

'Why you sendin' 'im a note?'

'Ask no questions.'

'You after a job there?'

'Don't be silly. Just do as you're told.'

'Should I wait for an answer, Moll?'

'Indeed you should not! Get out of there as soon as you've knocked. The note explains itself.'

If young Tommy Haggerty was mystified by the letter his sister had written, Andrew Morris was deeply troubled. Why on earth would Frank Latchford, a member of the Miners' Federation and a particularly eloquent and dangerous opponent of his father's, express a desire to meet

215

with him?

As he travelled by carriage to the appointed destination, he reflected on its significance: surely Latchford couldn't possibly know that only last Saturday, he and Molly had finally consummated their desires in that very place? The colliery manager's office?

No, he reassured himself. *He's chosen the office as a meeting place because of its symbolism. It's where the colliers' shift records and pay details are housed, and only a matter of a few yards away from the lamp room, where all lamps are tallied and recorded. It's the ideal venue for those who wish to be reminded of what the coalfields are actually there for.*

Although the snow had temporarily stopped, there lay a thick layer on the roads that made progress difficult as the two horses forced their way through. It was by now late afternoon, and already the darkness had fallen. Once he had skimmed the edges of town, the street lamps glimmered feebly, irregular droplets of ice hanging from their arms and frosting the glass of the lamp housing. Few people were abroad, several shops choosing to close early in the face of precious little trade. It was beginning to seem now that the town itself was facing a deadly conspiracy of enemies – the coal dispute and the bitter, merciless cold – and the best way to fend off such a relentless onslaught was to retreat to the cold sanctuary of hearth and home.

It took Andrew forty minutes from the moment he left the house to arrive at the colliery gates. They were hanging open – a consequence of the fury engendered in the strike's early days by his father's inflammatory words – and, as the carriage made its slow way along the road towards the manager's office, he noticed how still and menacing the head frames seemed now, silhouetted against the dark sky and the mocking stars.

When he finally reached his destination, he climbed down and stood outside the door. The small office seemed different from his last visit. Then it had been not only a refuge but also a trysting place. Now it stood there, a heavy layer of snow on its sloping roofs, still and silent in the dark yard which months ago would have been a hive of activity, of raucous shouts, obscene curses and the scene of a thousand complaints. The sinister black stillness was made all the more ghastly by the outline of the head frames fringed in white against the night sky, giant cobwebs waiting motionless for their next victim. Morbid fancies began to grip him, of pale, dead faces lying just beneath the layer of snow at his feet, all glaring in accusation. The sins of the father...

The horses snorted, lifting their heads in unison as if they both sensed that something was wrong in this dark and silent place.

Suddenly, a lamp flared from inside the office, and a shadow was projected, large and distorted, on the thin curtains of the window.

Then the door began to open, slowly, and not one, but two figures emerged from the gloom within.

A bitterly cold night. The streets of the town and the outlying districts were deserted, and a disturbing stillness settled upon the thousands of houses throughout the borough. Many of their inhabitants huddled before small fires where fragments of wood, scavenged from the rear premises of shops and warehouses, helped to replenish the rapidly dwindling supplies of coal slack that had themselves been the product of nefarious raids on the many slag heaps adjoining the dormant collieries. Some of them glanced furtively at their children, looking for the signs of malnourishment and approaching starvation and exchanging fearful and unspoken glances as the wood cracked and shifted above the smoky slack.

Yet one person that night lay unconcerned about the cold and the hunger. For him, the dispute in the colliery held no fear, no anxiety at all. For he lay on his front with his skull smashed into several pieces, and no one could possibly imagine the agony he had gone through before Death took him in his arms.

No one, that is, except the murderer.

CHAPTER THIRTEEN

'It's an evil night,' said Herbert Lythgoe as he watched James Cox divest himself of his outer clothing.

The Conservative Club was surprisingly three quarters full, its members preferring the subdued and smoke-filled atmosphere of the members' lounge to anything their womenfolk could offer them at their variously grand homes.

'Bloody right there,' Cox agreed with an accompanying cough. He ordered a drink at the bar and sat beside his friend, offering the other members who had hailed him a cursory wave of the hand. In better days he could buy and sell the lot of them, they all knew that, but he wasn't so thick-skinned that he couldn't sense a certain benign vindictiveness lurking beneath their cigar-wreathed bonhomie.

Herbert Lythgoe was a successful businessman too, but on a far lesser scale. His Lythgoe's Aerated Water Company began life as a herb beer factory, but in less than ten years it had grown into a large concern producing gingerade, lemonade, horehound and soda water. Yet even he had been affected by the long dispute in the coalfields: such sweet and refreshing drinks as he bottled had been swiftly consigned to memory as purse strings tightened and families were forced to purchase what meagre supplies they could with none of the fripperies they or their children had once enjoyed.

'You all right, James?'

Cox took the drink – a large whisky and soda – from the waiter and took a sizeable sip before responding. His hand was shaking. 'Been up yonder.' He gave a nod in the general direction of his extensive works.

'This time of night?'

'Aye.'

'Yon manager of yours – what's his name?'

'Walsh.'

'Aye, that's the bugger. Shouldn't he be doing the checking? 'Specially on a bloody awful night

219

like this.'

Cox took out a cigar and guillotined the head, lighting it with a match and moving it slowly round in his mouth to achieve an even burn. As the glow grew brighter, his hand trembled far less until, after a minute's slow, warming inhalation, he was quite himself again.

'I spoke to him this afternoon. I like to check things for myself, Herbert. There's a bloody expensive locomotive up yonder just stranded on its tracks. Wouldn't put it past some of those striking buggers to derail it and send it hurtling into the canal. Ice or no ice. And a four-coupled saddle tank doesn't come cheap.'

Lythgoe laughed out loud. 'So you went up there to play bodyguard to a bloody train? In this weather?'

'Locomotive, Herbert. Not a train. And we built the bugger. No. I couldn't rest until I'd made sure she was blocked in securely.'

'You're a careful man, James Cox. I'll grant you that.'

'I am,' he said with a long and luxurious pull on the cigar which Ambrose Morris had given him only last Saturday.

Despite her mother's assurances that Frank Latchford meant Andrew no harm, Molly Haggerty had a deep sense of foreboding, a hollow sensation at the pit of her stomach that had nothing to do with hunger. She had made the arrangements as Frank had told her, and the letter had been delivered, according to little Tommy. But she had spent the whole of the evening and most of the night warding off the demons that danced in the dwindling coal flames, mocking, evil little devils that hissed and spat at her every time she tried to think beyond the wintry misery of the moment.

Her mam had told her once of a distant relative who had the *rare sense*. She had a way of knowing when someone was going to die, and she always lit a candle and placed it in the window as a sign to the neighbours that another one of them would soon be winging his or her way to the Great Unknown. To little Molly, the thought of seeing a candle flickering in a window had been enough to keep her awake for weeks, and she almost screamed every time an altar boy held one aloft with no trace of fear in his sparkling eyes.

Now, as she lay in bed and listened to little Tommy wheezing and snoring beside her, his feet resting on her legs to keep warm, she felt that those tales of long ago had blended together to form a terrifying incarnation, where she was both the mystic with a sense of impending doom, and her childish self shaking with fear beneath the bedclothes.

She had been mad to do it. To send Andrew, dear, loving Andrew, to a dark and lonely place to meet the man who once felt he owned her.

And yet her mam had been so sure...

She thought of last Saturday night. Andrew's father, lying there in the alleyway with his blood draining onto the icy cobbles.

Her brother groaned and turned over. In the shaft of moonlight that sliced through the gap in the curtains she saw the lids of his eyes flicker and a half-smile spread across his face. He was content, for a while at least.

Michael Brennan, too, lay with disturbed thoughts. Ellen was beside him, her face calm in repose, and from Barry's room he could hear the gentle rise and fall of his breathing. He had told him a story after Ellen had warmed the boy's bed with a hot brick wrapped in cloths, and Barry had asked him if there really were dragons that breathed fire and chased innocent young women.

''Course not,' he had replied, stroking his dark hair.

'So where do they come from then? Dragons?'

'I make them up.'

'Can anyone breathe fire?'

'No.' He had thought to make a humorous reference to his superior, Captain Bell, but that might have scared the boy.

'Dragons are bad, though?'

'Oh yes.'

'Could you fight one?'

'But they're not real. I told you.'

'Aye but if they were, you'd be able to fight 'em, wouldn't you, Dad?'

''Course I would.'

Reassured, Barry had snuggled deep into the bedclothes then, and gone instantly to sleep.

Now, Brennan watched his own cold breath drift upwards against the dull glow of the moon.

The Davy lamp door knocker at the Morris residence had given him an idea, that was all, but he couldn't get it out of his head, because if he were right about that, then it would lead him down pathways that could prove hazardous indeed. But the more he thought about it, the more he felt convinced that it explained one thing, at least, and if he could follow the suggestion logically then...

At that moment, with the greatest of ironies, there was a tremendous knocking at his front door which was below his bedroom window.

Ellen stirred but didn't wake immediately. He clambered out of bed, cursing beneath his breath as the bitter chill of the night assailed him.

More knocking. Heavy. Insistent.

Narrowly avoiding the chamber pot at the foot of the bed, he made his way to the window, where he pulled the curtains open and slid the catch to allow him to slide open the lower frame.

He stuck his head out, the icy wind blasting his face and causing him to close his eyes and catch his breath for a second. Then he peered downwards and yelled, 'Who the bloody hellfire...?'

But he stopped when he saw Constable Jaggery standing there, hugging himself with his arms beneath the great black cape he had wrapped around his huge frame.

'Constable? Do you realise...?'

'Sorry, S-sergeant.'

Even from this distance, Brennan imagined he could hear the constable's teeth chattering.

'What is it?'

'There's been another m-murder, S-sergeant.'

'So? Couldn't it wait?'

'N-no, Sergeant. C-Captain B-Bell hisself sent me. S-said he's f-fed up of dead bodies all over the p-place an' you'd b-best put a s-stop to 'em.'

'Wait there!' he snapped, and closed the window, turning to find not only Ellen awake and sitting up in bed with a less than delighted expression on her face, but also a bedraggled-looking Barry standing in the doorway, rubbing his eyes and mumbling something about dragons.

For once, Brennan was grateful for the weather. The ice that had trapped the canal boat had also been thick enough to prevent the body that now lay face down, a few yards from the boat's stern on its eerie, moonlit surface, from sinking down into the murky depths. If the waters of the canal had been free-flowing, then his job would have been immeasurably harder. For one thing, a murder on board a narrowboat in normal weather conditions could have taken place anywhere along, say, a ten mile stretch of the Leeds–Liverpool Canal. Unlike a land-based murder, where the place where the body was found wasn't under dispute, with a boat the surrounding area would most certainly be an open question. For another, the fact that the body was lying there in all the misshapen indignity of death would enable them to act much more speedily than if it had sunk into the water without trace, to resurface at sometime in the future when time of death and possibly even its cause would be a matter of considerable doubt.

Furthermore, the first policeman to arrive on the scene, Constable Davies, had shown sufficient presence of mind to ensure the surrounding area be kept clear of any interference. With his bullseye lamp, he had even spotted a few footprints embedded deep in the crusted and frozen snow that lay near the edge of the canal bank alongside the gunwale, footprints of varying sizes and impressions. He was quite pleased when Sergeant Brennan praised his foresight, although he spoilt it somewhat by adding, 'We'll make a policeman of you yet, lad.'

Before he did anything else, Brennan sent Constable Davies back into town, giving him the address of a monumental sculptor and instructions to bring him to the scene of the crime with all haste, making sure he brought with him a plentiful supply of plaster of Paris and all the necessary paraphernalia to make a cast of the footprints before the snow returned, thus wiping out any hope of an impression of the footwear. He gave orders to a second constable to find as many pieces of wood or metal he could to cover the footprints just in case the snow began to fall again.

Careful now to avoid the possibly incriminating footprints, he stepped gingerly across the ice, conscious of the cold, dark waters that lay beneath its surface. When he reached the body, he stooped and held a lamp close to the man's head. The man had been bludgeoned to death from behind. A dark crust of blood had already formed around the base of the skull, and his eyes were open, as if death had been so instantaneous he didn't even have time to close them. Brennan remembered something his grandmother – a superstitious old devil from the old country – had told him when he was around seven years old.

When ye die, Micky, sure it's said that the last thing ye see on God's good earth is stamped on your eyes forever. Like one o' these photograph things. So you

225

make sure ye're beside a statue of one of the holy saints when ye breathe yer last. That's a heavenly image to take with ye, now!

Wouldn't it be a boon to detection if such an image were imprinted on a victim's pupils!

The murder weapon – a heavy iron windlass, used for turning the canal lock gates – lay a few feet away, still glistening with blood. Jaggery stood above it, illuminating its sinister presence with the oil lamp he had found inside the boat's cabin.

With a sigh, Brennan brought the lamp closer to the dead man's face. He didn't recognise him, guessing his age at anything from thirty to forty. He was quite small – around five foot five – and his clothes seemed smart: dark checked suit with a brown cravat and polished boots. He wondered what had brought him to such an ignominious end.

A few minutes later, Brennan stood inside the canal boat and looked around. The small cabin was bathed in shadows. Jaggery was holding his lamp aloft, moving it round in a slow arc to show the gloomy details of its interior.

The cabin was, he had to admit, a testament to man's ingenuity in finding a place for everything. The stove took centre stage, but around it in a tiny curve was a low padded bench. Above the bench a narrow ledge ran the length of the makeshift cabin, a home for all manner of ornaments and illuminated prints depicting sturdy horses and an array of impossibly colourful boats. One framed print, smaller than the rest but taking pride of place in the centre of the others, showed a profile of the Duke of Bridgewater, with the legend 'Father of the Canals' etched along the bottom. Mugs, plates, and several items of cutlery lay on the tiny table stretching out from the stove.

'There!'

Brennan held up a hand to stop Jaggery's slow movement of the lamp. He pointed down to the small slender table. As the light from the lamp grew brighter, he could make out a thick splattering of blood that coated not only the surface of the table but also the small plates that rested there. He was surprised that none of the contents of the table had been disturbed. No struggle, then. The victim – and according to the bargee who found the body his name was Bragg – must have known his assailant, or been completely taken by surprise so that he had no chance to defend himself.

'Seems a bit of a simple sort, don't he?' Jaggery said with a nod in the direction of the window.

Through its murky narrow pane, they could see two more constables standing on the canal bank, while between them Josiah Sweet, a heavy greatcoat wrapped around his shoulders, sat on the edge of the canal staring at the iced surface and its gruesome contents, its cracked and ridged fretwork turned a murky grey by the pale moon. He was swinging his legs, kicking his heels against the crumbling stonework of the bank, and his head was bowed low, swaying from time to time to the rhythm of an imagined melody.

'Simple or not, he has some questions that need answering,' Brennan replied. 'I want to know everything he can tell me about our friend here. Everything.'

It seemed an interminable length of time before Constable Davies returned with a surly-looking individual, tall and unusually thin, who carried what looked like a large canvas bag.

'Jonathan Crombie, Sergeant,' the young constable said by way of introduction, but the tone of his voice suggested the newcomer was a man with an axe to grind.

'You're the sculptor, then?' Brennan asked, extending a hand and leaving it in mid-air, unshaken.

'*Monumental* sculptor,' came the reedy response. 'Dealing in Sicilian marble and Scottish granite,' he said with a flourish, then added, 'not dead bodies. They're normally all tucked up nice and warm in a coffin when I get to work.'

'I'm not asking you to have anything to do with a dead body,' Brennan snapped. His tone was surprisingly sharp, bordering on intolerant. 'I'm simply asking you to make a few plaster casts.'

With a grunt, Mr Crombie held up his canvas bag. 'Where?'

Brennan escorted him over to the stretch of land near the edge of the canal bank.

With Jaggery standing there holding the lamp – *I felt more like a bloody street lamp than an officer of the law,* he later moaned – the monumental sculptor adopted a businesslike air. 'I need water,' he said briskly, and Brennan gave orders to one of the constables standing beside Josiah Sweet.

Over the next few minutes, as he gathered together the materials he needed, Crombie provided a commentary on his work.

'This is snow,' he said, rather unnecessarily.

228

'And though it's frozen I need to act fast. As you can see, I'm pouring the plaster into the water container gradually. Two minutes stirring should do the trick. You'll notice I'm adding salt. This will encourage a more rapid hardening. There. That should do it.'

Thus he moved from footprint to footprint, adding an initial pouring of plaster before inserting a length of twisted rope 'to get the cast out,' he explained, then filling the impression to the brim until each one had been treated. 'Now we wait,' he said, standing up and wiping his hands, glistening with wet plaster, on a thick cloth.

While he was thus engaged, Brennan moved back to the cabin and gave orders for the boat's owner to be brought to him.

Josiah Sweet had begged not to be taken down to the police station. There was genuine terror in his eyes at the thought of being placed in a cell or an interview room. Buildings didn't do for him, he explained pitifully, not when he'd spent most of his life in a canal boat measuring sixty foot long and fourteen foot wide. Why, whenever he set foot in a public house or a shop, he would look at all that empty space above his head, space stretching all the way to a ceiling. It didn't make sense. And churches! They were the worst of all, they were. Who on earth needed all that openness? It was impossible to reach up and stroke the ceiling, even with the tallest ladder, and he loved to do that on the *Wellington,* just stretch out his arms and press them flat against the wooden curves of the cabin.

'No need to take you down into town, as long as you answer my questions truthfully,' Brennan stated firmly. He noted the relief on the boat-man's face. 'You've known the victim how long?'

'Months. He's me friend.'

Brennan knew that some of that, at least, was a lie. Josiah Sweet was a simple enough fellow – five minutes in his company would tell anyone that – but there was an innate deviousness in his eyes, a symptom both of mistrust and being mistrusted, that told him that whatever the nature of their re-lationship, it certainly wasn't based on friendship.

'Where is he from?'

Josiah frowned. 'Manchester, I reckon. Talked about Manchester a lot any road. Said I should moor up there next year when they open the Ship Canal. Told me he'd make me rich.'

'What was he doing on your boat?'

'Told you. Visitin'.'

'In this weather?'

'Aye.'

'And how long had he been staying with you on your boat?'

'Didn't say 'e 'ad.' Josiah held one hand in the other tightly, as if it were a bird ready to spread its wings and fly away. 'Didn't say 'e 'adn't, neither.' A stern look from Brennan made him lower his eyes. 'A week or so, that's all.'

'You say he'd asked you to make yourself scarce?'

'What?'

'He asked you to leave him alone for a while.'

'Aye.'

'Did he say why?'

'Said he were expectin' a *guest*.' He almost spat out the word.

'Name?'

Josiah gave a derisory snort.

'But he wanted you off the boat at five o'clock?'

'Aye.'

Although there was nothing to connect the murders of Morris and Bragg, the fact that this latest victim came from Manchester, and the one-eyed man they were looking for spoke with an accent 'not from round here' according to Latchford, gave Brennan a vague feeling that there was a link.

'Did Mr Bragg ever bring a one-eyed man with him?'

Unexpectedly, Josiah began to giggle.

'Something funny?'

'What you said.' Josiah saw the annoyed expression on the policeman's face and immediately pursed his lips.

'What did I say?'

'Mr Bragg bringin' a one-eyed man wi' 'im. That'd be impossible.'

'Why?'

''Cos it were 'im. Mr Bragg was the one-eyed man.'

Brennan sighed. 'And I could've sworn he had two when I saw him a few minutes ago.'

'Oh aye. He had two right enough. Only when he left 'ere 'e'd put a patch round his eye. Thought it bloody daft meself.'

Brennan thought about that for a second or two then resumed his questioning.

'And you got back at ten?'

'He'd said till closin'. Gave me some money for a few pints. I went to t'Star.'

'Anybody see you in there?'

Josiah smiled at what he thought was a ridiculous question. ''Course they did. They all know Joss.'

'Tell me what happened when you found the body.'

He sighed. 'I thought Bragg'd gone out. 'E 'as habit o' doin that. Lamp weren't lit. Cabin were in darkness. So I walks in an' reaches up for t'lamp only it's not there where it should be. I reaches forward thinkin' Bragg'd left it on t'table. Wouldn't a bin t'first time. But it weren't there, so I fumbled around for a bit till I found t'matches. I allus keep 'em in yon cupboard. Keeps 'em dry, see? Things get damp on boats. Any road, when I lit one, I could see he weren't 'ere. Then I looks outside an' sees 'im lied there on th'ice, arms an' legs all sprawled to buggery. Even then I thought, evil bugger's drunk. Dead drunk.' He laughed out loud. 'I were half right any road, eh, Sergeant?'

Brennan gave a weak smile of acknowledgement. 'Go on.'

'I went out, slitherin' all over t'show, but I knew 'e was a goner before I reached 'im. So I ran back to t'pub an' they sent someone down to you lot.'

'When you got back to the boat – the first time – did you see anyone on your way back from the pub?'

'No. Not a soul.'

'Did Mr Bragg ever speak of why he was ... staying with you?'

Another slow shake of the head. 'Just said 'e 'ad a job on.'

Josiah then screwed up his face and slammed his eyes shut, and Brennan thought at first he was in great and sudden pain. But then he opened his eyes once more and said, almost shouting, 'I remembered summat else!'

'Go on.'

'Aye! We were sat there in t'cabin an' we'd 'ad a few drinks an' 'e turns to me an says, "You know what, Joss, old pal?" An' I says, "What?" An' he says, "When sinners need to pay, it's me they pay".'

'Sinners pay? What did he mean by that?'

Josiah shrugged. 'But it's what I remember,' he said proudly. 'An' you asked for everythin'.'

'Where are his belongings?'

Josiah pointed towards a small cupboard below the windows. 'Didn't 'ave much.'

Brennan bent down and extracted a small valise that had seen better days. He took a quick glance inside a shirt, a few toilet necessities and a note-book. He flipped open the pages, hoping to find a list of addresses, dates, names of contacts, all the literary paraphernalia one would expect to find in such a book – but, apart from the single word *Bragg* on the inside cover in elaborate script, there was nothing. Another dead end.

CHAPTER FOURTEEN

The first thing Andrew Morris did that morning was to make an appointment at the bank. The meeting the previous evening with Frank Latch-ford and his associate had taken a completely unexpected turn, and what he was being asked to do was nothing short of blackmail. Yet he had little choice but to agree, and so he made the journey into town ready to put things into motion.

It was lunchtime, and Brennan was on his way out of the station with a warming vision in mind of a beef and onion pie and a pint of best bitter, a quiet corner of the Crofter's and half an hour's uninterrupted solitude in which he would make an attempt to piece together several elements of the two murders.

But he only managed to reach the front desk when Captain Bell's voice echoed down the corridor.

'Sergeant Brennan? Perhaps you would be so kind...'

A minute later he was sitting opposite the chief constable, food and drink consigned to unsatiated memory.

'Is there a connection between the two murders?'

'The victim had a habit of wearing an eyepatch. I'm sure they're linked.'

'From Manchester, you say?'

'Yes, sir.'

Captain Bell leant back in his chair and eyed Brennan for a good few seconds. Then he said, 'When I was in India, the grey-headed crow was a pest, did you know that?'

'I don't think I did, sir.'

'It got everywhere. Walls. Alleys. Temple courts. And prying into everything. No matter how many times it was shooed away the blighter always came back, never letting go until he found something of value, then he'd fly off and devour it.'

'Really?'

Brennan tried not to sigh. The chief constable had a very heavy hand as far as symbolism was concerned.

'But then there was the ubiquitous cow, slow and lazy but always giving the impression it was ruminating deeply about something. Which one are you, Sergeant? A prying crow – or a ruminating cow?'

'I rather think a mixture of both, sir.'

'I beg your pardon?'

'Well, at the risk of incurring your displeasure, I would like to speak to Andrew Morris again.'

'Why?'

'The one-eyed man was, we know, making enquiries about Andrew Morris's relationship with young Molly Haggerty.'

The chief constable raised an eyebrow. 'What did you say?'

'A young woman from Scholes.'

'A *relationship?*'

'Exactly so, sir. I have spoken to them both. They admit it.'

'Did his father know of this?'

'He told me that *somehow* his father had found out about them.'

'And she lives in Scholes, you say?'

'Yes. With her mother and brother.'

'No father, eh?'

'Killed down the mine, sir. The explosion five years ago. At the Morris pit.'

Captain Bell's eyes opened wide. 'Two motives

for the price of one then.'

'I beg your pardon, sir?'

'Many of the miners and their families blamed poor Arthur for that accident. That's motive number one, isn't it? Then when Arthur mysteriously appeared in Scholes, this Haggerty girl had the perfect opportunity to end his opposition to the match, didn't she?'

'As did Andrew Morris.'

'He and Molly had been ... together on the Saturday night. He drove her by carriage back to Scholes late at night. It meant they were both in the area when the murder was done.'

'You aren't seriously suggesting young Andrew killed his own father because he opposed a blatantly obvious mismatch? Preposterous.'

Brennan shrugged.

'So,' Captain Bell leant forward and pressed a bony finger on the table, 'where does all this leave us?'

'We know that this Bragg fellow made sure the boat's owner, Sweet, was out of the way from five o'clock. He'd obviously arranged to meet someone. I'd like to know who that someone was.'

The chief constable's eyes lit up as an inspired thought hit him.

'This Molly character has a brother, you say. Surely he has an equally strong motive? And he could have written that dastardly note that was found on the body.'

'Well yes, sir, but...'

'But me no buts, Sergeant! Never underestimate the force of a sibling's anger, his sense of protection, his desire for revenge on the man who upsets his sister and thwarts her chance of happiness.'

'All quite true, sir, but for one thing.'

'What?'

'The brother's only ten years old. And the murder of Arthur Morris was long past his bedtime.'

The chief constable slammed his fist down once more. 'Are you taking a rise out of me, Sergeant?'

'No, sir,' Brennan replied hastily, underpinning his irony with alibi. 'It's just that Bridie Haggerty – she's his mother – swears he was tucked up in bed alongside Molly herself.'

Captain Bell frowned and sat back. 'Mothers have been known to lie before.'

'They have indeed.'

Time to steer away from such nonsense, thought Brennan.

'But there are some aspects of the case that interest me greatly. The note, for instance. I've been giving that note a lot of thought recently. Doesn't it strike you as odd that...?'

But before he could finish, the chief constable clapped his hands together and studied him closely. Brennan wondered if he were in receipt of another shaft of illumination.

But then Captain Bell said, 'What did you say the woman's name was, Sergeant?'

'Who? Bridie Haggerty?'

'Yes. Now why is that name familiar? The first name I mean.'

'She has no record, sir. Neither of them has. I checked.'

An irritable shake of the head. 'No, it isn't that. I wonder...' Then he leant forward, opened a drawer and took out a sheaf of writing paper. Then he prepared his pen and wrote a few sentences which he blotted before handing it to his sergeant.

'What's this, sir?'

When he spoke, there was an air of triumph about the chief constable. 'You indeed have my permission to return to the Morris residence, Sergeant. Please hand this note to Isaacs, the butler. It may turn out to be nothing, of course, but the name Bridie is a familiar one, made me think of someone by that name who worked there at one time. A maid of some sort, dishonourably discharged, as we would have described it in the army. Apparently she became the stuff of legend. I remember Arthur Morris regaling us one night with a parody of her dismissal. "Bridie's Lament", he called it. Very funny it was, too. See what Isaacs has to say about it, will you? If I'm right, then we have yet another motive for killing poor Arthur.'

Brennan read the note and placed it in his pocket. It was only as he was leaving the station that he realised he hadn't shared with his superior his musings about the letter found on Arthur Morris and the acrostic message it contained, or the idea the door knocker had given him.

But the more he thought about it, the more convinced he was that he was right.

'Did you do as he asked?'

Molly Haggerty looked around her nervously. There were several people in the Silver Grid on King Street, but they were mainly travellers who had just alighted from the LNWR station and were eager to cradle a hot cup of tea and allow the steam to remind them of warmer times, for outside the snow was once more falling thickly. None of them knew her.

It was early afternoon, and she had told Mr Birch, the overlooker, that she thought she had a fever and didn't feel very well at all. At the ominous word 'fever' he had ushered her out of the weaving room and warned her to stay away until she posed no danger to the others. The message the boy had brought her, from Andrew, had filled her with both relief that he was indeed safe, and fear – for she was desperate to learn of what took place at the colliery the previous night.

Andrew looked at her and smiled, reaching out to clasp her hand. 'Yes, I did.'

'And you're certain?'

'I am.'

'He didn't try to harm you?'

'No.'

'I was so worried. And this morning, there's been talk of another murder.'

He creased his brow. 'Who?'

'Nobody knows. But there's been a lot of rumours. They say whoever it was was found in the canal.'

'You mean on top of it. The canal's frozen solid.'

He had tried to make his voice sound light, but somehow, in the subdued atmosphere of the Silver Grid, with the windows half covered by a curvature of freezing snow, it sounded false.

Molly changed the subject. 'When does he want the money?'

He patted his inside pocket. 'I'm to meet him later.'

'Were you afraid of him?'

239

He shook his head. 'If it means we can carry on, I'd face Medusa herself.'

'Who's she?' she asked with more than a hint of jealousy.

'Oh, you needn't worry about her.'

He gazed at her for a while, no words passing between them, and then he said, 'In a way, what Latchford has done has only worked to speed things up. I wanted to ask what you thought before I did anything.'

'What is it?'

He lowered his voice even more, so that now he spoke with a whisper. 'Giving him money is only delaying the inevitable. Soon, everyone will know about us.'

'I know.'

'And when they do, it'll be impossible for you to stay in Scholes.'

'What are you sayin'?'

'I'm asking if you'll let me paint your portrait.'

She looked at him dumbly, and wondered briefly if Frank Latchford had after all struck him a blow on the head.

He gave a short laugh. 'I want to paint you sitting by the ice watching the skaters.'

She too laughed at that. 'Where? The canal?'

'No. Central Park.'

'Where's that?'

'New York.'

Bridie looked at her daughter with astonishment, horror and, if she were honest, just a tiny sliver of envy.

'He can't be serious about this?'

'He is, Mam.'

Such a momentous topic would have been impossible for Molly to keep contained, and she sat on the threadbare carpet, resting her arms on her mother's knees, the glimmer of an impossible future in the United States of America shining in her eyes. She saw the intricate artwork of ice on the windowpanes and, beyond the glass, sharp needles of snow caught in slanted waves before vanishing into the afternoon gloom.

'He strikes me as a very impetuous sort o' fellow.'

'He's an artist, Mam. They feel things differently.'

'He's also the son of Arthur Morris, child. He has responsibilities.'

Molly's voice rose a little, and Bridie realised that despite her grand age of nineteen, she was still a naïve and very trusting wee girl.

'He says his uncle will run things.'

'His uncle is the town's MP. D'ye know how much work that involves?'

'He could give it up.'

'Aye, he could.' She leant forward and stroked Molly's dark, flowing hair. 'Ye know, we almost lost you, when you were born.'

'I know.'

'"Touch and go," the doctor said. Well I touched you an' I wouldn't let go. I nursed you and held you and felt your tiny wee heartbeat. I even counted the beats, sayin' to meself, if she gets to fifty beats, she'll be fine. An' then a hundred, an' two hundred...You know how hard I prayed? Sure I never stopped. An' if you pray for somethin' long an' hard enough, it'll come true.'

She gave a long, heavy sigh and glanced over at little Tommy, who was asleep in his dad's armchair and still holding the wooden boat Seamus had carved out for him a long time ago. She frowned a little when she saw the right side of his face catch the meagre heat from the glowing coals in the grate. She wouldn't disturb him. Not much chance of a burn rash with the flames having long since died down.

'But America, child? Sure I'd never see you again.'

''Course you would.'

Bridie shook her head and pointed to Tommy. 'No, an' ye'd never see that wee fella either.'

But Molly was single-minded that night. 'I wish you could meet him, Mam.'

Bridie swallowed hard. Perhaps it was time to tell her after all. 'Oh, I've met young Andrew Morris, child.'

'What? When?'

'About nineteen years ago.'

She sat upright and gazed at her mother with a curious amusement in her eyes. 'Mam?'

'I used to work for the Morrises.'

'Work?'

'I was a maid. Only young, an' fresh from the oul' country.'

'But you never said.'

'No.'

She lowered her voice and once more glanced across at Tommy, whose expression held all the serenity of sleep.

'Only worked there a short while. And young

master Andrew was a mere child. Three, four years old.'

'You knew him *then?*'

'Oh I didn't have much dealings with him. He had a governess. Very grand, d'ye see?'

'What was he like?'

'He was a child, an' all childer are special, now, aren't they?'

'I'd love to see inside that house. Where he grew up. Though there's as much chance of that happenin' as...' her voice trailed off into the world of thwarted fantasy for a while. 'It must've been good, workin' in such a lovely place.'

'No, child. It wasn't good at all.'

There was a gentle crunching sound as some of the ash-frosted coals shifted and dropped through the iron grate into the pan below.

'Why not?'

Bridie glanced once more at young Tommy, still sleeping. She took a deep sigh, and then told her daughter what had happened to her all those years ago.

CHAPTER FIFTEEN

It was Constable Jaggery's first visit to the Morris residence, and, despite the thickly falling snow that had forced the cabbie to stop half a mile before his destination, pointing to the steam from the horse and the deep snow ahead of them as evidence, he was impressed when he stood on the front steps and took in the size of the place.

'Makes my little 'ouse favver a matchbox, Sergeant,' he said.

'The rewards of capital, Constable. Now, if you please, tell me what you notice about that door knocker.'

'What?'

'Has the cold affected your ears?'

He shrugged and gazed at the object for a while. 'Looks like a pitman's lamp.'

'A Davy lamp. Well spotted. Anything else?'

What had got into the man? Jaggery thought, blowing out a billowing cloud breath just to emphasise how cold it was out here. What the bloody hell did it matter what the door knocker looked like?

'It's brass.'

'Good. Now lift it and knock on the door. It's what it's there for.'

Jaggery did as he was told. He blinked as the heavy sound echoed throughout the house.

'Makes a noise, doesn't it, Constable?'

'Bugger of a racket, Sergeant.'

The butler Isaacs opened the door and gave a look of mild surprise when he saw Brennan.

'Remember me, Isaacs?'

'Indeed, sir.'

'Good. This hulk of a fellow is Constable Jaggery. Is Master Andrew at home?'

'I'm afraid not, sir. He went out this morning and has yet to return.'

'I see. Then I may as well speak with the lady of the house first.'

He made to step in, but Isaacs pulled the door

244

half shut.

'I'll see if madam is at home.'

Jaggery, who had taken an instant dislike to the fellow, gave a raw laugh. 'Call yourself a butler an' you don't know if the missus is in? Need to look at yourself, lad.'

As a ploy to gain entry it failed miserably, for the door was immediately slammed shut in their faces.

It was another five minutes before they gained admittance.

As Isaacs was leading the way to the drawing room, Brennan, his teeth still chattering, tapped him on the shoulder. 'Before we see the mistress, Isaacs.'

The butler turned round with a quick glance at his shoulder to see if the policeman's finger had left any residue. 'Yes, sir?'

'I have a note for you, from Captain Bell himself.'

Isaacs looked confused. He took the proffered note and, without looking at it, placed it carefully in his pocket. *Duty before curiosity,* Brennan reflected.

'I will, of course, need to speak to you later about it.'

'Of course, sir. This way, please.'

Within minutes they were seated, not in the more comfortable armchairs that flanked the hearth, but on high-backed library chairs, whose leather upholstery was firm rather than welcoming. Prudence Morris was once more dressed from head-to-toe in mourning, although this time her face wasn't hidden beneath her veil, which was folded back on her head. She sat in one of the armchairs facing them. A blazing fire roared lustily in the grate, its dancing flames reflected in the polished rosewood of the upright Steinway, its upper frame and ornate fretwork concealed beneath a black mourning drape.

Once again, Brennan was struck by the expression of pain on her face – not the passive suffering of grief bravely borne, but almost a sense of chronic physical pain. He recalled the rheumatism the maid Grace – and her acolyte Captain Bell – told him of, and her proud independence in dealing with it herself. He imagined he could detect a faint whiff of the arnica she regularly applied, and felt sorry for the woman, coping as she did with not just the grief of loss but the misery of a constant pain.

'Now, Sergeant, what is this all about?' Her voice was thin, but there was control there, too.

She's strong, thought Brennan.

'I need to ask a few more questions, ma'am. I really do apologise, but...'

'Please. Continue.'

'The night of the dinner party. You were in the dining room when the knocking was heard?'

'As I told you before.'

'So then you heard the knocking? It was done with some force, I gather.'

'Indeed. It sounded like a madman.'

'He used his fists, I gather.'

'Yes. A sign of an uncouth creature who cannot be bothered to use the conventional means.'

'It is a heavy door knocker. A small child, for instance, would be unable to lift it.'

'It isn't meant for small children.'

'No. Of course not. Tell me, after your husband left, what happened then?'

'The events haven't changed since I last told you.' She gave an impatient sigh, but went on. 'The Coxes left at the same time. The dinner party was quite ruined by the intrusion. My brother-in-law made some attempt to salvage the evening by offering to share some more of his Westminster tales, but I have little interest in the foibles of great men, Sergeant. So I retired for the night.'

'And your brother-in-law?'

'Fell asleep in the smoking room and had to be woken by Isaacs. Though whether the sleep was induced by tiredness or brandy is a moot point.' She spoke sharply, her dislike of Ambrose Morris barely concealed.

What has he done to displease her so? Brennan wondered once more, then cast the thought aside. *Families bring their own tortures,* he mused, recalling briefly the rows he had heard between his father and two brothers when they had declared their intention of taking a job down the pit. The months of gruff silences were followed by the relief he felt at Christmas when the three of them rolled in drunk and singing and declaring undying love for all the Brennans in the entire world.

'Do you know of a man named Bragg, Mrs Morris?'

She frowned at the name. 'Bragg? Who is he?'

'Just someone who may have been known to your late husband. Then again, he may not.'

'And why would Arthur have any dealings with this man?'

'I was hoping you would be able to tell me.'

247

She gazed into the flames. 'If it were business then I wouldn't be consulted. I'm sorry. The name and the man mean nothing to me. Is there a reason they should?'

Brennan hesitated. He shied away from the field of speculation. 'I shouldn't think so.'

'Well? Is there anything else?'

Before he could answer, he heard the front door slam shut.

'That will be my son. He is kept quite busy now that my husband ... and I barely see him.'

'This dispute has caused so much pain,' Brennan said.

'Yes. Yes, it has. Now if you will excuse me, I shall tell Andrew you await his pleasure.'

She stood up, not without difficulty, and walked stiffly to the door. Both men stood and Jaggery went to hold the door open. With a curt bow, the widow exited.

They heard some quiet murmuring in the hallway, then the doors opened and Andrew Morris walked in, giving the two policemen a curt nod. His face was flushed with the cold and he moved quickly to the roaring fire, where he bent low and warmed his hands close to the flames.

'My mother used to warn me against that,' said Brennan.

Andrew, still bent low, turned his head. 'What?'

'Warming my hands after being out in the snow. Said it causes chilblains. Something about the alternation of cold and heat.'

'And my nurse told me the same condition is aroused by the wearing of sleeping socks. Conflicting advice, Sergeant Brennan.'

'Quite, sir.'

'Now, I take it there's a purpose to the visit? Mother told me you were here to ask yet more questions.'

'I'm afraid so.'

Andrew stood up and, instead of sitting down, walked over to the Steinway and lifted the mourning drape before exposing the keys. Then he touched several in a slow, meandering collection of notes. 'We only recently had the hammer heads renewed. And the dampers and leathers replaced. It's almost angelic in its clarity now, don't you think?'

'Yes, sir.'

'Do you play the piano, Sergeant?'

Brennan heard Jaggery cough. 'Alas, no.'

'You should learn. I find it almost as soothing as painting. Though nowhere near as productive. With the piano I merely emulate the work of others. With painting, I'm a god.'

Again, Jaggery coughed. Brennan made a mental note to remind his constable that a cough was no indicator of subtlety.

'I understand. But I must press on.'

'Of course.'

While Brennan spoke, Andrew played a series of notes, a melancholy counterpoint to the sombre words in the room.

'Do you know of a man named Bragg?'

Andrew seemed to hesitate before the next note. 'Should I?'

'I have no idea.'

'Then I must disappoint you.'

'Or perhaps a one-eyed man who's been asking

249

questions about you and Molly Haggerty.'

'Ah.'

'He would be hard to miss. He wore an eye-patch.'

Again, a slight hesitation. 'Why would he be asking questions?'

'I think you can guess that, Mr Morris.'

He watched his fingers intently, concentrating on each delicate touch of the keys. 'You mean my father paid him to?'

'I do.'

'Well, then. What is there to say? You know we argued over Molly. He expressed a desire for me to marry a girl I have met a handful of times but whose father is a man of immense wealth. I often wondered how he found out about us. Now you may have solved a puzzle.'

'And created a much larger one, I'm afraid.'

'What do you mean?'

'Where were you last night, Mr Morris?'

'Last night? Why?'

'Please answer the question.'

'What time?'

'Oh, let's say from five onwards.'

The pressure on the keys became suddenly greater, a heavy pounding that was more suited to high drama.

'I was out.'

'Where?'

'At the colliery.'

'And what were you doing there?'

'I had a meeting.'

'I see. With whom?'

He gripped the lid of the piano and slowly

closed it. 'Before I answer any more of your questions, can you tell me what this is all about?'

Brennan looked at him carefully before responding. 'The man I mentioned earlier, Mr Bragg, was found last night. Murdered.'

Andrew turned pale. 'Murdered?'

'He was found on the ice, near a canal boat.'

Andrew nodded, as if the news had merely confirmed something. Then he smiled involuntarily at the surreal nature of the detail. 'I'm sorry, Sergeant. You're saying you now have two murders? And you think they're linked?'

'It's too early to tell.'

'Good God.'

'So can you tell me who you were with last night at the colliery? And what time you returned home?'

He walked over to the fire and stood with his back to the flames. 'I was with a man named Frank Latchford and a friend of his.'

Brennan assimilated the information with no trace of the surprise he felt. What on earth were these two men, from opposite sides of the dispute, doing last night? 'Who was the friend?'

Andrew smiled weakly. 'A priest.'

Now he did express surprise as his eyes opened wide. 'I beg your pardon?'

'Frank Latchford met me in the manager's office with Father McFarlane from St Mary's Church.'

'I thought Mr Latchford would have reason to dislike you?'

'He does. Besides the current situation with the dispute, he used to be with Molly. Before I came along.'

'So what on earth was he doing meeting you last night with a Catholic priest? Waiting to give you the last rites?'

At this Andrew laughed out loud. 'Nothing as fatalistic, I assure you. Mr Latchford is, as you know, a very – shall we say – disingenuous member of the Miners' Federation. He combines altruism with an eye for the main chance. I gather he's something of a champion of the labouring classes.'

Brennan recalled the incident outside the house of Jem Muldoon, and Latchford's intervention.

Jaggery, who was now lost in a sea of unfamiliar vocabulary, began to watch the flames, looking for the devil as he used to as a child.

'He has, of course, known about Molly and me for a while. Biding his time, I suppose. Now, he is blackmailing me.'

At that emotive word, Jaggery glanced up.

'How?' Brennan asked.

'A simple matter, really. He will make it common knowledge in Scholes and the wider Wigan area that Molly Haggerty is not only seeing the son of the demon Morris, but she and her family have been granted generous funding to tide them over the hardships of the time.'

'Is this true?'

'No, Sergeant. It's a complete lie. Molly is a proud girl, and, although at first I admit I made a small offer of support, she almost chewed my head off. Apparently there's a relative in Liverpool who provides support. But you see? If the gossip about Molly and me were made known, then the lie accompanying it would be accepted as truth. And you know what would happen to the whole family then.'

Sadly, he did.

'So he wanted money?'

'Well, yes and no. He certainly wanted money, but not for himself. That was the reason Father McFarlane was there. Latchford wanted me to provide relief funding for the miners and their families to the tune of five hundred pounds.'

'Bloody 'ell, that's some tune!' Jaggery said, preceding his interjection with a whistle.

'You aren't going to hand over such a sum, are you?'

Andrew sighed. 'I actually think it's a master stroke from Latchford. He will tell the Federation that I gave the money with good heart, out of a sense of shame at my father's wickedness, and that the gift is a result of delicate negotiations he has undertaken to persuade me to such a philanthropic act. Thus giving him a reputation as a skilful mediator, a saintly defender of the downtrodden, and a rising star in the Federation firmament. It also paints me as someone they can do business with and paves the way to opening further negotiations. It's masterful. I have already passed him the money. In banknotes.'

'I see. Well then, that can't be helped, unless you wish to lodge a formal complaint.'

'Which would produce the very effect I am anxious to avoid.'

'Of course. So, if we return to yesterday evening. You left the colliery at what time?'

'Around seven o'clock. I actually gave them both a ride back into the centre of town.'

'That was most gracious. That would be seven-fifteen or thereabouts?'

'Yes.'

'So you arrived home at what time?'

'About half past eight. The going was quite hazardous and I had to stop several times for the horses.'

Enough time to travel to the canal boat and commit murder, Brennan thought.

Isaacs was waiting for them as they entered the hallway. He handed them their outdoor coats and stopped at the doorway.

'The note you gave me, sir. From the chief constable.'

'Yes?'

'May I commend his memory.'

'So there was a maid who worked here named Bridie?'

'Yes, sir. Bridie Hanlon.'

'And she was dismissed?'

'Yes, sir.'

'What was the reason?'

'"Gross insubordination" it says in the servant book.'

'You weren't here at the time?'

'It was nineteen years ago, sir. No.'

'Is there anyone on the staff who was here back then?'

'Yes, sir. Mrs Venner, the cook. I anticipated your question and have arranged for her to meet us down in my office, below stairs.'

Because she was away from the place she knew best – her kitchen – and instead sitting on a small chair in the butler's office, Mrs Venner looked much less comfortable. Her red hair was still neatly tied back in a bun, but there were traces of flour in the red hair that gave her a flustered look. Besides, it was obvious that she wasn't looking forward to the interview.

'Mr Isaacs tells me you knew Bridie Hanlon?'

'I did.' She sat erect, primly, and with her lips pursed.

'Do you know what her married name was?'

'No. Only that he was Irish. They don't make good workers, the Irish. They're feckless.'

'My father was from Cashel,' said Brennan, barely able to conceal his anger. Or his pride. 'That's in Tipperary.'

'Yes. Well. I take folk as I find 'em.' She clasped her hands together and at least had the decency to blush.

'So. Isaacs tells me she was discharged for – what was it – "gross insubordination"?'

'Yes.'

'That covers a multitude of sins, does it not?'

She looked him straight in the eye. 'Can I ask what this has to do with the master's murder? The foolish girl was dismissed nineteen years ago.'

'Please humour me.'

'Very well. Bridie Hanlon made some very serious and damaging allegations.'

'About what?'

She held her back even straighter. 'She made a complaint to Mr Booth. He was the butler back then.'

A complaint about what?'

'There was a Christmas celebration here. Young

master Andrew was four. Everyone was having such a good time. Then the Hanlon girl came running down those stairs.' She threw a nod behind her. 'Told Mr Booth she'd been attacked.'

'Attacked?'

'That was the very word she used. Screaming like a wildcat she was.'

'Who had attacked her?'

'No one, of course.'

Brennan breathed out patiently. 'Who did she *claim* had attacked her?'

'It was slander of the most wicked kind. She said it had happened in the laundry room where he had tried to ... force himself on her.'

'Who? Arthur Morris?'

Mrs Venner did a double take. 'Oh no, sir. Not the master. If you must know, she said it was Mr James Cox, and him only recently married and all.'

CHAPTER SIXTEEN

'Beats me, Sergeant.'

'What does?'

The carriage and driver that Andrew Morris had kindly made available to them was having great difficulty negotiating the tight bend in the road at the Boar's Head. The snow, which was now falling in sharp bursts made all the more stinging by the strengthening wind, had built up along the tram tracks, and large ridges of churned up slush had earlier been created by the trams and the farmers' carts, laden with heavy milk churns, stubbornly making their way towards the town's market square for the weekly market.

'I mean, this James Cox. He's rollin' in cash, got a wife and children, an' 'e tries it on with a kitchen maid.'

'It was nineteen years ago. He would have been around thirty then. No children.'

'But just married. Takes all sorts, I suppose.'

'What concerns me is where the hell he fits in. I mean, is it just a coincidence that he was a guest at Morris's dinner? He's an old friend, he told me that, so it's hardly surprising he was invited to the farewell dinner for Ambrose Morris last week. These businessmen tend to stick together. And then Arthur Morris receives a letter which sends him haring up to Scholes.'

'Why didn't Arthur Morris tell anyone what was in the letter?'

Brennan shrugged. 'Maybe he didn't want any of them to know – whoever sent the letter must have been known to him, otherwise where did he expect to find the sender once he'd got to Scholes? And if he wished to keep this person's identity a secret, well then, there must have been a reason for doing so. His wife, remember, was there.'

'You sayin' it could've been a woman?'

'Could've been. Or a veiled threat, the significance of which only he would know.'

'All the more reason for him to tell somebody. His brother, or Cox, his old friend. Again, why keep it to himself?'

'It's one of the key questions, Constable. Why go there at all?'

Jaggery thought for a moment, letting the heave and sway of the carriage calm the swirl of ideas in his head.

Finally he said, 'Did Cox go home when the dinner broke up?'

'No, he says he went to the Conservative Club. His wife then travelled on alone.'

'So he could've done the dirty deed, eh? If he left straight off. Could've gone to Scholes, stabbed meladdo an' then back to the Con Club for a stiff brandy.'

'He could. But why? What would his motive be?'

''S always summat to do wi' business with that lot, Sergeant. You mark my words. Or summat to do with Bridie Whatsername. She was fired and no bugger believed 'er. He tries his hand an' gets burnt, so to speak.'

'But why wait nineteen years? And if it did have anything to do with Bridie Haggerty, surely James Cox would've been the one with a knife sticking out of his chest? It doesn't make sense. Although I'm convinced the Haggertys have some connection with this thing. Otherwise why would Bragg be asking questions about them?' Brennan shook his head. 'No, it's a curious thing.'

A thought suddenly struck him.

'Constable. Tell the driver we wish to go to Scholes.'

Jaggery rubbed his head in despair. 'Bloody 'ell, Sergeant, we might as well take up lodgings in that bloody place. Remember last time we went up yonder?'

When he saw Brennan glaring menacingly at him for daring to question an order, he tapped on the trap above his head and passed on his sergeant's instructions.

It took them another twenty minutes of slipping and sliding through the thick snow before they got as far up the hill leading into Scholes as they could.

'It's no use, sir,' the coachman called down to them. 'It's too deep up here. This is as far as the horses can make it.'

Brennan called out his thanks and stepped down from the relative warmth of the carriage's interior, Jaggery slumping down with ill-concealed displeasure. There were few people on Scholes, the street that gave the area its name. Some of the shops were still open, their lamps lit inside, giving them an eerie and haunted look, and they could see clusters of beshawled women standing at the various counters making what few purchases they could afford and entertaining each other with the trivia of gossip. A small, ruddy-faced group of children were screeching delightedly as they hurled snowballs at all and sundry – including the large uniformed policeman across the road – and it was obvious that they, at least, were making the most of the terrible conditions and making merry whenever they could, even if it were at the expense of the local constabulary.

'Little bastards!' Jaggery yelled as a snowball struck him squarely in his left ear.

When they reached the Rose and Crown on the corner of Scholes and Scholefield Lane, Brennan gave a sideways glance through the window, just in case anyone there should show an interest in Jaggery's uniform, but the place was empty, and the barman was leaning on the bar smoking a pipe and reading a newspaper.

When they knocked at the door of number 7, it was Bridie Haggerty herself who answered.

'If it's Molly ye've come to see, she's out.'

'No, Mrs Haggerty. It's you. May we come in?'

She looked at Brennan curiously, but ushered them both inside. 'Ye'll be givin' me a bad name, police 'ere again.'

'It's just a few questions, Bridie.'

'Well ye'll have to ask 'em as I'm workin'.' She made her way through to the tiny kitchen, where a mound of dough was waiting to be kneaded. 'My wee lad is out on the street with his pals.'

'Aye,' said Jaggery, rubbing his left ear. 'I think I spotted 'im.'

Bridie began to press forward, kneading the pliant dough with firm fists. 'He likes a nice cob o' hot bread. Soakin' up the butter. Well, margarine, but it's better than nothin'. We make do.'

'Bridie, I want to ask you about the time you worked for Arthur Morris.'

For a second the fluid movement of kneading was broken. She gave a blank look, then continued.

'It's about the time you were ... let go.'

'Sacked, ye mean?'

'Yes. What happened?'

She lifted her head and rested her hands on the dough. 'I was, as they say, "grossly insubordinate".'

'You made allegations against Mr James Cox.'

'Allegations!'

She gave a sneer, then began to shape the

dough into a large ball. She busied herself placing it gently in a cracked ceramic bowl before placing a towel across its exposed rim. Then she brushed past the two policemen and went into the front room, where she bent low to place the bowl in front of the fire, which was glowing with no sign of a flame.

'Will ye pass me that bucket?' she said as Brennan stood beside her. He reached to the left of the hearth where a coal bucket lay half-filled with coal slack.

Bridie held it, took out the iron poker that lay inside, and emptied some of the contents onto the glowing coals. Immediately, thick smoke billowed out and she waved it from her face, giving a little cough in the process. Then she gently prodded the coals, prising some of them apart to allow the glowing embers beneath to breathe.

'There. That'll give a fair blaze in a while. It's needed, ye see, to make the dough rise.'

'Bridie?'

She stood up, wiped her hands on the makeshift apron she was wearing, and gave a slow nod. 'I was asked to fetch some clean linen from the laundry room. I heard someone's steps on the stairs but I thought it was another of the servants. Then the door swung open an' he was stood there.'

'James Cox?'

'Aye. Said he had little time an' could we please *forego the pleasantries*. Sure I hadn't a bloody clue what he meant but I knew what he wanted. Then he reached out an' ... he touched me. Where he shouldn't.'

'What happened then?'

Bridie gave a bitter laugh and swung the poker in the air as if she were conducting an orchestra from hell. 'D'ye want me to paint you a picture?'

Brennan paused for a second, then said, 'What I'm about to suggest ... I can assure you, it won't go any further. But there's something I need to know. It might have a bearing on this case.'

'Go on.' Bridie licked her lips.

'Is James Cox the father of your daughter Molly?'

There was a gentle knock on Frank Latchford's door, and when he looked through the window he saw three men shifting from foot to foot with their hands stuffed deep in their pockets. Thick mufflers hid their faces, but he knew them right enough. He opened the door and, without a word, ushered them in.

'We thought tha' should know,' said one.

'They're theer agen,' said the second man. 'That swine Brennan and the fat bastard.'

Latchford pressed his lips together. What the hell were they doing back there?

The third man, more thick-set than the others and whose broken nose and scarred face were legacies of the clog-fighting he was most proficient in, spoke in a gruff voice. 'We should've finished the swine off when we had the chance.'

Latchford shook his head. 'That would have got us nowhere. Apart from the gallows. No, he got a warning and that's the end of it.'

'We can make sure this time,' the first man snarled.

'No!' said Latchford sharply. 'That would be a

disaster.' He thought for a moment. 'I'll go to see Bridie Haggerty when they've gone. See what they wanted.'

'They're nowt but bloody spies!' the clog-fighter growled, but when Latchford glared at him he became silent, like a slavering but obedient dog.

Brennan sat slumped in the armchair, ignoring the pain from the toy wooden boat he'd just sat on. A far greater pain concerned him just then, and he winced in agony as he watched Constable Jaggery wrestle the poker from Bridie Haggerty's grasp.

She had swung the weapon with admirable speed. It caught him completely unawares, and the shaft of the poker slammed him full on the shoulder before he could blink an eye. It took his breath and, as he fell backwards onto the armchair, he saw her raise it again in what appeared to be a heavy downward swing. That was when Jaggery, with an urgency not often seen in the big man, launched himself forward and grabbed the raised arm, forcing the poker, and her right hand, backwards with such strength that she could either drop the offending object or listen to her wrist bone snap.

'You bloody mad cow!' Jaggery grunted when her outrage had finally subsided and she sat on her knees before the still dormant dough. 'You all right, Sergeant?'

Brennan nodded and had gained his breath sufficiently to reach beneath him and remove the tormenting toy. 'That's quite a temper you have there, Bridie,' he said, somewhat hoarsely.

'An' that was quite an insult,' she snapped

263

back, rubbing her wrist as Jaggery stood over her like a poker-wielding Colossus.

'I'd still like you to answer my question though.'

Her shoulders seemed to sag, as though suddenly all the fight had left her.

'Then the answer is no, Sergeant. James Cox attacked me. I never said he got what he wanted.'

'He wasn't intimate with you?'

She gave a sad smile. 'Oh the devil tried, right enough. He touched me, if you know what I mean. But I just went limp till he got close. Then I kicked him in the balls.'

'You did what?'

'Man can't work without his tools, now, can he?'

'So Molly isn't the result of the attack?'

'Well if she is I'd like to know how.'

Brennan reached up and touched his shoulder, which was throbbing violently. Perhaps some of the pain came from the fact that, if Bridie was telling the truth – and he suspected she was – then he had made an erroneous assumption earlier in the carriage, and that did his self-esteem no favours at all.

'Can I get up?' Bridie asked.

Brennan nodded to Jaggery, who, reluctantly and without offering her his hand, allowed her to rise.

'Now it's my turn,' she said.

'What do you mean?' Brennan watched her warily as she moved to the side of the fireplace. Was she about to sally forth once more? He gave Jaggery a quick glance, but he was already holding the poker aloft, ready for a sideswipe at his command.

'You're not the first to suggest that,' she said. 'And it's somethin' that's been eatin' away at me conscience ever since. I suppose now's as good a time as any to get it off me chest. Ye see, Sergeant, a few weeks ago I had a visitor. A messenger from someone who needed to speak to me urgent like. The messenger had a patch over one eye.'

'So you did know him.'

'Aye, I did. He worked for Morris, right enough. I was to meet Arthur Morris in Mesnes Park, where he had a proposition for me.'

Brennan's eyes grew wide. 'You met Arthur Morris?'

'Aye. He told me he wanted to talk about Molly. And his son Andrew. He'd found out an' wanted to put a stop to it.'

'What exactly did he say to you?'

'Oh, he said he could make life very hard for us. The strike was biting hard and it would be no trouble for him to have us evicted.'

'He wouldn't have done that. Not then anyway. It would have made him even more of a demon than he already was to some people.'

'Oh I know that. I told him I didn't approve of them bein' together any more than he did, but I'd be damned if he was goin' to dictate to me an' mine who we should or shouldn't be seen with. Then he grabbed me.'

'Grabbed you? There in full view of everyone?'

'He's a violent swine, Sergeant Brennan. An' he's got a strong grip. I saw him once do the same to his wife when I worked up yonder, an' I know a lot of the women round 'ere get a leatherin' at times, but you don't expect to see it from the moneyed lot, do ye? Anyways, he was squeezin' the life out of me arm an' grinnin' all at the same time. I couldn't believe it. So I let rip at 'im. An' it was then, when I flared up an' yelled at him there an' then in the middle of the park, that he sat back, eyes bulgin'. "I know you, don't I?" he said. An' it was only then he recognised who I was. All the time we'd been sittin' there he had no idea I was that maid he dismissed so long ago. An' then he gives a big smile, as if somethin' had just occurred to him.'

'What was it?'

'Oh, he was quick, I'll give the devil that. He said he had the means to make sure we left the area. I said, "What are you talkin' about?" an' he said, "If people knew who Molly's real father was, wouldn't that get the tongues blabbin". "What do you mean, *real* father?" I says. "She had a real father an' he died in one o' your dangerous pits." He just laughed an' said it was amazin' what people would say if he paid 'em enough. He said he knew a great deal about that swine Cox an' he was sure he could make folk swallow a tale like that.'

'But that's ridiculous. James Cox has two young children. He would never allow Arthur Morris to suggest such a thing. It would ruin his reputation.'

Bridie sighed. 'I know, an' I told him just that, almost spat it in his face. Then he smiled an' said there'd be more than one person willin' to put the story round about Mr James Cox bein' Molly's father, an' if he wished to sully the reputation of a swine who'd been plottin' against him anyway, then that was his business.'

'What did he mean, "plotting against him"?'

266

'Sure I haven't the foggiest. But I got the impression he didn't give a flyin' hoot about Mr James Cox's reputation. An' them such close devils an' all. An' at the time he was so convincin'. I believed him. But I didn't know what to do.' She paused and glanced down. 'So I prayed.'

'You *prayed?*'

'I know it's an evil thing to do, but as sure as I'm standin' here today, I prayed every night and at every Mass for God to strike him down and take him from this world. I was brought up to believe absolutely in the power of prayer, Sergeant. An' then God answered me prayers. Or I thought he had, anyways. An' when they found his dead body not far from me own back yard, well ... I nearly did somethin' terrible. A mortal sin. The guilt of prayin' a man dead...'

Her voice trailed off as the coals began to show some flicker of flame.

Despite repeated attempts to persuade the woman to explain what she meant, she remained silent. Brennan knew he would get nothing more of value out of her.

'So Arthur Morris would do anything to prevent his son and Molly from being together, including the ruination of James Cox's character,' Brennan said, half to himself.

'He was a selfish man, Sergeant.'

'And a violent one.'

You're no sheep, Bridie Haggerty, he said to himself as he stood up, gingerly holding his shoulder. *Arthur Morris had met his match with you. But would you have the strength of will to kill a man in cold blood?*

'How do we get 'er down to the station, Sergeant?' said Jaggery, still keeping a wary eye on the mad Irishwoman.

'What?'

'It'll be a bugger draggin' 'er down Scholes in all this snow.'

'What on earth are you talking about?'

Exasperated, Jaggery held up exhibit number one. 'Assaultin' a police officer in the pursuance of his duties.'

Brennan smiled. 'Oh, accidents will happen, Constable Jaggery. You put it down before you do yourself an injury.'

The poker made a clanging sound as it was thrust, somewhat peevishly, back into the coal bucket.

Instead of seeing them to the door, Bridie moved over to the bowl resting before the fire. As they were leaving, Brennan looked back at the hearth. He saw, with some satisfaction, that the dough was already beginning to rise beneath the cloth.

Ten minutes after her visitors had left, there was another knock on the door. When she opened it, Frank Latchford was standing there.

'Frank!' she said, and there was genuine fear in her voice.

'Can I come in, Mrs Haggerty? I gather you've had company?'

Bridie stepped to one side and ushered him in.

CHAPTER SEVENTEEN

The following day, Donald Monroe presented Brennan with a copy of the post-mortem report into Bragg's death at Wigan Infirmary.

'You will see that the main thrust of the report centres around the ecchymoses at the base of the neck.'

'Ecchymoses?' Brennan had never got used to the good doctor's fondness for medical terminology. It had its place in a report, of course, but a verbal digest should be uncluttered, as it were, by such embellishments.

'Bruises. From blood vessels that are ruptured and spread into subcutaneous tissue. That's beneath the skin, Sergeant.'

'Thank you.'

'He was struck most forcibly from behind. No attempt to protect himself is apparent, and death would have been quite rapid. When I detached the skull cap from the subjacent membranes – not an easy matter, let me tell you, especially with those used to hard knocks – I made an opening in the *dura mater* and...'

'What are you getting at?' Brennan asked impatiently.

'The brain, Sergeant Brennan. That's what I was getting at. There was a great deal of haemorrhaging. I'd say the one who wielded the murder weapon intended his victim to die – this was no struggle that went wrong. A blow of such force could only have one result.'

'I see.'

'There was also some redness around the right eye, or rather, the surrounding socket.'

'Redness?'

'Had no bearing on his death, but it appears to be some sort of rash. An irrelevance, but I thought I'd mention it.'

Brennan thought quickly. 'The eyepatch.'

Monroe looked at him curiously and scratched his chin.

'Well, Sergeant, if that is all, I have a ward full of patients. Living ones, at least for the time being.'

'Of course.' He gingerly rubbed his shoulder as a prelude to standing.

'How are the bruises?'

'I beg your pardon?'

Dr Monroe sat back and pretended to glower. 'Now don't tell me they have healed up already. A brutal attack like that will take time to heal.'

It dawned on Brennan that he was referring to the injuries sustained in the attack he suffered a week or so ago in the alley near his home, not the more recent assault with a poker. He hadn't forgotten the brutality, nor the words of his unseen assailant as he lay there bleeding.

'Oh, the bruises will fade in time, I'm sure.'

'Might I suggest friction with soap liniment? That should remove any residual swelling. Outward application of arnica, too, should help, though there's a new remedy from America, Hazeline, prepared from wych hazel, they say will soon supersede arnica.'

Brennan thought of Prudence Morris. 'I've smelt arnica on Prudence Morris, doctor. It's not the most pleasant of aromas.'

'Mrs Morris? Has she suffered an injury?'

Brennan smiled. 'No, she uses it for her rheumatic condition.'

Monroe frowned. 'Oh, that won't do at all. Tell her she would be far better advised to apply a hot bran poultice regularly. Or perhaps a liniment of camphor oil with soap and opium. And there are a whole gamut of electric or galvanic appliances. No, Sergeant, arnica won't do. It won't do at all.'

With this further demonstration of his vast medical knowledge hanging in the air like a disinfectant, he stood up and escorted his visitor to the door.

Once outside, Brennan stood in the cold corridor that led to the wards and watched Monroe breeze his way down towards his patients, while he turned in the opposite direction and headed for the porticoed entrance. He had a lot to think about. Especially concerning a picture that was beginning to emerge of Arthur Morris.

What was it Mrs Venner, the cook, had hinted at? That he was like a Jekyll and Hyde character, pleasant one minute 'and a brute the next'. And he had played rough with Bridie when he met her in the park. What's more, many years ago, she had seen him grab his wife roughly once while she was working there. If she saw it once, then how many more times might such a thing have happened? Could that be why she applied arnica? Not for rheumatism, which was a convenient way of disguising the pain associated with bruising,

271

but for the bruising itself?

He stood in the entrance to the infirmary, on the very spot where he had stood with Andrew Morris over a week ago when he had come to identify his father's body. He had quoted Shakespeare then. What was it he had said? 'Fear no more the heat of the sun, nor the winter's furious rages'. Had he been referring, not to the suggestion that death brings with it almost a liberation from the vagaries of life, but to the dichotomy within his father's personality – the warmth and the rage struggling within him?

Arthur Morris, Brennan mused. *The more I find out about you, the less I like.*

He thought also of the rash on Bragg's right eye socket. Why wear a patch when he had two perfectly good eyes? But then he answered his own query almost at once – it's a perfect disguise. If he was out and about in Scholes and Wigan, asking questions that would inevitably arouse interest, what better way to draw attention away from the face? For those with a morbid disposition, a black eyepatch, with its suggestion of something gruesome lurking beneath, provides a compelling focus of curiosity, not to mention the hint of something sinister and devilish. You're more likely to remember the patch than the face.

The sky, he noted, was grey, but there were a few glimpses of blue in the distance. Perhaps the elements, too, were fighting a battle.

'Any joy with the post-mortem, Sergeant?' Constable Jaggery asked once he got back to the station. The man was fidgeting quite badly, moving his balance from one foot to the other, as if he had St Vitus's Dance.

'A post-mortem hardly brings joy, Constable,' Brennan responded harshly.

'Aye, well, there's summat you should know. It's like good and bad.'

'What?'

But before he could get an answer, he saw Captain Bell bearing down on him hard, a satisfied smirk on his face.

'Sergeant Brennan!' he said as Jaggery, never comfortable in the presence of greatness and also aware of what was coming, slouched away. 'I hear the butler Isaacs confirmed what I suspected?'

'It was Mrs Venner, the cook, actually, sir.'

'Notwithstanding. The Haggerty woman was the selfsame maid who was dismissed?'

'Yes, sir.'

'Capital!'

'But I have spoken to her and it appears…'

'Forget appearances! While you were at the infirmary with Doctor Monroe, I took the opportunity to have Constable Jaggery supply me with what I required.'

'Sir?'

'He is a bovine fellow, isn't he? Still, like the buffaloes of Agra, he gets there in the end.'

Brennan caught sight of Jaggery's back disappearing into the canteen. 'He supplied you with what, sir?'

'Oh, he told me all about your little adventure yesterday in Scholes, at the home of that Irishwoman.'

'He did?'

'He told me what she said to you. It was a plodding recital, but nevertheless...'

'I could have given you a full report just as soon as I...'

'No matter, Sergeant!' He slapped Brennan on the shoulder, causing him to wince in pain. 'Ah, that will be the assaulted area. Terrible business, and a good job Constable Jaggery was there to prevent further injury.'

Brennan made a mental note to strangle Jaggery.

'Still, it only confirms what I suspected.'

'And what's that, sir?'

The chief constable raised a finger, as if to forestall any further questions, and indicated that his sergeant should follow him. They passed along the corridor to the door at the end that led down to the cells. As Captain Bell unlocked the heavy wooden door, he turned to Brennan and said, 'After Constable Jaggery's report, I felt it incumbent upon me to keep you from further injury, and it was made apparent that you were in an invidious position yesterday, being injured and no doubt your judgement somewhat impaired.'

What was the idiot talking about?

They both descended the dark stairway, a single gas lamp at the top of the stairs the only illumination.

'So I sent a few constables up to the mad woman's house and had her arrested and brought here. She is in the cells awaiting our pleasure. Assaulting a police officer, as Constable Jaggery so loyally pointed out, is a serious business. Besides, the woman has motive – more than one, too, I gather, what with her dismissal from the Morris residence...'

'Nineteen years ago.'

'Women like that have long memories, Sergeant. And Constable Jaggery tells me she had some outrageous notion that Arthur Morris was intending to blackmail her.'

They reached the dark, narrow corridor that was flanked on both sides by heavy wooden doors inlaid with small iron grilles.

'*And* her husband was killed in the explosion five years ago. There were some in this town who had the audacity to blame poor Morris. I'm sure she was in the vanguard.'

'So she waited five years before gaining her revenge?'

'They're patient, insidious creatures, sometimes. Never be fooled by feminine submissiveness.'

'But sir, I really think...'

'Tell me, Sergeant, how many motives does one need to present a solid prosecution? The woman has motives coming out of her ears!'

Captain Bell stopped outside the furthest cell from the stairway. A constable was standing behind a small table, the newspaper he was reading before the sound of their approach carefully tucked beneath his chair.

'If you will be so kind, Constable Davies.'

The constable took out a large bunch of keys and unlocked the cell door.

Captain Bell abjured seniority and allowed his sergeant to enter first. Bridie Haggerty was kneeling by the small aperture that lay high in the outer wall, through which a shaft of grey light filtered through from the pavement above, and was praying fervently with eyes tightly closed.

'I'll leave you to do your job, Sergeant.'

With this implied rebuke hanging in the cold, damp air of the cell, he closed the door quickly and left.

Brennan stood there for a full minute, unwilling to interrupt the poor woman at prayer. It was likely to be her sole comfort for a while yet, until he could at least give a display of carrying out the chief constable's orders. Only then would he be able even to attempt to have her released. If necessary, he thought, he would swear on oath that the attack with a poker was nothing more than an accident caused mainly by his reckless and sudden movement in the small front room, and any testimony to the contrary given by the sole witness would be dismissed as – to echo Captain Bell himself – 'bovine inexactitude'.

'This wasn't my doing,' he said when she had finished with the sign of the cross.

Bridie said nothing but moved to the wooden slab that was firmly attached to the left-hand wall. She sat down slowly and gazed at the floor. A rat suddenly scurried out from beneath the makeshift bed and disappeared through a gap in the opposite wall. The only reaction from Bridie was a wry smile.

'Don't worry. You'll be out soon enough.'

'They didn't even give me time to sort my wee Tommy out.'

'I'll send someone round to make sure...'

'Don't bother yerself. It's what neighbours are for.'

Instead of taking up an interrogative stance opposite her and glowering down with stern authority, which would be his usual method, he sat beside her and leant forward. She shifted her position slightly, a physical sign of her displeasure.

'Sometimes the chief constable can be a pain in the arse,' he said in a low voice.

She turned and looked at him curiously.

'I know you had nothing to do with Arthur Morris's death, Bridie.'

She shrugged her shoulders, then looked away.

'Just as I know you had nothing to do with the second murder.'

'The man on the boat?'

'Yes. But if you hadn't been so cruelly dragged here, I would have been paying you another visit.'

'Why?'

'To ask you more about the time you worked for Arthur Morris.'

'It was a lifetime ago. I was just a young colleen, green as Ireland.'

'Something you told me struck me as interesting. You said Arthur Morris had a temper, and you'd seen him act violently towards his wife, Prudence.'

'So?'

'What happened that time you saw him?'

'Sure I can't remember. Not really.'

'Anything you can think of.'

She sat there for a while, watching the rat which emerged from the wall opposite and scurried back beneath the wooden bed.

'I'd been told to go to the nursery. Master Andrew had been ill and had been eating his food either in his room or in the nursery. I was taking a tray of food...' she broke off and shook her head.

'What is it?'

'Jesus, Sergeant. To think that sickly wee thing would grow up to... Molly thinks she loves him. But Frank Latchford has the measure of the man, I reckon. At least he's makin' him pay to...' she immediately looked down, as if she could have bitten her tongue.

Brennan recalled what Andrew Morris had told him. He scrutinised her for a while, then returned to his original line of questioning. 'Please go on.'

'There's not much more. I was going past the master bedroom, an' the door was open. I heard a short scream, y'know, like when you hurt yerself? An' I saw the master grippin' her arm, an' his face was purple.'

'Did he say anything?'

'He said somethin' but it was like a whisper through gritted teeth. I couldn't stay any longer because Mister Ambrose – he'd been in the nursery lookin' in on his nephew – came out to see where I was with the food an' he gave me a right shallickin' for lettin' the food go cold, though I'd hardly been there more than a minute.'

'You never saw a recurrence?'

'What?'

'Did you see him do it again? Assault his wife?'

'No. But the way she just stood there reminded me of a dog used to the boot. D'ye know what I mean?'

Brennan, who had seen too many examples of husbands abusing their wives in the vilest of ways, nodded. It always struck him as odd that some of these women, victims of the cruellest brutality, would steadfastly refuse to give evidence, as if their spouse would by some miracle learn the error of his ways.

'Did he ever treat you in such a way? Apart from the time he met you in the park and threatened you?'

'I've always been taught to look after meself, Sergeant Brennan. An' if he'd raised a finger against me he'd have got the same treatment as the swine Cox did.' Her face darkened at the mention of James Cox. 'But I'll tell you summat. Back then, those two were as thick as thieves.'

'Arthur Morris and James Cox?'

'Aye. Money sticks wi' money. It's the way of the world, right enough.'

When he got to the door of the cell, he was surprised to see tears in her eyes. 'What is it, Bridie? What's troubling you?'

She was on the verge of saying something, but then whatever it was remained unspoken, and she lowered her head once more.

He left the prisoner with her melancholy reflections, and sought out the traitor in his camp.

He thought first about going in to see Captain Bell and tell him that the woman downstairs might justly claim to be the victim of wrongful arrest, but he decided he had better assemble his thoughts more rationally if he were to arrange for Bridie to be released. Besides, he had a score to settle with the bovine inadequate who would now be skulking in a corner of the canteen nursing a steaming hot mug of tea and a grievance.

Sure enough, Jaggery was in the canteen, but he was sitting erect, facing the doorway, and appearing for all the world to be looking forward to the tongue-lashing he must surely expect. Four or five others were watching a couple of the older constables playing snooker, lounging with their top buttons undone, talking in desultory fashion and, apart from giving Brennan a subservient nod, showed no other sense of the fusillade he was about to fire.

Is the fellow truly a fool? Brennan wondered as he saw the confident look on Jaggery's face. He prepared to unleash his broadside.

But as he approached the table where he was sitting, it was Jaggery who spoke first.

'Before you begin, Sergeant, I had no choice. Old Ding-Dong had me in a corner.'

'That'll be nothing compared to what...'

'But I've been doin' a bit of detectin' on me own, like.'

'What?'

By way of an answer, he produced a notebook from his pocket as if it were a rabbit from a top hat. Brennan recognised it as the one he had found in Bragg's valise on the boat.

'Bragg's notebook?'

'The very same.'

'There's nothing in it but his name.'

'Aye.'

'And you've detected that, have you?'

Jaggery leant forward and invited him to sit down. With gritted teeth, Brennan did as his constable asked.

'I have a confession, Sergeant.'

'I'm listening.'

'When we brought this stuff to the station last night, did you or did you not say that the contents of the valise could be burnt?'

'I did. A shirt and a few bars of soap, a flannel and *that*.'

'Aye, well, I have a little 'un at home likes drawin'.'

Brennan saw at once. 'So you took the notebook instead of burning it?'

'I did.'

'And I presume you found something inside it that I'd missed? Some incriminating words scrawled in invisible ink?'

'No, Sergeant.'

He was beginning to seethe once more.

'But my lad's learnin' how to write. So he copies the name inside – *Bragg* – over and over again till he fills a couple of pages. An' I'm showin' him where he's goin' wrong, like.'

'Well?'

'But he's a good copier, see? Missus reckons he'll work with his head, not his hands, when he's all growed up. Any road, it's when he's writin' his letter r, with a little squiggle on the end like it's curlin' up, see?' He opened the notebook and showed him the endless column of 'Bragg's in a childish scrawl. All of them with an upturn at the end of the *r*. Then Jaggery turned back to the original name on the inside cover and showed him the same characteristic. 'I'd seen that somewhere before, Sergeant. And guess where it was?'

Brennan blinked at the name again. Then he stood up, quickly left the canteen and returned within a minute, holding in his hand the letter and envelope that were found on the body of Arthur Morris. He sat down and placed the notebook, the letter and the envelope all together in a line.

A. Morris...
Strike causes hell – O Lord end suffrin
Or die...
Bragg...

Why hadn't he seen it on the boat? His only excuse would be the dim lighting, although even as the thought struck him he dismissed it. He should have checked it. But it was clear as day now. The letter *r* was identically formed in all three locations.

Which meant that the letter Morris received was written by Bragg.

'Am I right, Sergeant?'

Brennan, all thoughts of bovine strangulation forgotten, looked up and uttered what sounded like a symphony to Constable Jaggery's ears.

'Good work, Constable. You've done well.'

CHAPTER EIGHTEEN

'You intend to do what?'

Prudence Morris stood at the foot of the garden looking across the valley towards the straggling maze of pit houses in the distance. They had looked so pretty with their white rooftops all in a row, thin straggles of smoke curling into the grey sky. The all-too-brief glimpse of blue had long since gone from the sky, and heavy snow clouds had drifted overhead, cumbersome and menacing in the stillness they brought.

She was wearing a thick black coat trimmed with fur, a mourning bonnet fastened with ribbon that partially concealed the string of black beads around her neck, delicately carved and made of Whitby Jet. Despite the snow which had begun to fall half an hour earlier, she had insisted on Andrew taking her around the outside of the house and along the meandering pathways that led ultimately to the rear garden and its domineering aspect. She had been inside interminably, she had argued when he demurred, and besides her rheumatism was showing signs of abating.

Finally he had agreed, on the understanding she lean on him throughout and they walk at a most leisurely pace. The snow underfoot was treacherous, he had told her.

Now, as he stood beside her and saw her gazing forward, as if she dared not look him in the eye, he repeated what he had just told her.

'I intend to marry and to pursue my work – my art – in America.'

'Marry?'

'Yes.'

'Whom?'

He told her.

'A mill girl? Is this the artistic temperament manifesting itself in lunacy?'

'I had the wildest idea that you already knew.'

'Knew about this? How?'

'From Father.'

'*He* knew?'

'Yes. And tried to prevent it, in his own inimitable way.'

She appeared to consider this for a moment, then shook her head slowly. 'No, Andrew. It was an intimacy he did not share with me.'

'But when we spoke the other day, when Uncle Ambrose was here, you said something that made me think you knew.'

'What was that?'

'After you both brought up the subject of my responsibilities concerning the coalfields and the strike, you said something about "the other thing" you wished to speak to me about. I was afraid that meant you already knew.'

He watched her lips purse, and noticed, perhaps for the first time, tiny creases along her lips. Had the pain she had endured all these years formed those cracks?

'No. That was something else altogether.'

'Please, explain.'

She shook her head, expelled a small cloud of breath. 'The time isn't quite right. But don't worry. The time will come.'

He frowned at the cryptic comment, but recognised the moment had passed.

Slowly she turned to face him, and he saw her eyes were moist with tears.

'America?' she whispered.

He took a deep breath. 'You must understand we can't stay here. She would hate being the constant object of scorn and hatred, even if she were to come and live here.'

The lips tightened once more. 'That will never happen.'

'I don't want it to. That's why I want us to go where we can be free.'

She gave a half-smile. 'You sound like a refugee fleeing persecution.'

'In a way that's what we'd be.'

'Nonsense! Fanciful nonsense. Besides, you have duties here.'

He shook his head. 'I'll speak to Uncle Ambrose.'

'Ha! That man won't leave his precious Westminster. It would be easier extracting a tiger's tooth.'

'Then we could appoint an executive to take responsibility for the day-to-day running of the collieries.'

'That's what your dear father would have wanted, is it?'

Andrew was on the verge of responding but thought better of it.

She placed a gloved hand on his arm. 'Promise me one thing.'

'What is it?'

'Do not act precipitously. Let me send a telegram to your uncle in London. See if he will return to speak with you. At least promise me that.'

He saw, in her glistening eyes, something beyond the usual façade of rectitude, the primness she invariably adopted whenever their discussions seemed to drift away from her high-principled moorings. It was that rarest of glimpses into her inner self – the woman beneath the mother.

Sometimes he felt like a man standing on the edge of the world, looking down and seeing nothing but darkness – a cold, Stygian gloom wherein all manner of vengefully malignant spectres swirled in their loathsome circles just waiting for him to take one more fatal step; while behind him a fireball was fast approaching, consuming all in its path, its ferocious heat far more ruinous than the most powerful blast furnace in existence.

James Cox walked down Market Street, leaving the insidious warmth of the club behind him, the sickly chatter of fireside commentators who predicted not only a change in the weather but a freshening wind of common sense soon to sweep the land, rendering miners and owners close bosom friends shaking hands and sharing a convivial and conciliatory drink.

Optimistic poppycock! A scene only to be found in a *Punch* cartoon.

Perhaps he shouldn't have rounded on them. After all, they were suffering too in their several ways: manufacturers of aerated water, of clothing and mantles, of general house furnishings, of cotton spinners and hatters, of paint and varnish, of corn, flour and provender, even of tobacco and cigar dealings, all of them feeling the cold pinch of penury.

Yet their infernal optimism, their self-deceiving assurances that salvation was just round the corner, like a tram stuck in the snow just waiting for the thaw, had irritated him beyond measure.

None of them faced the scale of bankruptcy he faced.

It was early evening. Thankfully, the clanging of

the mill girls' clogs he would normally hear at this time was muffled by the thick, unyielding snow. He ignored the groups of them giggling behind him, arms linked and rejoicing with an eldritch whoop every time one of them slid almost to the horizontal, only to be saved by the human chain.

Sometimes he envied them. They had to worry about nothing but the mill remaining open, and so far every cotton mill in Wigan had shown a stubborn resilience he found distasteful. They could go home to their stinking hovels and eat their gristle or pigs' feet or whatever it was they consumed, and sit in their dingy little front rooms talking inanely about the latest gossip from the spinning room or the weaving shed or wherever they plied their dusty, shabby little trade.

But what did he have? His children, of course, and his wife. And his large, imposing house on the edge of Lord Crawford's estate.

But if the contracts were broken...

He shook his head and turned round, glowering at the giggling witches behind him.

'Why, Mr Cox! A pleasant surprise!'

Standing between him and the mill girls, who had stopped to gaze in awe at a shop window displaying some colourful fur capes priced at seven guineas, was Frank Latchford.

Cox blinked twice before recognising the Federation man. 'Latchford. What do you want? I'm busy.'

He turned to go but felt a large hand press down on his shoulder. Once more he turned round, his eyes blazing with anger now. 'How dare you!'

'Now that's no way to speak to someone who

might be able to do you a favour, is it?'

'What the blazes are you talking about?'

'There's the Bricklayer's Arms round the corner, in Hallgate. Let's me and you go and have a drink, shall we?'

The thought of entering that establishment, a place of dubious and violent repute, filled Cox with horror.

'Go to hell!' he resumed his progress down Market Street.

'Someone who can do a favour can do a bad turn an' all,' Latchford said, lowering his tone to a whispered growl.

There was something in his voice, in his manner, that forced Cox to stop and listen.

'Go on,' he said.

'I'm on a sort of mission of mercy. Seeking out the great men of the town and asking for, shall we say, an investment?'

'For God's sake what are you talking about?'

Latchford smiled. 'Imagine how your star would rise, Mr Cox, if it were made known you subscribed to a relief fund that would...'

Confusion gave way to understanding, which manifested itself in a sneer spread across Cox's face. 'Taken to begging, have we? That's a crime, don't you know?'

'You have the most amazing ability to turn goodness into evil, Mr Cox. A sort of alchemist in reverse.'

'Have you been drinking, Latchford?'

'Not one drop.'

'Well then there can only be one other explanation for your ramblings – you've lost your mind.

It's we who need relieving, not the ones who rely on our industry. We bestow charity with every wage packet. Good evening!'

He swung round and resumed his progress down Market Street, his shoulders hunched and his head bowed low like a menacing bull.

Latchford drew his muffler closer to his throat and stuck both hands into his pockets. *Worth a try,* he thought. He shrugged and was about to cross the road when someone called his name. He turned to his right and saw Detective Sergeant Brennan standing on the steps of the Crofter's Arms. What the bloody hell did he want now?

'I thought it was you!' Brennan said as he got near.

'Sergeant Brennan. A surprise.'

'I like the beer in the Crofter's,' he said with a nod behind him.

Thin snowflakes swirled around the two men like insects.

'You finished for the day?' Latchford asked.

He looked across the road, anxious to be away.

'Oh, I never finish. Not really. Was that James Cox I saw you with just then?'

Latchford glanced down Market Street. He could just make out the man's stooping form as he reached the corner of Market Square. A line of hackney carriages stood waiting, with little hope of business, for early evening customers. Cox addressed the first cabbie and clambered inside.

'It was.'

'I didn't realise you two were acquainted.'

'He knows me and I know him. If that's a definition of acquainted, then I suppose we are.'

'Can I buy you a drink?'

Latchford's eyes narrowed. 'Why?'

'Oh, I could lie and say I like your company, but you wouldn't swallow that now, would you?'

'Hardly.'

'Well then. Let's say I have a few questions and seeing you just now has saved me the trouble of disturbing you in your home.'

'Didn't stop you disturbing Mrs Haggerty in her home this morning, did it?'

'That wasn't my idea. In fact, I've just arranged for her release. She's on her way now back home, in a carriage paid for by the chief constable himself.'

Who had only done so when Brennan presented him with the evidence of Bragg's writing of the letter to Arthur Morris and the unfeasibility of Bridie being in league with a nefarious character from Manchester.

'The least you could do.'

'So? Shall we sample – or in my case further sample – the delights of the Crofter's ale? At least we'll be out of the snow for a while.'

Once ensconced in a small corner booth, the two men sat with their foaming glasses and allowed the smooth sharpness to slither down before Brennan began.

'How did you know about the way Arthur Morris died? With a knife through the heart. It wasn't exactly common knowledge now, was it?'

Latchford laughed out loud. 'And you think it was a slip? Saying something only the murderer would know?'

'Possibly.'

'When you say it wasn't common knowledge, Sergeant, you're reckoning without the loose tongue of a certain priest.'

Brennan nodded slowly.

'Tell me about your dealings with Andrew Morris.'

Latchford smacked his lips, licking the froth. 'I have no dealings with the man.'

'You and Molly Haggerty were courting at one time.'

'It's no secret.'

The man was definitely hiding something, but he wasn't the type of character to succumb to threats. There was a confidence about Frank Latchford that bordered on arrogance.

'I hear you're making him pay.'

That brought a reaction. Latchford gave him a sharp look, but said nothing.

'How are you making him pay, Frank?'

Latchford seemed to come to a decision. 'I'm not making him do anything. He's made a contribution to the relief fund. Magnanimous, unlike his father.'

'Were you asking for a similar gesture from James Cox just then?'

There was a new expression in Latchford's eyes, respect tinged with wariness, the way you'd watch a tiger prowling behind its bars. 'It wouldn't have done any harm, would it? And I'm not too proud to *beg* for help.'

A sneering note entered his voice.

'I can see that. With Arthur Morris out of the way, do you think things will begin to move now?'

'There's every chance. If the colliery owners

don't do anything rash. Doesn't help the immediate suffering though, does it?'

'They'd hardly be rash at a time like this,' Brennan replied. Then he smiled. 'Speaking of rashes, Frank, I'd like you to do me a favour.'

Latchford looked at him warily. 'What is it?'

'Call it a favour you owe me.'

'I owe you nothing.'

'Oh I think you do. I can't prove who organised the attack on me last week which put me in the infirmary, but I have a good idea.'

Latchford looked blankly at him and said nothing.

'It's always wise to avoid making enemies if you possibly can.'

'Is it?'

'And if you carry out this small favour, perhaps I can see my way to foregoing the desire for revenge. Believe me, Frank, if I want to get someone, no matter how long it takes...'

Latchford appeared to weigh up his options. Perhaps the prospect of continually watching his shadow persuaded him. Finally, he came down on the side of self-preserving pragmatism. 'What's the favour?'

'I want you to come up to the infirmary with me right now.'

'Why?'

'To look at a body.'

CHAPTER NINETEEN

Two days later, Ambrose Morris stepped off the train at Wigan North Western and handed the porter his case. He hadn't packed much, for he didn't intend to stay any longer than it would take to persuade young Andrew of the error of his ways. Ambrose hadn't shared his late brother's determination to see Andrew married to some eligible but distinctly unattractive heiress, but to see him throw his life away on some mill girl... Still, he had an idea that might work.

The telegram had come at a most inopportune time. His duties within the party had begun to assume greater significance since the tortuous progress of the Parish Councils Bill – over fifty folios of print covering the amendments alone – which provided a very real threat of forcing the House to sit until Christmas. Balfour, bless him, had offered to withdraw much of the opposition if the government split the bill in two, leaving the poor law elements until next year, but Gladstone was fixated on the bill, the whole bill, and nothing but the bill.

Damn the man.

Nevertheless, despite the pressing demands of the Commons, and Salisbury's insistence on strategy – a quality Ambrose was admired for – he relaxed as the carriage made its slow advance through the built-up snow. The events of the previous fortnight even now seemed unreal, consigned to that storehouse of the past, where the memory of his brother's murder sat alongside happier times when the two of them had been youngsters unencumbered by the obligations of adulthood. Strange, he reflected, how, since Arthur's death, his thoughts had been drawn to those innocent days, times he hadn't given a moment's thought to in years. All of his brother's faults, indeed all of his own, too, seemed to fade away like dried-out stains when they were once more climbing trees and rocking on wooden horses.

'When do we change?' he said out loud, and he laughed when the coachman, misunderstanding the rhetorical question, slid open the wooden trap and told him there would be no need to change, the horses could cope.

When they finally arrived in Standish and the family home, Ambrose stepped down from the carriage and saw his sister-in-law's face framed in an upper window. He gave her a cheery wave, but even at this distance he could see the deep worry lines etched on her face. She had told him, in her longer than usual communication, about the second murder in the town while he was in London – a man named Bragg, whom Sergeant Brennan felt had a connection with the family.

He wondered if her 'rheumatism' had gone?

Brennan had been busy these last two days. Firstly, he had sat down to put on paper everything to do with the two murders, but the smooth cursive flow of his writing soon became interspersed with footnotes, interpolated suggestions, question marks and exclamation marks, words and phrases underscored, some almost obliterated in frustration. Finally, he had placed the pages and pages of jumbled thoughts and speculations on one side of his desk, and beside them he placed a blank sheet of notepaper and wrote the following:

1. The letter found on Morris's body with the message:

His hand shal be agenst evryman and evryman's
hand agenst him
Strike causes hell – O Lord end suffrin
Or die

No name or address of sender. But Bragg's handwriting.
2. How did A.M. know where to go in Scholes? Again, no address. How? How?
3. Letter and envelope filthy. Yet maid at Morris home says envelope was white and clean. How did it get dirty if he put it straight into pocket?
4. If Bragg wrote letter, did he lie in wait for A.M. in alleyway?
5. Why would A.M. go in alleyway? Invited by Bragg?
6. But if Bragg wrote letter, how did he get back to Scholes ahead of A.M. after posting letter? Carriage? None seen.
7. But did Bragg post letter??? If not, who then?
8. Accomplice? Josiah Sweet? Possible. But seems feeble character. Would Bragg trust such a fool to deliver letter?

9. Back to three.

10. The Davy lamp door knocker. Heavy, loud, yet the one who posted the letter used his fist. Why? Was the knocker too high for him? A child? Again, would Bragg entrust such an errand to a mere child?

11. Bragg. Bragg. Bragg. Asking questions about Andrew and Molly. For Arthur Morris? Likely. So Bragg was working for A.M. [Frank Latchford confirmed at the infirmary mortuary that he was indeed the one who had been asking questions – so no room for doubt.]

12. Yet if Bragg was working for Morris, why should he kill the golden goose?

13. Unless he were acting for a third person to become a paid assassin? But who? Why? Who would benefit most from A.M.'s death? And who would then have to kill Bragg, probably in order to shut him up for ever?

14. Back to three. Always the letter. Is there an explanation? Yes! Yes! Yes!

Brennan had sat back with a satisfied expression on his face. Not smug, no, because that implied a certain amount of pride, too, and pride was the last thing he felt. He had been blind, he knew – the formation of the letter *r* for one thing, and it had been Jaggery who showed genuine initiative then. Helped by his four-year-old son, of course. Furthermore, if he were right, and his answers to the questions he had posed, especially to questions three, ten, and thirteen, were correct, then he would have to tread very carefully indeed.

The next thing Brennan did, following on his

assumption that he was right in his deductions, was to initiate discreet investigations. The person he had in mind had been very clever, and he had to be absolutely certain of his facts if he were to proceed. A telegram communication to the chief constable in Manchester, signed by Captain Bell as protocol dictated, had been followed by inquiries much closer to home, inquiries he kept from his superior for the time being.

He also had the plaster casts of the footprints taken at the murder scene by the canal all lined up in a neat row along one wall of his small office.

Naturally, he had had the impressions photographed as well, and an initial search of Josiah Sweet's boat had unearthed a foul-smelling pair of the latter's hobnailed boots that matched one set of prints. Another set had corresponded with the soles of Bragg's boots, as was to be expected seeing that he had been staying on the boat for a while. But it was the third set of footprints that caused him some interest. There was no match with anything on the boat. Could these be the footprints of the murderer? If so, all he had to do was search every house in Wigan for a match.

And yet the tread on the soles was quite unusual, quite distinctive.

The final task he had given himself, and in some ways the most arduous, had been to arrange a private meeting with the chief constable during which he wished to present his findings. He wouldn't, of course, describe them as *findings*, as he knew full well that Captain Bell would assert they were no such thing. But he would be as convincing an advocate as he could in order to impress upon him the force of his logic, a thread binding all of his questions together, but which depended upon the slender thread retaining its strength at its most tenuous spot – the answer to question number three.

It was a matter of seconds before he went to fulfil his appointment with Captain Bell that Constable Jaggery came rushing up the steps of the police station, slipping on the thick snow on the topmost step before regaining his precarious balance with the aid of the iron railing. He had a flushed and excited expression on his face. Brennan met him at the entrance, watched by a curious brace of individuals about to be entered into the arrest book.

'Got 'im, Sergeant!' Jaggery said after a few deep breaths.

'Got who?'

'The witness. Says he can identify meladdo.'

Thus armed with a stronger case, Brennan turned and marched towards the office of the chief constable.

James Cox sat in his study and shook his head once more. From the nursery upstairs came the sounds of his children yelling at each other, one of them pleading that it was his turn on the rocking horse. He leant forward and read once more the communication he held in his still-quivering hands. The letter, from the Blackpool Tower Company, was unequivocal. Two weeks. That was all they would allow him to resume production and go some way towards making up the *lamentable delay* he had shown in completing his *rather substantial* contract.

Did they think he was a magician? Conjuring iron and steel from a gigantic top hat with a wave of a giant wand? They were only thirty odd miles away. Hadn't they heard about the devastation wrought by the damned miners and their refusal to accept the economic realities of life?

Did they think he could stroll down to the nearest colliery, clamber into a pit cage and lower himself down to hew tubfuls of coal, then haul them to the surface where he could lift them with little effort onto the coal wagons which he would attach to a convenient locomotive, its steam already billowing into the blue, sunny sky, and transport them to his works where they would be swallowed by beehives and then furnaces that hadn't been fed for weeks?

Or were their heads already high above the clouds swirling around a tower – a bloody castle in the air – that had yet to be built?

A pity about Bragg, he told himself. Bragg would have shown initiative and somehow organised what he would need. But Bragg was dead, wasn't he? Dead and therefore useless.

He looked at the photograph on his study wall, a posed studio portrait of himself and Agnes in the early flush of marriage, and he saw the sparkle in his eyes that was soberly hidden beneath the rigidly stern expression and the well-trimmed moustache. He saw, too, the naïve optimism in Agnes's eyes, only the slight incline of her mouth suggesting she had retained any thoughts of the ridiculous accusations of the Irish slut that had been made only a few days before the photograph was taken.

Looking at these ghosts from the past, he was struck, only momentarily it must be said, by a shaft of regret. His younger self had shown only the nascent spark of the conflagration that would later consume him in his middle age.

Bragg had organised that, too.

It struck him as therefore more than a coincidence when he heard the front door bell and, in a few minutes, admitted Detective Sergeant Brennan into his study who, within thirty seconds of sitting down, brought up the name of Theodore Bragg.

'Theodore Bragg?' he said after a few seconds' thought.

The ever so slight emphasis he had placed on the Christian name told Brennan all he wanted to know.

'You knew the man, of course?'

'What makes you say that? I'm a very busy...'

'I know he did some work for you.'

'Oh? How do you know that?'

'The Manchester police have been very helpful. He is, shall we say, known to them?'

'So?'

'When we informed them of his death, they searched his addresses. He had several.'

'Go on.'

'And he was a businessman. He kept records. Not incriminating in any way, I don't think Mr Bragg would ever have been that reckless.'

Cox appeared to breathe out a very slow sigh of relief.

'But he did record names and dates, I suppose

to remind him of who owed him what and why. They found your name there.'

'Did they now?'

'Yes, sir.'

Cox waited for Brennan to continue, but the detective remained silent. He glanced over Brennan's head at the photograph once more, then looked out of the window, where the glass was thick with frost. After what felt like an age, he said finally, 'Perhaps the fellow did some work for me, I seem to recall a name something like that.'

'Good. Now, sir, when I told you they found names and dates, I should have explained that the names and the dates became quite extensive.'

'What do you mean?'

'I mean, Mr Cox, that Bragg recorded, against your own name, the names of all the prostitutes and servant girls he had managed to procure for you over a course of years. Perhaps I misled you when I said he kept nothing incriminating. I was, of course, referring to nothing incriminating to Bragg himself. To others, he was less benign.'

Cox gave the study door a furtive glance. He could hear, from upstairs, the raucous screams of his children at play in the nursery.

'I resent the implication!'

'I implied nothing, Mr Cox. I came straight out with it. You have been using women for a number of years, some willing and paid, some unwilling and unpaid. It's the latter that interest me, but in a rather different way from how they interested you.'

'This is an outrage!'

Cox slammed his fist down on the table, creasing the letter he had been reading when Brennan walked in.

'The Manchester police are even now putting together sworn statements from the young girls whose identities they can discover from the extensively documented records of Theodore Bragg.'

Cox slumped back in his chair. 'Are you here to arrest me?'

Brennan waited a while before replying. 'Not as yet, sir.'

'Then why are you here?'

'I need you to tell me all you can about your dealings with Mr Bragg. And the dealings of others.'

'Others?'

'And,' Brennan went on without elaborating, 'I am assured that if you cooperate fully, then there's every likelihood that charges may be dropped. Or at least diluted to an unscandalous degree.'

The carrot worked.

Cox began to talk, which was a source of great relief to Brennan, whom the Manchester police had informed only that morning that the names of all the women ascribed to James Cox in Bragg's notebook were written entirely in code – a code they found indecipherable and of no forensic use whatsoever.

Sometimes, he thought with a smile as he stepped into the freezing cold of the gloomy afternoon, *the game of 'Bragg' involved a calculated amount of bluff.*

'Mam! Mam!'

Tommy Haggerty burst through the front door and ran into the kitchen. She wasn't there.

Quickly he darted back and hurtled upstairs, where he found her with a bundle of bedsheets in his and Molly's room.

'What in the name of all the saints is the matter, child?' she said, her voice muffled by the sheets beneath her chin.

'You'd best come quick.'

'Come where, child?'

'Outside, Mam.'

'Why? It's freezin' cold.'

'There's a man says he wants to see you.'

Bridie frowned and moved into her own bedroom, the one she had shared with Seamus so long ago, and placed the sheets on the bed. Then she peered through the curtains at the carriage on the street below.

What was going on?

She told Tommy to wait upstairs, a futile instruction, for as soon as she set foot on the bottom stair she heard him clattering his clogs on the stairs behind her. She stood in the still-open doorway and looked out. Across the street she could see some of her neighbours already standing in their own doorways, looking across with folded arms and murmuring wild speculations to each other. Some of Tommy's friends were climbing on the rear of the carriage, one of them almost reaching the top before the coachman leant back and gave him a sharp swipe with his whip.

The carriage door was flung open and a man Bridie dimly recognised sat there, one leg extended in the act of exiting. He wore a black armband and a thick black topcoat. His cravat was similarly hued, and his gloves and hatband completed the picture of mourning.

'Mrs Haggerty?' he said.

It came to her, then. This was a most illustrious visitor indeed – Ambrose Morris, Arthur Morris's brother and the town's MP. What could he possibly want with her? But then, almost before the question had shaped itself in her mind, she knew the answer.

'May I come in?' he said after formally introducing himself.

Other neighbours were now outside, the expressions on their faces ranging from simple curiosity to outright hostility. *A lot of questions to be answered on a lot of doorsteps, she thought, before the street would be satisfied.*

She stepped aside and let him enter. Tommy, standing now with a wary eye on the strange visitor, at first refused to go outside and play, but when the man reached into his pocket and pulled out a shiny sixpence he decided that honour had been satisfied and he had shown enough filial concern for one day.

'I presume you know why I'm here?' Ambrose Morris said once the door had closed and he had been invited to sit down.

'Would it have anythin' to do with my daughter an' your nephew, by any chance?'

'Yes, it would.'

'Go on.'

'Two days ago I received a telegram from my sister-in-law informing me of Andrew's plans to go to New York. With your daughter.'

'About the same time I found out an' all.'

'And your feelings?'

'Like yours, I expect.'

'Good. His mother doesn't want him to go any more than you want your daughter to go. So it seemed only sensible if we could decide upon a solution.'

'Oh?' Suddenly, Bridie became wary. If this man were anything like his late brother, solutions only worked out if they favoured himself. She told him about her meeting with Arthur Morris in Mesnes Park. The next few minutes therefore came as something of a shock.

'Ye don't recognise me, do you, Mr Morris?'

He shook his head.

When she explained, he looked astounded. 'Good Lord! I remember you coming down those stairs screaming as if it were yesterday! But I wouldn't have recognised you now.'

Because the world is a wearying place, she reflected sadly.

'Did Arthur – my brother – know? Who you were, I mean?'

'After I told him, yes.'

'I see. Still, it makes no difference, does it, to our situation?'

'No, sir.'

'The solution I propose is this. I will impress upon Andrew the vital necessity of his remaining here in Wigan, at least until this damnable coal strike is at an end. It would do the company no good whatsoever if he were to leave now. I think I can persuade him to delay things until then.'

'What about my Molly?'

'Your daughter is how old?'

'Nineteen.'

'A minor. In order for her to be able to marry, she would need to obtain your written permission. You could use that threat to cool her ardour, although it is in reality an empty threat if she swears on oath before the vicar general that you have consented, even if you haven't. Still, she won't know that, will she?'

'Hold on. It's true I don't want her to go sailin' off to America, but there's a world o' difference between that an' plottin' to keep 'em apart.'

Ambrose smiled. 'I'm not doing that. Merely delaying things until later. When the world is a more settled place. I also propose to offer you a small annuity that would help you bring up that impish son of yours, something I am willing to do whether you agree to what I ask or not.'

'Why would you do that? Sure 'tis nothin' but a bribe.'

Ambrose opened his hands in a gesture of honesty. 'I know how badly you were affected when your husband lost his life in one of our collieries. It's a belated payment of insurance, if you like, something you are perfectly entitled to. Bribery it most certainly isn't.'

She glanced at the window, where Tommy was standing with a small group, doubtless showing them his booty. 'And what then?'

'If they both still feel the same way, then neither his mother nor myself will stand in his way. By that time, many things will have changed, believe me.'

Hopefully the men will be back to work and the town back on its feet, thought Bridie.

'Have you spoken to your nephew, Mr Morris?'

'I am about to do that, after I leave here. But I wanted to speak with you first. As a matter of courtesy.'

He wanted her to ask Molly to be patient. Once he had gone and the carriage, and the neighbours, had disappeared, she sat in the gathering gloom, hoping she would be doing the right thing. And wasn't it only right that she receive some sort of remuneration for Seamus being taken away from her so cruelly?

But then she thought of Frank Latchford, and what she had told him over a fortnight ago. The guilt was always there, hidden sometimes by the events of the day, but it came rushing back, like now, with all the force of a raging toothache.

She should have listened and said nothing when he told her about the man who had been asking all those questions. She should never have told him about Arthur Morris and his threats. Nor should she have accepted his offer of help, an offer designed, she knew full well, to force her into acting as advocate for Frank when he next decided to pursue her Molly.

What had he done?

Had he lain in wait for the man who was threatening her and Molly? She cast her mind back to the moment she stood on the railway track with the speeding train a matter of seconds away, when she felt, with absolute and terrifying certainty, that Frank Latchford had carried out her unspoken wish and ridden her of Arthur Morris. But there, with the vibrations of the tracks beneath her feet, certainty had suddenly become doubt: Frank Latchford couldn't have killed Arthur Morris – or he was a bloody fool if he had – because in doing so he would simply be removing an obstacle to the union of Molly and Andrew Morris.

He would, in effect, have cleared the way for the girl he still loved to marry another.

He wouldn't have done that, surely?

CHAPTER TWENTY

Constable Jaggery sat atop the carriage alongside the cabbie, and rammed his fists deep in the pockets of his greatcoat. He had his helmet pulled close around his ears, and his thick muffler, strictly speaking not part of the official uniform, wrapped firmly around his throat, but there was only so much he could do to ward off the bitter cold.

The snow of the last weeks had now turned into a ferocious blizzard stinging wherever it made contact with his bare flesh. How the cabbie could see more than a yard in front was beyond him: the front bullseye lamps only highlighted the relentless force of the elements, and from time to time on the journey from the police station up to Wigan Lane – a slow and merciless incline that gave free vent to the fierce howling of the wind-borne blizzard – Jaggery could do nothing more than close his eyes and hope fervently the horses would see them safely to their destination. He also muttered curses that were thankfully swept away by the powerful blast, curses that brought down all manner of plague on Ding Dong Bloody Bell, who even now was seated *inside* the carriage with Sergeant Brennan and enjoying the relative warmth afforded by the thick blanket provided by the cabbie.

Inside, Bell leant back and stared at his detective sergeant.

He admired the way Brennan had argued the case; that was beyond doubt. The strength of his argument, a chain forged with iron links of logic, was undeniable and powerfully suggestive of guilt, but what he had uncovered had disgusted and horrified him in equal measure; a reaction, he knew, that was unfair, tantamount to blaming a doctor for his diagnosis of a malignant tumour. Furthermore, his absolute belief in the rightness of law, a belief reinforced beyond measure during his service for Queen and country, transcended any personal sense he might feel of loyalty or even sympathy. The guilty had to be punished. But first they had to be caught.

Prudence Morris sat at the dinner table and watched her son and brother-in-law with keen interest. She knew, of course, that Ambrose had been to see the Haggerty woman, but until now, Andrew was unaware of the visit. She wondered how the subject would be broached, and how her son would respond. Since Arthur's death, he had been more and more enervated, but whether that were some kind of natural reaction to the bereavement or due to the romantic interest in his life, she couldn't tell.

Ambrose's strategy – that was what he called it – was to divide and conquer. Keep them apart for a short while and he would guarantee the two would not marry, and therefore the American dream would remain just that. He told her the Irishwoman was at least partially in agreement – she would persuade her daughter to wait until the strike had ended, which gave Ambrose time at least to work out his strategy in full.

One thing was sure – she could not lose her son. And Ambrose had promised.

But she was totally unprepared for what her brother-in-law was about to say.

'You realise, of course, Andrew, that any suggestion of emigration must wait.'

'Why? I have already made preliminary enquiries. It will be a place where I can breathe.'

'Not from what I hear.'

'You know what I mean. Here, my work as an artist is stifled by other considerations. The onerous duties of the coalfields, for one. I'm unsuited for that.'

'I know. It is why I have an eye on a certain property in London that might solve a problem.'

'Property?'

'You've heard of Tire Street, in Chelsea? It's near the Embankment and has a wealth of studio houses specially designed for artists. Whistler himself lives there.'

Andrew's eyes widened.

'It might be a sound investment, Andrew. Both as a property and a working environment.'

'But why would you buy such a place?'

Ambrose shrugged. 'It would keep you in the country, for one thing.'

'And Molly?'

'Once the strike is over, there would be ample opportunity for you to take her down there to see the place. Artists are more bohemian in their response to – shall we say – imbalanced liaisons?'

'But I'd set my heart on America.'

'Take a smaller step first, Andrew. London is far enough away from the tittle-tattle of this town, and Chelsea is a place where your art can breathe the fresh air of inspiration.'

Andrew smiled. 'Poetically put, Uncle.'

'And, once you are established – who knows? An exhibition at the Royal Academy?'

'I think Molly would find London – unnerving.'

'Nonsense! At least they'd have a stab at understanding her. In New York she'd be as lucid as a Cherokee squaw.'

Andrew flinched at this, and it was his mother who came to her brother-in-law's rescue.

'Ambrose was simply putting himself in the girl's shoes. How alien would such an environment be to her? What he suggests would have the added bonus of accessibility. She would at least be able to see her mother, and I would be able to see my son.'

He looked from one to the other and a confused frown creased his forehead. 'This is an unusual alliance.'

'What do you mean?' his mother asked.

'The usual atmosphere between you two is frosty, isn't it? Is this an alliance formed out of necessity? A treaty of convenience?'

A sharp exchange of glances occurred just then. The wind howled like a banshee all around the house, and the windowpanes rattled with the force of the elements creating a blizzarding frenzy outside.

Both Ambrose and Prudence opened their mouths to speak, but it was Ambrose whose voice was heard above the rising storm. 'Andrew, there is something that you need to know.'

'What is it?'

He looked at his mother's face, but she had her head bowed very low, and it was difficult to make out the expression on her face. Was this the *right time* for her to speak of the mysterious *other thing?*

'Strange. I have stood in the House and faced down the lions of the opposition when in government. In opposition I have stood strong against those members of my own party when conscience has taken me on a different course.'

Ambrose dabbed at his lips with a napkin and placed it gently beside his plate. He laughed bitterly. 'Conscience. A wonderful thing, isn't it?'

'Uncle Ambrose?'

Andrew shifted uncomfortably in his chair. He had no idea what was going on, and his glance towards his mother brought no explanation.

'I'm sorry, Andrew. Where was I?'

'You were praising your conscience,' his sister-in-law said quietly.

'Ah yes, so I was. I have done all those things, as I say, in the full glare of parliamentary scrutiny, of howling insults and fierce criticisms. But now, here, tonight, I find it very difficult to say what I have to say.' He looked at Prudence Morris and took a deep breath. 'You see, my boy, there's something you need to know.'

Suddenly they heard a strange sound emanating from the hallway; someone was hammering at the front door with his fist, a loud and disturbing racket that, seconds later, was followed by the clanging of the Davy lamp knocker.

Whatever Ambrose Morris had to say to his nephew would have to wait. They had visitors.

'Now, sir, to demonstrate.'

Sergeant Brennan, Captain Bell and Constable Jaggery were all standing on the steps before the front door of the Morris residence. Behind them, the cabbie had clambered quickly down from his seat, rubbed his gloved hands together with some violence before climbing gingerly into his carriage and closing the door, wrapping the blanket around his legs with a resentful grunt.

Brennan leant forward and, with clenched fist, began to pound rhythmically on the door, ignoring for the moment the less arduous appeal of the heavy brass knocker. After a fusillade of blows, he stepped back and invited Jaggery to make the more conventional mode of announcing one's presence, which he did with gusto.

'You see, sir,' Brennan went on when Jaggery had finished with the Davy lamp, 'it struck me as rather odd that someone should stand here with a letter in his hand, a letter which *had* to be read immediately otherwise the strategy wouldn't work, and for some reason refuse to use the door knocker. It's heavy, and it does the job it's supposed to do with literally alarming efficiency. So why not use it?'

Jaggery, who had not been privy to the sergeant's exposition to Captain Bell, merely scratched his head. Thumping, knocking – what was the bloody difference?

But the chief constable nodded in understanding.

The door swung open, and a rather irate-looking Isaacs stood there and performed the perfect butler's trick of glaring submissively at these unexpected visitors. When he recognised the chief constable, however, his demeanour altered and the hostility in his eyes retreated.

Once they were inside the hallway, he asked if they would mind waiting there while he went to find the mistress.

Jaggery, unwrapping his thick muffler, took the opportunity to ask a question.

'Are you saying there were two people at the door, Sergeant?'

Brennan shook his head. 'I assure you, Constable, there was only one person standing at the door when the hammering was heard.'

'Who was it then?'

Before he could respond, Isaacs reappeared and escorted the three of them into the drawing room where they should make themselves comfortable until the mistress was ready to receive them.

But five minutes later, it was Ambrose Morris, accompanied by his nephew Andrew and his sister-in-law Prudence, who entered the drawing room.

'My sister-in-law insisted on coming, Alexander, although I told her not to concern herself.'

Ambrose had naturally addressed his remarks to the senior policeman.

'A pleasure, ma'am,' said Captain Bell with a

314

slight bow.

Brennan noted how easily she was moving now – the pain she had been under for so long seemed to have eased a great deal. The lingering smell of arnica had also vanished.

'It must be important to bring you out on a night like this,' Ambrose remarked as they all waited for Prudence to be seated.

'Yes, Ambrose. It is.'

There was a melancholy resonance in the chief constable's voice.

Andrew seemed to have caught the tone of his words. He shifted uncomfortably in his seat before standing up and moving to the fireplace. Out of the corner of his eye, Brennan watched him carefully, noting the nervous way he placed one arm on the mantelpiece and stared at the series of landscapes he himself had painted. In particular, he was examining the wintry scene, where the solitary young man was still sitting by a frozen stream, his hand pressed flat against the hard ice.

'Well then. Make it snappy, can't you?'

A distinct note of irritation had entered Ambrose's voice. 'We have a great deal of unfinished business – family business – to attend to.'

Brennan wondered what *unfinished business* they had interrupted.

'And I really do have to be back in London by tomorrow night.'

'Sergeant Brennan will explain things.' Captain Bell raised his chin, as if he were ready to inspect the troops.

'This is all rather mysterious!' Prudence Morris said, and glanced at her brother-in-law with annoyance and curiosity in equal measure.

'What I have to say, ma'am,' said Brennan, 'will not be pleasant.'

'Then wouldn't it be better if my mother were removed from the room?'

There was a note of rising panic in Andrew's voice.

'Removed?' she snapped back. 'Like a salver of half-eaten scones?'

'Sergeant!' the chief constable hissed impatiently. *Get this over with*, his tone demanded.

'I'm afraid we need to return for a while to the night your husband was found in Scholes, ma'am.'

'Really, Alexander,' Ambrose Morris began, but he was met with a stony expression.

'Go on, Sergeant.'

Brennan took a deep breath. 'Mrs Cox and yourself remained in the dining room while your husband and Mr Cox moved into the smoking room?'

'That is correct.'

'And Mr Morris here had left the room to get some cigars from his room.'

'Cubans,' Ambrose added inconsequentially.

'Quite. While you were out of the room, Mr Morris, a hammering of fists was heard at the front door.'

'Yes.'

'And when the maid answered the door, you were halfway down the stairs with your cigars and you say you saw a figure lurking in the bushes.'

'Yes. Though it was very dark and...'

'Nevertheless, you pointed this figure out to the maid.'

'Yes.'

'Who thought she saw someone but wasn't sure.'

'Correct.'

'Still, putting that to one side for a while, the result was a letter that had been dropped into the post basket behind the letter box.'

'Yes.'

'Addressed to Arthur Morris. And your brother-in-law opened it and reacted angrily, did he not?'

Andrew pushed himself away from the mantelpiece and moved towards Brennan.

'Do you intend merely to go over old ground, Sergeant? Do you realise how distressing this must be for my mother?'

'Yes, sir. And I'm very sorry for it.'

Suddenly he turned and faced Prudence Morris. 'For how many years had your husband been physically abusing you, Mrs Morris?'

There was uproar. Andrew almost screamed his protests, Ambrose made an immediate and impassioned plea to Captain Bell to foreclose this outrage to decency at once, while Prudence Morris lowered her head and clasped her hands gently together. The chief constable had a depth of compassion on his face that Brennan feared might erupt into anger, but mercifully he kept silent.

Brennan, meanwhile, remained steadfast, his gaze never leaving her.

At last, she spoke. Her voice was barely a whisper, but there was steel there, a quality Brennan had recognised in her on a previous occasion. 'Arthur was a man who used physical strength to assert his authority.'

Andrew made a step towards her but she held

317

up a hand to forestall him.

'No, Andrew. Please. Let me finish.'

She looked up at Brennan and smiled feebly. 'He was a brutal man, Sergeant. But only in private. He would never mistreat me in full view of our son. Never. There was always a discretion in his violence towards me.'

She presented that lamentable fact as evidence for the defence, Brennan reflected, and thought of a time when Morris *was* seen. By a kitchen maid named Bridie Hanlon.

'Which is why,' she said quietly, 'I am amazed at the acuteness of your observation. How did you know?'

'Your maid told me you never let her assist you when dressing. You never allow her to apply arnica, for your rheumatism. It has its own aroma, does it not?'

'It does.'

'But arnica is used to treat bruises, rather than rheumatism.'

'It can be used for rheumatism.'

'I'm assured that any reputable physician would recommend some concoction involving camphor oil, soap and opium. Not arnica.'

'And that was your only evidence?'

Brennan hesitated slightly. He had the testimony of two people: the cook, Mrs Venner, who compared Arthur Morris with Jekyll and Hyde, and Bridie Haggerty, who not only saw him on one of the rare occasions he let the domestic mask slip, but who also suffered first-hand his penchant for brutality. But he said nothing. No good would be served by referring to either woman now that the

318

truth was exposed.

'So,' he went on, ignoring her question, 'you had suffered a great deal. Your son appears never to have seen this side of his character.'

'Never!' said Andrew firmly.

'Yet you saw his intransigence when he discovered your relationship with Molly Haggerty.'

At the mention of her name, and the painful memory of his father's outburst, he bit his lip.

'Violence manifests itself in different ways,' Brennan said softly to Andrew. 'What he threatened you with I have no idea, but he made it perfectly clear you were to break off your dalliance with her, didn't he?'

'Yes.'

'Right. So we have a situation where your mother is systematically abused over a period of many years; we have a situation where you are in danger of losing the girl you are deeply in love with; and we have a situation where the whole town is haunted by the spectre of starvation conjured up, many believe, by your father.'

At this point he reached into his pocket and took out the filthy envelope with its equally filthy contents that were found on Arthur Morris's body.

'It struck me as odd, you see, the circumstance of this letter.'

'Why?' Ambrose Morris asked, staring at it in confusion.

'The maid and yourself, Mrs Morris, said that the letter that dropped into the post basket was a clean white envelope, and that the letter your husband extracted was equally pristine, or at least unremarkable.'

319

'So?'

'Three things: one, how did it come to be in this state?'

'It was a filthy night, Sergeant,' Ambrose interposed. 'Perhaps my brother took it out and examined it while on his way to Scholes.'

'Perhaps. Which brings me to my second point: how did he know where to go? There's no address on the letter, no indication whatsoever as to who sent it.'

'You said it contained some clue.'

'Ah yes, the acronymic reference to Scholes: *"Strike causes hell – O Lord end suffrin."'*

'There you are then.'

'Where are we, sir? The reference to Scholes is clear, but where in Scholes?'

'Perhaps my brother recognised the reference and acted accordingly.'

'Well I think you're partly right, sir. I think he recognised something, but not the reference. I think he recognised the name of the sender of the letter.'

Both Ambrose and Andrew laughed out loud at that.

'But there is no name in that letter!' Ambrose cried out in exasperation.

'No, sir, but there was a name in the letter your brother received that night.'

'What? You speak in ridiculous riddles, man!'

Prudence Morris's voice was low but carried an air of authority. 'You must explain the conundrum, Sergeant.'

'The letter your husband received was not the one we found on his person.'

'I beg your pardon? How can that be?'

'Mrs Morris told me that she was quite capable of recognising her husband's name on the front of the envelope. *Arthur Morris*. But the letter we found on his person was addressed simply to "A. Morris". A mistake. If you're going to substitute one letter for another, at least make them superficially the same.'

'This is nonsense!' Andrew cried out.

'If the letter your father opened contained his full name – and your mother stated that it did...'

Prudence Morris gave a sharp nod and stated firmly, 'It most definitely had his name, "Arthur Morris", on the envelope.'

'Then he wouldn't have hesitated to open it. Whereas "A. Morris" could be Andrew, or Ambrose. It is my belief that the letter that dropped through that post basket also contained a name and an address. I believe it contained a threat that so enraged Arthur that he would inevitably respond the way he was expected to – with anger and with impulse. He would go to Scholes at once and have it out with the person who supposedly wrote it.'

'Who was that?'

Brennan shrugged. 'I can only guess the writer claimed to be Mrs Haggerty, or perhaps the popular agent for the Miners' Federation, Frank Latchford. Someone he had had angry dealings with in the past. Neither of those two know anything about this, of course.'

Andrew cleared his throat. 'You mean you don't have this supposed letter? The one that was taken from my father's body and *that* left in its place?'

'I don't have it, sir, no.'

'Then you can say what you like about it, can't you? You can speculate to your heart's content! Why, it could have contained a recipe for strawberry jam for all you know!'

'True, Mr Morris, but a recipe for strawberry jam would hardly send your father up to Scholes in a furious temper.'

'Let me get this straight,' Andrew went on. 'Someone comes all the way to Standish to post a letter – with a name and address – and then returns forthwith to lie in wait for my father on the off-chance he responds?'

'Not quite, sir. Nobody "came all the way to Standish" as you put it.'

'Well then, he sends a messenger who posts it for him.'

Brennan shook his head.

'Well how in God's name...'

'The one who was standing at that front door with the letter to post was already here.'

'This is ridiculous!' Ambrose exclaimed with a raising of his arms as if both contained order papers and he was fulminating across the despatch box.

'No it isn't, sir. It's quite simple. Someone hammered on the door with his fists instead of using the heavy door knocker.'

'Why didn't he use the knocker?' asked Andrew.

'Because he couldn't.'

'Why ever not?'

'The man standing at the front door couldn't possibly use the knocker or post the letter *because he was inside at the time.'*

'What nonsense!' Ambrose almost yelled.

'No it isn't, sir.'

Brennan turned fully to face the Member of Parliament now and spoke in sombre, heavy tones.

'You couldn't risk opening the door and using the Davy lamp knocker in case you were seen. Besides, opening the door on such a night would have brought a flurry of snow on the hall carpet. Difficult to explain, I would have thought. Far simpler to hammer on the inside of the door with your fists after you'd dropped the letter in the basket, again from the inside, thus ensuring someone would immediately find the letter. If not, it may have lain there unnoticed for the rest of the evening.'

'What is this?' Prudence whispered in horror, her hand moving to her mouth.

'Your brother-in-law, Mrs Morris, then moved quickly back to the stairs where he gave every appearance of coming down rather than rushing back up when the maid dashed out to see who was at the door. Then, when she flung the door wide open, he persuaded her that he had seen a dark figure in the bushes. His forceful insistence was nothing more than the power of suggestion. Therefore she said she saw it too.'

At that moment a strange sound was heard in the room. Ambrose Morris was clapping his hands together.

'Bravo, Sergeant. Masterful performance. But deep in the realms of speculation. I see no proof of any of this wildness.'

Brennan could see that the man wasn't a poli-

323

tician for nothing – he had that outer shell of confidence bordering on arrogance, and the absolute conviction that anyone involved in the making of laws could also be involved in manipulating them.

Suddenly there was movement, unexpected and shocking. Prudence Morris stood up and moved quickly to where her brother-in-law was standing, and then she threw herself into his arms.

Andrew gasped to see his mother and uncle in what appeared to be an embrace of passion and fear. Even Captain Bell appeared shocked to his very core. Yet when Brennan spoke, his voice was low, and calm, and certain.

'That's where the masterful performance can be found.'

He nodded towards Ambrose and Prudence. He was holding her in his arms and she had her head buried in his chest.

For Andrew, this was in the realm of fantasy. Never, in all his life, had he witnessed anything but a tolerant distance between the two of them. Now they were embracing as lovers.

'It isn't true!' she said, her voice muffled and cracked. 'Ambrose was here when Arthur was killed. In this very house! He was found asleep in the smoking room. Ask Isaacs. He'll tell you! How can he be in two places at once? Tell him, Ambrose.'

'Uncle Ambrose?'

Ambrose looked at his nephew and touched Prudence's head, a gentle, loving gesture. But he remained stolidly silent.

Brennan went on. 'You hired Theodore Bragg, did you not? Paid him a handsome sum to get rid of your brother.'

Ambrose slowly shook his head. 'Speculation, Sergeant Brennan. Merely speculation. In a court of law...'

At that point, Brennan held up a notebook.

'What is that?' Ambrose asked, his voice losing a little of its equilibrium.

'It's Theodore Bragg's insurance policy. Or rather, his notebook with an account of how much you paid him for his work that night. It was sent over from Manchester this morning.'

But again, Ambrose shook his head. 'Numbers scrawled on a page, Sergeant? Really! I never even met the man.'

But Brennan went on, ignoring the man's calm protestations. 'I have a sworn statement from James Cox that you not only knew Theodore Bragg but you availed yourself of his services on more than one occasion.'

'Nonsense!'

At this, Prudence detached herself from his arms and moved a few steps back, surveying him closely.

'Mr Bragg was a man who lurked in the darker corners of society, Mrs Morris. Men like him are necessary, sometimes, when men like your husband need unpleasant or discreet services carried out. I'm aware of Mr Cox's arrangements with the man, and I can guess that your husband used him to gather whatever information he could on his enemies, members of the Miners' Federation, rival businessmen, and so on, including finding out all he could about your son's relationship with Molly Haggerty. But your brother-in-law used him in quite a different way. According to the sums he received from you, Mr Morris, he performed very great services for you. Such as murder.'

'Ambrose! This is madness, is it not?'

Prudence Morris's hands went to her forehead, and for a moment Brennan thought she was about to faint as she did the first time he saw her. Andrew, as if he read Brennan's thoughts, dashed over and placed an arm around his mother's shoulder, leading her back to the armchair she had previously occupied. Once she had settled back down, Brennan resumed his relentless narrative.

'But then perhaps Bragg got greedy. Perhaps, having killed Arthur Morris and swapped the letters for one which was designed merely to confuse the police, he felt he should be better rewarded for the enormity of what he had done. I'm not sure whether the note he left with the acronym of Scholes was his idea or yours, Mr Morris. No matter; what isn't in any doubt is that Mr Bragg wrote it. The horror of the gallows casts a very long and dark shadow, does it not? So then you decided to kill Bragg and eliminate all of the links connecting you with your brother's death. Or it may be that the killing of Bragg was your intention all along once Arthur had been taken care of.'

He paused and allowed a softness to colour his next words.

'You had your brother killed because you could no longer stand by and watch his systematic brutality destroy the woman you have loved for a very long time.'

Ambrose Morris whispered the single word, 'Speculation,' but it contained none of the forceful denial of earlier.

It was Prudence who spoke next, a new note of desperate optimism in her voice. 'But that cannot be! Ambrose could not possibly have killed this man Bragg!'

'Why not?'

'Because he was in London, wasn't he, when the vile man was killed? He was found on the ice near a canal boat on the very night Ambrose had travelled to London earlier in the day. You had a committee meeting that night, Ambrose, remember? The reason you had to return to the capital?'

Ambrose nodded, a look of gratitude on his face. It was soon wiped away.

Brennan said quietly, 'I'm sure the committee meeting would have been recorded, and an agenda, together with a record of all those present, distributed?'

'There!' Prudence exclaimed, as if she had pulled Ambrose from a torrential flood.

One look at his face told her all she needed to know.

'But I saw him on to the train!' said Andrew. 'I watched the train leave the station. He definitely travelled to London. Again, how could he be in two places at once?'

His voice had the tone of a child, not only eager to believe in the whimsy of a faery world, but also filled with despair as fantasy was fast becoming delusion.

Brennan nodded. 'It took me a while to work it out, and it was indeed something you yourself said to me that put me in mind of how it was done.'

'Something *I* said?' Andrew's eyes were wide

and rimmed with tears now.

'You said to me, "Sometimes I feel the world revolves around journeys and destinations. Not enough time for the stops in between." Do you recall?'

'Yes, but I don't see how...'

'Once I became convinced your uncle was guilty, I knew there was some way, some elusive stratagem, that would enable him to return to Wigan having left you on the station watching him depart for London. The London train stops at Warrington Bank Quay. It's entirely possible to leave the train at that station, having previously purchased not only a ticket to London but a single ticket to Warrington – or, if this were planned weeks in advance, even arranging for Bragg himself to buy the ticket so suspicion wouldn't fall on him, possibly with the promise of a final lucrative payment – then travel by carriage to Culcheth, near Warrington.'

'Why Culcheth?' Andrew asked.

'If your uncle were to travel back from War-rington Bank Quay to Wigan North Western – the station he had just left – on the next train back, then there would be a very tangible risk of being spotted. Station porters are very adept at noticing passengers, especially the first-class ones who might grant them a sizeable tip. No, he had to return to Wigan quickly – but by a different train and a different station. Wigan Central Station is on the MS & LR line – the Manchester, Sheffield and Lincolnshire Railways. Culcheth is a stop down the line. The other benefit of travelling back to Wigan Central is that, as you are well aware, despite its name it is far from central – it lies down Station Road and is off the beaten track as far as the town centre is concerned. Less risk of being seen and recognised.

'He probably left his case at the left luggage office at Warrington so he could make the journey to the canal boat unencumbered by anything other than the single-minded determination to be rid of the one person who could ruin him. The thickly falling snow would have helped, of course. No one spends long looking at you when everyone is hunched and eager to find some warm, homely place whether it be home itself, a public house, or a canal boat stuck on the frozen ice. He found Bragg alone on the boat – as he had instructed, probably with the promise of bringing payment – and, possibly when he turned round to offer him a drink, he struck him with the implement he had doubtless picked up on arrival – the windlass.'

Brennan allowed the full horror of his words to settle on the room. He looked at Prudence Morris, whose head had slowly drooped like a flower wilting in a hard frost. She reached up and touched her son's hand, which was resting gently on her shoulder.

'My guess is you dragged the body outside with the intention of hurling him into the depths of the canal. But the ice proved too thick, so you left him there and made your way back into town. You returned to Central Station, caught the next train back to Culcheth, whereupon you travelled back to Warrington Bank Quay and, after collecting your luggage, resumed your journey to London.'

He stopped and looked at Ambrose, who was

now staring back at him with obvious agitation.

'Had you arranged to meet Mr Bragg on the pretext of paying him some more money? Or had he himself made the first move in demanding, shall we say, a bonus for such a murder? He may well have heard of the progress of our investigations.'

But Ambrose said nothing, merely stared at him, his mouth set and rigid. The coals, burning in the grate, were reflected in his eyes, tiny flames flickering above hotly glowing embers.

'You see, Mr Morris, I sent my constable here down to Central Station and he showed the ticket collector there your photograph. I obtained it from the posters you used to proclaim your candidacy in the last election. The man recognised the face, even if he hadn't known you at the time. He's what you might call a witness, sir. A witness to your otherwise inexplicable return to your constituency when you were officially supposed to be at a committee meeting in London later in the day.'

Ambrose seemed to sag, a look of defiance still in his eyes, but something else there, too – a sense of impending doom.

Prudence began to sob. 'All these years,' she said, 'all the words we exchanged whenever he was away. All the glances, the shared intimacies... All for nothing, Ambrose. Why? Why?'

As if he had come to a decision, Ambrose Morris rose to his full height and thrust out his chest. Immediately, Brennan was struck by the force of the man's personality, and could see him dominating some Commons debate, imposing his will on others with his eloquence and his physical presence.

'The evidence you have, Sergeant Brennan, while sufficient I suppose to damage irrevocably my political career, is hardly sufficient to bring me to a court of law and effect a conviction. Even you must see that the arguments counsel would use are specious and speculative and open to the most fierce denunciation by the expensive barrister I would, of course, employ. You do see that, don't you? To miss a committee meeting is hardly proof of anything. And so what if I was seen at Wigan Central by a ticket collector or even the stationmaster himself? You have no sightings of me anywhere near a – what was it? A *canal boat?*'

The expression, not only in Brennan's eyes but also in the chief constable's, told its own story. Both of them knew that without an outright admission of guilt, Ambrose Morris would remain a free man.

'So if you expected me to fall upon my sword, metaphorically speaking, you are quite wrong.'

'Ambrose...' Prudence began, but when he turned to look at her she reverted to a silence that was rendered voluble by the glistening tears in her eyes. She, at least, was in no doubt as to his guilt.

'But there are categories of incarceration, are there not, Alexander?' he said, addressing his remarks to Captain Bell but looking with infinite sadness at the woman he had loved for so long. He took a long, deep breath, then exhaled slowly. 'I shall apply for the office of Crown Steward and Bailiff of the Chiltern Hundreds and resign my seat as soon as the process can be established.'

Jaggery was about to make some protest about

allowing this murderer to resign from one job and apply for another. Only a signal from Brennan, and a promise to explain things later, prevented an outburst.

'This strike will soon be at an end. When I left the House, the rumour was strong on the side of reconciliation. I gather the prime minister is putting in place a strategy of intervention the like of which has never been seen before now. Things change, do they not? I will absent myself from the collieries and perhaps leave the country. India, Alexander! What do you say to that, eh, old friend?'

But Captain Bell was inwardly seething. The thought of this man, of whom he had grown so fond despite his innate reluctance to get close to anyone, getting away with fratricide and murder was more than he could bear. He grunted an apology to Prudence Morris and was about to storm past Brennan, when the latter placed a restraining hand on his chest.

'Sergeant Brennan?'

'Sorry, sir, but it won't do.'

'What won't do?'

'Mr Morris can't get away, literally, with murder, and since he won't confess, then we will have to see that our evidence is, shall we say, cast in stone?'

Captain Bell looked nonplussed.

'Or rather,' Brennan went on, 'cast in plaster.' He turned to Ambrose Morris and looked down at his shoes. 'I see your shoes are well trimmed and highly polished, sir?'

Ambrose gave a sigh of exasperation.

'Perhaps you'll allow my constable here to look in your room for some footwear more suited to the elements?'

Before Ambrose could object, Brennan barked out an order and Jaggery quickly left the room. They heard some mutterings and raised voices as Jaggery threw the full weight of his authority at Isaacs, who eventually and reluctantly led him to Ambrose's room. No one spoke for the several minutes it took for Jaggery to return, giving his sergeant a confirmatory nod. He was holding up a pair of black boots in one hand and a large photograph in the other.

Brennan took the objects from Jaggery and held them up to scrutinise them closely.

'Unless I am completely in error, the soles of these boots, with their rather unusual tread, provide a perfect match with footprints found at the scene of the murder. In short, Mr Morris, this is proof positive that you were there after all.'

It was Prudence Morris who spoke next. 'Ambrose?'

When he turned to her, the expression on his face was that of a man ravaged by grief and horror.

'Do you recognise those boots?'

He nodded slowly, resignedly. Then he said, 'They are Hyer boots, from America, Sergeant. They were a gift from Arthur.'

No one uttered the thought they all shared – that the gift of a dead man had helped ensnare the one who had him killed – but Ambrose Morris gave a shrill laugh that contained a bitter eloquence of its own.

Captain Bell moved back and clasped a hand

on his shoulder.

'Might I say something?' Ambrose said quietly.

His old friend nodded, and released his hand from his shoulder.

'Andrew, I know that there's been much, far too much, for you to take in tonight. I'm not proud of what I did to my own brother. But I have watched him abuse your mother for years. She was growing weaker and weaker. Surely you have seen that for yourself? I decided that this could go on no longer, so I did what has been revealed here tonight. I admit it. And it so nearly worked, did it not? Knowing him as I did, a letter – supposedly from Mrs Haggerty, informing him her daughter was with child and there was a very large price to pay for her silence – produced the desired effect. And once I got him there in Scholes, with Bragg lurking in the shadows ... why, no one would be blamed because everyone could be blamed!'

His voice began to crack at that point, and he stared at Andrew for a long time before emitting a long, low sigh.

As he turned to go, Andrew spoke up. 'What were you going to say? Earlier, before the police came?'

Ambrose Morris, his back now to his nephew, straightened and turned to face him. 'It doesn't matter now. Nothing matters now.' He paused, then added, 'My boy.'

With the last phrase his voice cracked, and the reflections of tiny flames in his eyes were broken up by the tears welling there. He gave Prudence a smile, and then the Member of Parliament for Wigan, with the chief constable at his side, was escorted quietly from the room.

Andrew Morris gave a husky cough and stared at the closed door for a long time. At last, he sighed.

'You must leave my mother and me to assemble our broken pieces and either attempt to glue them together or hurl them into the blazing fire, Sergeant. There's nothing more you can do here, is there?'

As Brennan signalled to Jaggery to leave, he made his way to the door and stopped, turning to Prudence Morris who was sitting in her armchair with her head bowed low. He could find nothing to say, and saw her son standing with one arm on her shoulder.

What would happen now? he wondered. The humiliation of a public trial would be almost too ghastly for them to bear, coming so soon after the murder of Arthur Morris, the still-unresolved anguish of the lockout, and the similarly unresolved issue between Andrew and Molly Haggerty. Perhaps that particular liaison would wither and die with a sad inevitability, and Frank Latchford would once more be seen around the streets of Scholes with the young mill girl on his arm.

A part of him did feel sorry for Ambrose Morris, too. He had arranged for his brother's death to prevent any further suffering on Prudence's part. An act of love? Using the bitterness of a miners' strike to conceal the real motive for his murder. Getting Arthur to go to Scholes that night was, in one sense, a master stroke – no shortage of suspects in that district, and conversely no chance of convicting anyone with no evidence to hold against them.

It would have been perfect. And after a suitable period of mourning, Ambrose and Prudence would finally have been able to show their true feelings after all these years.

As he stepped outside into the blizzard once more, he saw the chief constable sitting upright in the carriage, with Ambrose Morris seated beside him, staring fixedly ahead. Jaggery had already climbed onto the seat beside the cabbie, and Brennan pulled his collars close to him. He glanced back at the house and saw Andrew Morris and his mother through the drawing-room window. They were talking animatedly, and then, after his mother had spoken, Andrew suddenly raised his head and walked over to the window, pressing both hands flat against the glass. He stared out, seeking his uncle half-concealed in the carriage with Captain Bell beside him. Brennan saw a look of absolute horror on the young man's face.

Whatever she had told him, it had affected him very badly indeed.

Still, it was none of his business now, he told himself as he climbed up and sat alongside Constable Jaggery. The cabbie cracked a whip and slowly the wheels crunched forward into the howling wind.

Soon, he would be warm again. He would be home with Ellen, and Barry would be asleep upstairs, confident that his dad would slaughter any dragon that dared show its face that night.

AFTERWORD

The 1893 miners' strike – or lockout, as the miners insisted on calling it – was caused by the owners demanding that the miners accept a twenty-five per cent reduction in their wages, something the Miners' Federation flatly refused to contemplate. The dispute lasted from the end of July to the middle of November, and saw the establishment of soup kitchens throughout the affected areas of the strike. It was, indeed, a time of great hardship, and one can only wonder at the resilience and determination of all those caught up in such a desperate struggle, where survival was a close-run thing.

The dispute is of historical significance. It marked the first occasion that the British government intervened in an industrial dispute, with the Prime Minister, William E. Gladstone, arranging a meeting between the two sides under the chairmanship of the Foreign Secretary Lord Rosebery, KG.

Eventually, on the 17th November at the Foreign Office, it was agreed that the miners could return to work under the old wages. Yet the victory, though celebrated, was far from sweet after all the suffering it had engendered. The Reverend William Wickham, who was vicar at St

Andrew's Church in Springfield, Wigan, and who himself provided soup kitchens for the needy, recorded his own views of the suffering he had witnessed:

Where, then, is the men's victory? Their losses are evident, and they have been terrible. It will take many a long month to get over even some of these losses; some never can be got over... Bad blood has been stirred, hard words have been spoken, and, sometimes, hard blows hit (though the behaviour of the men generally has been excellent).

Notwithstanding, the settlement of the dispute was met with great rejoicing: there was singing and dancing in the streets, and in some districts the occasion was marked by the celebratory ringing of church bells.

It would be nice to imagine them celebrating that Christmas of 1893 in good spirits, now that the lockout was over and the men had returned to work. But somehow I doubt there was much cheer that winter.

ACKNOWLEDGEMENTS

I should like to thank my agent, Sara Keane, of the Keane Kataria Literary Agency, for having faith in me and helping enormously to get this novel published. She deserves a medal!

I should also like to express my eternal gratitude to Sophie Robinson, editor at Allison & Busby, for her astute and meticulous editing of *Striking Murder*. She helped me avoid embarrassing errors. Any mistakes are therefore my own fault.

I wish especially to express my respect and admiration to the numerous mining communities, who over the years have worked so hard and made so many sacrifices to bring coal to the surface. This country owes them a huge debt.

Finally, I'd like to thank the people of Wigan, my home town, both past and present. The friendliness and proud history of the place is something to treasure.

The publishers hope that this book has given you enjoyable reading. Large Print Books are especially designed to be as easy to see and hold as possible. If you wish a complete list of our books please ask at your local library or write directly to:

Magna Large Print Books
Magna House, Long Preston,
Skipton, North Yorkshire.
BD23 4ND

This Large Print Book for the partially sighted, who cannot read normal print, is published under the auspices of

THE ULVERSCROFT FOUNDATION

THE ULVERSCROFT FOUNDATION

… we hope that you have enjoyed this Large Print Book. Please think for a moment about those people who have worse eyesight problems than you … and are unable to even read or enjoy Large Print, without great difficulty.

You can help them by sending a donation, large or small to:

**The Ulverscroft Foundation,
1, The Green, Bradgate Road,
Anstey, Leicestershire, LE7 7FU,
England.**
or request a copy of our brochure for more details.

The Foundation will use all your help to assist those people who are handicapped by various sight problems and need special attention.

Thank you very much for your help.